BLOOD MUSIC

"A dazzling flight of disciplined imagination! One of the most interesting stories to come along in years!"
—Poul Anderson

"One of the most entertaining and intellectually stimulating sf novels I've read in a good long while."
—Paul Preuss

"A compelling variation on themes of destruction and rebirth . . . with a finality that's both exalting and disconcerting. Like Clarke in CHILDHOOD'S END, Bear goes to the limits."
—Locus

"Greg Bear is one of tomorrow's up and coming authors!"
—Ray Bradbury

"A powerful, vivid novel whose poignant imagery exists outside the boundaries of the sf genre."
—Booklist

"Greg Bear is one of the best of this generation's idea writers. He explores the very edge of tomorrow . . ."
—David Brin

"Bear's unique novel about the nature of thought and reality solidifies his position as a writer of remarkable talent and fresh vision. Highly recommended!"
—Library Journal

BLOOD MUSIC

GREG BEAR

ACE SCIENCE FICTION BOOKS
NEW YORK

This Ace Science Fiction Book contains the complete
text of the original hardcover edition.
It has been completely reset in a typeface
designed for easy reading, and was printed
from new film.

BLOOD MUSIC

An Ace Science Fiction Book/published by arrangement with
the author

PRINTING HISTORY
Arbor House edition/April 1985
Ace Science Fiction edition/March 1986

ISBN: 0-441-06796-4

Ace Science Fiction Books are published by
The Berkley Publishing Group,
200 Madison Avenue, New York, New York 10016.
PRINTED IN THE UNITED STATES OF AMERICA

NOTES AND
ACKNOWLEDGMENTS

My sincere appreciation to Andrew Edward Dizon, Ph.D., John Graves, Ph.D., Dr. Richard Dutton, Monte Wetzel, and Dr. Percy Russel for access to their laboratories and their valuable time and help. For special details, thanks also to Marian McLean at the World Trade Center and Herbert Quelle at the German Consulate in Los Angeles, as well as Ellen Datlow, Melissa Ann Singer, and Andy Porter.

John F. Carr and David Brin suggested that the original short story should become a novel, some years ago. Stanley Schmidt, in his capacity as editor at *Analog*, suggested I should work out the original idea in more detail and see if it was more than just a fantasy. Beth Meacham expressed editorial enthusiasm for the proposed novel and provided crucial support and encouragement.

While dropping by a San Diego convention on Hybridoma and Scale-Up research, I spotted Vergil I. Ulam's red Volvo sports car in the hotel parking lot. At this moment he is a young graduate student looking for part-time employment.

For Astrid—
Luxury, necessity, obsession
With all my love

INTERPHASE

Each hour, a myriad of trillions of little live things—microbes, bacteria, the peasants of nature—are born and die, not counting for much except in the bulk of their numbers and the accumulation of their tiny lives. They do not perceive deeply, nor do they suffer. A hundred trillion, dying, would not begin to have the same importance as a single human death.

Within the ranks of magnitude of all creatures, small as microbes or great as humans, there is an equality of "elan," just as the branches of a tall tree, gathered together, equal the bulk of the limbs below, and all the limbs equal the bulk of the trunk.

We believe this as firmly as the kings of France believed in their hierarchy. Which of our generations will come to disagree?

ANAPHASE

JUNE-SEPTEMBER

1

La Jolla, California

The rectangular slate-black sign stood on a low mound of bright green and clumpy Korean grass, surrounded by irises and sided by a dark cement-bedded brook filled with koi. Carved into the street side of the sign was the name GENETRON in Times Roman letters of insignia red, and beneath the name the motto, "Where Small Things Make Big Changes."

The Genetron labs and business offices were housed in a U-shaped, bare concrete Bauhaus structure surrounding a rectangular garden court. The main complex had two levels with open-air walkways. Beyond the courtyard and just behind an artificial hummock of earth, not yet filled in with new greenery, was a four-story black glass-sided cube fenced with electrified razor-wire.

These were the two sides of Genetron; the open labs, where biochip research was conducted, and the defense contracts building, where military applications were investigated.

Security was strict even in the open labs. All employees wore laser-printed badges and non-employee access to the labs was carefully monitored. The management of Genetron—five Stanford graduates who founded the company just three years out of school—realized that industrial espionage was even more likely than an intelligence breach in the black cube. Yet the outward atmosphere was serene, and every attempt was made to soft-pedal the security measures.

A tall, stoop-shouldered man with unruly black hair untangled himself from the interior of a red Volvo sports car and sneezed twice before crossing the employee parking lot. The grasses were tuning up for an early summer orgy of irritation. He casually greeted Walter, the middle-aged and whippet-wiry guard. Walter just as casually confirmed his badge by running it through the laser reader. "Not much sleep last night, Mr. Ulam?" Walter asked.

Vergil pursed his lips and shook his head. "Parties, Walter." His eyes were red and his nose was swollen from constant rubbing with the handkerchief that now resided, abused and submissive, in his pocket.

"How working men like you can party on a weeknight, I don't know."

"The ladies demand it, Walter," Vergil said, passing through. Walter grinned and nodded, though he sincerely doubted Vergil was getting much action, parties or no. Unless standards had severely declined since Walter's day, nobody with a week's growth of beard was getting much action.

Ulam was not the most prepossessing figure at Genetron. He stood six feet two inches on very large flat feet. He was twenty-five pounds overweight and at thirty-two years of age, his back hurt him, he had high blood pressure, and he could never shave close enough to eliminate an Emmett Kelly shadow.

His voice seemed designed not to win friends—harsh, slightly grating, tending toward loudness. Two decades in California had smoothed his Texas accent, but when he became excited or angry, the Panhandle asserted itself with an almost painful edge.

His sole distinction was an exquisite pair of emerald green eyes, wide and expressive, defended by a luxurious set of lashes. The eyes were more decorative than functional, however; they were covered by a large pair of black-framed glasses. Vergil was near-sighted.

He ascended the stairs two and three steps at a time, long powerful legs making the concrete and steel steps resound. On the second floor, he walked along the open corridor to the Advanced Biochip Division's joint equipment room, known as the share lab. His mornings usually began with a check on specimens in one of the five ultracentrifuges. His most recent batch had been rotating for sixty hours at 200,000 G's and was now ready for analysis.

For such a large man, Vergil had surprisingly delicate and sensitive hands. He removed an expensive black titanium rotor from the ultracentrifuge and slid shut the steel vacuum seal. Placing the rotor on a workbench, one by one he removed and squinted at the five squat glass tubes suspended in slings beneath its mushroom-like cap. Several well-defined beige layers had formed in each tube.

Vergil's heavy black eyebrows arched and drew together behind the thick rims of his glasses. He smiled, revealing teeth spotted brown from a childhood of drinking naturally fluoridated water.

He was about to suction off the buffer solution and the unwanted layers when the lab phone beeped. He placed the tube in a rack and picked up the receiver. "Share lab, Ulam here."

"Vergil, this is Rita. I saw you come in, but you weren't in your lab—"

"Home away from home, Rita. What's up?"

"You asked me—told me—to let you know if a certain gentleman arrived. I think he's here, Vergil."

"Michael Bernard?" Vergil asked, his voice rising.

"I think it's him. But Vergil—"

"I'll be right down."

"Vergil—"

He hung up and dithered for a moment over the tubes, then left them where they were.

Genetron's reception area was a circular extrusion from the ground floor on the east corner, surrounded by picture windows and liberally supplied with aspidistras in chrome ceramic pots. Morning light slanted white and dazzling across the sky-blue carpet as Vergil entered from the lab side. Rita stood up behind her desk as he passed by.

"Vergil—"

"Thanks," he said. His eyes were on the distinguished-looking gray-haired man standing by the single lobby couch. There was no doubt about it; Michael Bernard. Vergil recognized him from photos and the cover portrait *Time Magazine* had printed three years before. Vergil extended his hand and put on an enormous smile. "Pleased to meet you, Mr. Bernard."

Bernard shook Vergil's hand but appeared confused.

Gerald T. Harrison stood in the broad double door of Genetron's fancy for-show office, phone receiver gripped between ear and shoulder. Bernard looked to Harrison for an explanation.

"I'm very glad you got my message . . ." Vergil continued before Harrison's presence registered.

Harrison immediately made his farewells on the phone and slammed it on its cradle. "Rank hath its privileges, Vergil," he said, smiling too broadly and taking a stance beside Bernard.

"I'm sorry—what message?" Bernard asked.

"This is Vergil Ulam, one of our top researchers," Harrison said obsequiously. "We're all very pleased to have you visiting, Mr. Bernard. Vergil, I'll get back to you later about that matter you wanted to discuss."

He hadn't asked to talk to Harrison about anything. "Sure," Vergil said. He rankled under the old familiar feeling: being sidestepped, pushed aside.

Bernard didn't know him from Adam.

"Later, Vergil," Harrison said pointedly.

"Sure, of course." He backed away, glanced at Bernard pleadingly, then turned and shambled back through the rear door.

"Who was that?" Bernard asked.

"A very ambitious fellow," Harrison said darkly. "But we have him under control."

Harrison kept his work office in a ground floor space on the west end of the lab building. The room was surrounded by wooden shelves neatly filled with books. The eye-level shelf behind the desk held familiar black plastic ring-bound books from Cold Spring Harbor. Arranged below were a row of telephone directories—Harrison collected antique phone books—and several shelves of computer science volumes. His graph-ruled black desktop supported a leather-edged blotting pad and a VDT.

Of the Genetron founders, only Harrison and William Yng had stayed long enough to see the labs begin work. Both were more oriented toward business than research, though their doctorates hung on the wood panel wall.

Harrison leaned back in his chair, arms up and hands clasped behind his neck. Vergil noticed the merest hint of sweat stains in each armpit.

"Vergil, that was very embarrassing," he said. His white-blond hair was artfully arranged to disguise premature thinning.

"Sorry," Vergil said.

"No more than I. So you asked Mr. Bernard to visit our labs."

"Yes."

"Why?"

"I thought he would be interested in the work."

"We thought so, too. That's why *we* invited him. I don't believe he even knew about your invitation, Vergil."

"Apparently not."

"You went behind our backs."

Vergil stood before the desk, looking glumly at the back of the VDT.

"You've done a great deal of useful work for us. Rothwild says you're brilliant, maybe even invaluable." Rothwild was the biochips project supervisor. "But others say you can't be relied upon. And now . . . this."

"Bernard—"

"Not Mr. Bernard, Vergil. This." He swung the VDT around and pressed a button on the keyboard. Vergil's secret computer file scrolled up on the screen. His eyes widened and his throat constricted, but to his credit he didn't choke. His reaction was quite controlled. "I haven't read it completely, but it sounds like you're up to some very suspect things. Possibly unethical. We like to follow the guidelines here at Genetron, especially in light of our upcoming position in the marketplace. But not solely for that reason. I like to believe we run an ethical company here."

"I'm not doing anything unethical, Gerald."

"Oh?" Harrison stopped the scrolling. "You're designing new complements of DNA for several NIH-regulated microorganisms. And you're working on mammalian cells. We don't do work here on mammalian cells. We aren't equipped for the biohazards—not in the main labs. But I suppose you could demonstrate to me the safety and innocuous nature of your research. You're not creating a new plague to sell to Third World revolutionaries, are you?"

"No," Vergil said flatly.

"Good. Some of this material is beyond my understanding. It sounds like you might be trying to expand on our MABs project. There could be valuable stuff here." He paused. "What in hell *are* you doing, Vergil?"

Vergil removed his glasses and wiped them with the placket of his lab coat. Abruptly, he sneezed—loud and wet.

Harrison looked faintly disgusted. "We only broke the code yesterday. By accident, almost. Why did you hide it? Is it something you'd rather we didn't know?"

Without his glasses, Vergil looked owlish and helpless. He began to stammer an answer, then stopped and thrust his jaw forward. His thick black brows knit in painful puzzlement.

"It looks to me like you've been doing some work on our gene machine. Unauthorized, of course, but you've never been much for authority."

Vergil's face was now deep red.

"Are you all right?" Harrison asked. He was deriving a perverse pleasure from making Vergil squirm. A grin threatened to break through Harrison's querying expression.

"I'm fine," Vergil said. "I was . . . am . . . working on biologics."

"Biologics? I'm not familiar with the term."

"A side branch of the biochips. Autonomous organic computer." The thought of saying anything more was agony. He had written Bernard—without result, apparently—to have him come see the work. He did not want to hand all of it over to Genetron under the provisions of the work-for-hire clause in his contract. It was such a simple idea, even if the work had taken two years— two secret and laborious years.

"I'm intrigued." Harrison turned the VDT around and scrolled through the file. "We're not just talking proteins and amino acids. You're messing with chromosomes here. Recombining mammalian genes; even, I see, mixing in viral and bacterial genes." The light went out of his eyes. They became rocky gray. "You could get Genetron shut down right now, this minute, Vergil. We don't have the safeguards for this kind of stuff. You're not even working under P-3 conditions."

"I'm not messing with reproductive genes."

"There's some other kind?" Harrison sat forward abruptly, angry that Vergil would try to bullshit him.

"Introns. Strings that don't code for protein structure."

"What about them?"

"I'm only working in those areas. And . . . adding more non-reproductive genetic material."

"That sounds like a contradiction in terms to me, Vergil. We have no proof introns don't code for something."

"Yes, but—"

"But—" Harrison held up his hand. "This is all quite irrelevant. Whatever else you were up to, the fact is, you were prepared to renege on your contract, go behind our backs to Bernard, and try to engage his support for a personal endeavor. True?"

Vergil said nothing.

"I assume you're not a sophisticated fellow, Vergil. Not in the ways of the business world. Perhaps you didn't realize the implications."

Vergil swallowed hard. His face was still plum red. He could feel the blood thudding in his ears, the sick sensation of stress-caused dizziness. He sneezed twice.

"Well, I'll lay the implications out for you. You are very close to getting your ass canned and sold for bully beef."

Vergil raised his eyebrows reflexively.

"You're important to the MABs project. If you weren't you would be out of here in a flash and I would personally make sure you never work in a private lab again. But Thornton and Rothwild and the others believe we might be able to redeem you. Yes, Vergil. Redeem you. Save you from yourself. I haven't consulted with Yng on this. It won't go any further—if you behave."

He fixed Vergil with a stare from beneath lowered eyebrows. "Stop your extracurricular activities. We'll keep your file here, but I want all non-MABs experiments terminated and all organisms that have been tampered with destroyed. I'll personally inspect your lab in two hours. If this hasn't been done, you'll be fired. Two hours, Vergil. No exceptions, no extensions."

"Yessir."

"That's all."

2

Vergil's dismissal would not have unduly distressed his fellow employees. In his three years at Genetron, he had committed innumerable breaches of lab etiquette. He seldom washed lab glassware and twice had been accused of not wiping up spills of ethidium bromide—a strong mutagen—on lab counters. He was also not terribly cautious about radionucleides.

Most of the people he worked with made no show of humility. They were, after all, top young researchers in a very promising field; many expected to be wealthy and in charge of their own companies in a few years. Vergil didn't fit any of their patterns, however. He worked quietly and intensively during the day, and then worked overtime at night. He was not sociable, though neither was he unfriendly; he simply ignored most people.

He shared a lab space with Hazel Overton, as meticulous and clean a researcher as could be imagined. Hazel would miss him least of all. Perhaps it was Hazel who had penetrated his file—she was no slouch on the computers and she might have gone looking for something to get him into trouble. But he had no evidence for that, and there was no sense being paranoid.

The lab was dark as Vergil entered. Hazel was performing a fluorescent scan on a gel electrophoresis matrix with a small UV lamp. Vergil switched on the light. She looked up and removed her goggles, prepared to be irritated.

"You're late," she said. "And your lab looks like an unmade bed. Vergil, it's—"

"Kaput," Vergil finished for her, throwing his smock across a stool.

"You left a bunch of test tubes on the counter in the share lab. I'm afraid they're ruined."

"Fuck 'em."

Hazel's eyes widened. "My, aren't you in a mood."

"I've been shut down. I have to clear out all my extracurricular work, give it up, or Harrison will issue my walking papers."

"That's rather even-handed of them," Hazel said, returning to her scan. Harrison had shut down one of her own extracurricular projects the month before. "What did you do?"

"If it's all the same to you, I'd rather be alone." Vergil glowered at her from across the counter. "You can finish that in the share lab."

"I could, but—"

"If you don't," Vergil said darkly, "I'll smear your little piece of agarose across the floor with my wingtips."

Hazel glared at him for a moment and surmised he wasn't kidding. She shut off the electrodes, picked up her equipment, and headed for the door. "My condolences," she said.

"Sure."

He had to have a plan. Scratching his stubbly chin, he tried to think of some way to cut his losses. He could sacrifice those parts of the experiment that were expendable—the *E. coli* cultures, for example. He had long since gone beyond them. He had kept them as memorials to his progress, and as a kind of reserve in case work had not gone well in the next steps. The work had gone well, however. It was not complete, but it was so close that he could taste success like a cool, clean swallow of wine.

Hazel's side of the lab was neat and tidy. His was a chaos of equipment and containers of chemicals. One of his few concessions to lab safety, a white absorbent mat to catch spills, hung half-off the black counter, one corner pinned by a jar of detergent.

Vergil stood before the white idea board, rubbing his stubbly beard, and stared at the cryptic messages he had scrawled there the day before.

Little engineers. Make the world's tiniest machines. Better than MABs! Little surgeons. War with tumors. Computers with hu-capac. (Computers = *spec tumor* HA!) size of volvox.

Clearly the ravings of a madman, and Hazel would have paid them no attention. Or would she? It was common practice to scribble any wild idea or inspiration or joke on the boards and just be prepared to have it erased by the next hurried genius. Still . . .

The notes could have aroused the curiosity of someone as smart as Hazel. Especially since his work on the MABs had been delayed.

Obviously, he had not been circumspect.

MABs—Medically Applicable Biochips—were to be the first

practical product of the biochip revolution, the incorporation of protein molecular circuitry with silicon electronics. Biochips had been an area of speculation in the literature for years, but Genetron hoped to have the first working samples available for FDA testing and approval within three months.

They faced intense competition. In what was coming to be known as Enzyme Valley—the biochip equivalent of Silicon Valley—at least six companies had set up facilities in and around La Jolla. Some had started out as pharmaceutical manufacturers hoping to cash in on the products of recombinant DNA research. Nudged out of that area by older and more experienced concerns, they had switched to biochip research. Genetron was the first firm established specifically with biochips in mind.

Vergil picked up an eraser and rubbed out the notes slowly. Throughout his life, things had always conspired to frustrate him. Often, he brought disaster on himself—he was honest enough to admit that. But not once had he ever been able to carry something through to completion. Not in his work, not in his private life.

He had never been good at gauging the consequences of his actions.

He removed four thick spiral-bound notebooks from his locked desk drawer and added them to the growing pile of material to be smuggled out of the lab.

He could not destroy *all* the evidence. He had to save the white blood cell cultures—his special lymphocytes. But where could he keep them—what could he do outside the lab?

Nothing. There was no place he could go. Genetron had all the equipment he needed, and it would take months to establish another lab. During that time, all his work would literally disintegrate.

Vergil passed through the lab's rear door into the interior hall and walked past an emergency shower stall. The incubators were kept in a separate room beyond the share lab. Seven refrigerator-sized gray enameled chests stood along one wall, electronic monitors silently and efficiently keeping track of temperatures and CO_2 partial pressure in each unit. In the far corner, amid older incubators of all shapes and sizes (gleaned from lab bankruptcy sales), stood a buffed stainless steel and white enamel Forma Scientific model with his name and "Sole Use" scribbled on a piece of surgical tape affixed to the door. He opened the door and removed a rack of culture dishes.

Bacteria in each dish had developed uncharacteristic colonies— blobs of orange and green which resembled aerial maps of Paris or Washington D.C. Lines radiated from clusters and divided the colonies into sections, each section having its own peculiar texture and—so Vergil surmised—function. Since each bacterium in the cultures had the potential intellectual capacity of a mouse, it was quite possible the cultures had turned into simple societies and the societies had developed functional divisions. He hadn't been keeping track lately, involved as he had been with altered B-cell lymphocytes.

They were like his children, all of them. And they had turned out to be exceptional.

He felt a rush of guilt and nausea as he turned on a gas burner and applied each dish of altered *E. coli* to the flame with a pair of tongs.

He returned to his lab and dropped the culture dishes into a sterilizing bath. That was the limit. He could not destroy anything more. He felt a hatred for Harrison that went beyond any emotion he had ever felt toward another human being. Tears of frustration blurred his vision.

Vergil opened the lab Kelvinator and removed a spinner bottle and a white plastic pallet containing twenty-two test tubes. The spinner bottle was filled with a straw-colored fluid, lymphocytes in a serum medium. He had constructed a custom impellor to stir the medium more effectively, with less cell damage—a rod with several half-helical teflon "sails."

The test tubes contained saline solution and special concentrated serum nutrients to support the cells while they were examined under a microscope.

He drew fluid from the spinner bottle and carefully added several drops to four of the tubes on the pallet. He then placed the bottle back on its base. The impellor resumed spinning.

After warming to room temperature—a process he usually aided with a small fan to gently blow warmed air over the pallet—the lymphocytes in the tubes would become active, resuming their development after being subdued by the refrigerator's chill.

They would continue learning, adding new segments to the revised portions of their DNA. And when, in the normal course of cell growth, the new DNA was transcribed to RNA, and the RNA served as a template for production of amino acids, and the amino acids were converted to proteins . . .

The proteins would be more than just units of cell structure; other cells would be able to read them. Or RNA itself would be extruded to be absorbed and read by other cells. Or—and this third option had presented itself after Vergil inserted fragments of bacterial DNA into the mammalian chromosomes—segments of DNA itself could be removed and passed along.

Every time he thought of it, his head whirled with possibilities, thousands of ways for the cells to communicate with each other and develop their intellects.

The idea of an intellectual cell was still wonderfully strange to him. It made him stop and stand, staring at the wall, until he jerked back to attention and continued his work.

He pulled up a microscope and inserted a pipetman into one of the tubes. The calibrated instrument drew up the dialed amount of fluid and he expelled it into a thin circular ring on a glass slide.

From the very beginning, Vergil had known his ideas were neither far-out nor useless. His first three months at Genetron, helping establish the silicon-protein interface for the biochips, had convinced him the project designers had missed something very obvious and extremely interesting.

Why limit oneself to silicon and protein and biochips a hundredth of a millimeter wide, when in almost every living cell there was already a functioning computer with a huge memory? A mammalian cell had a DNA complement of several billion base pairs, each acting as a piece of information. What was reproduction, after all, but a computerized biological process of enormous complexity and reliability?

Genetron had not yet made the connection, and Vergil had long ago decided he didn't want them to. He would do his work, prove his point by creating billions of capable cellular computers, and then leave Genetron and establish his own lab, his own company.

After a year and a half of preparation and study, he had begun working at night on the gene machine. Using a computer keyboard, he constructed strings of bases to form codons, each of which became the foundation of a rough DNA-RNA-protein logic.

The earliest biologic strings had been inserted into *E. coli* bacteria as circular plasmids. The *E. coli* had absorbed the plasmids and incorporated them into their original DNA. The bacteria had then duplicated and released the plasmids, passing on the biologic to other cells. In the most crucial phase of his work, Vergil had used viral reverse-transcriptase to fix the feedback loop between RNA and DNA. Even the earliest and most primitive biologic-equipped bacteria had employed ribosomes as "encoders" and "readers" and RNA as "tape." With the loop in place, the cells developed their own memory and the ability to process and act upon environmental information.

The real surprise had come when he tested his altered microbes.

The computing capacity of even bacterial DNA was enormous compared to man-made electronics. All Vergil had to do was take advantage of what was already there—just give it a nudge, as it were.

More than once, he had the spooky feeling that his work was too easy, that he was less a creator and more a servant . . . This, after having the molecules seem to fall into their proper place, or fail in such a way that he clearly saw his errors and knew how to correct them.

The spookiest moment of all came when he realized he was doing more than creating little computers. Once he started the process and switched on the genetic sequences which could compound and duplicate the biologic DNA segments, the cells began to function as autonomous units. They began to "think" for themselves and develop more complex "brains."

His first *E. coli* mutations had had the learning capacity of planarian worms; he had run them through simple T-mazes, giving sugar rewards. They had soon outperformed planaria. The bacteria—lowly prokaryotes—were doing better than multicellular eukaryotes! And within months, he had them running more complex mazes at rates—allowing for scale adjustments—comparable to those of mice.

Removing the finest biologic sequences from the altered *E. coli*, he had incorporated them into B-lymphocytes, white cells from his own blood. He had replaced many intron strings—self-replicating sequences of base pairs that apparently did not code for proteins and that comprised a surprising percentage of any eukaryotic cell's DNA—with his own special chains. Using artificial proteins and hormones as a method of communication, Vergil had "trained" the lymphocytes in the past six months to interact as much as possible with each other and with their environment—a much more complex miniature glass maze. The results had been far better than he expected.

The lymphocytes had learned to run the maze and obtain their nutritional rewards with incredible speed.

He waited for the sample to warm up enough to be active, then inserted the eyepiece into a video pickup and switched on the first of four display screens mounted in the rack over the counter. There, very clearly, were the roughly circular lymphocytes in which he had invested two years of his life.

They were busily transferring genetic material to each other through long, straw-shaped tubes rather like bacterial pili. Some of the characteristics picked up during the *E. coli* experiments had stayed with the lymphocytes, just how he wasn't yet sure. The mature lymphocytes were not reproducing by themselves, but they were busily engaged in an orgy of genetic exchange.

Every lymphocyte in the sample he was watching had the potential intellectual capacity of a rhesus monkey. From the simplicity of their activity, that certainly wasn't obvious; but then, they'd had it pretty easy throughout their lives.

He had talked to them on as high a level of chemical training and had built them up as far as he was going to. Their brief lives were over—he had been ordered to kill them. That would be simple enough. He could add detergent to the containers and their cell membranes would dissolve. They would be sacrificed to the caution and shortsightedness of a group of certifiable flatworm management-types.

His breath grew ragged as he watched the lymphocytes going about their business.

They were beautiful. They were his children, drawn from his own blood, carefully nurtured, operated upon; he had personally injected the biologic material into at least a thousand of them. And now they were busily transforming all their companions, and so on, and so on . . .

Like Washoe the chimp teaching her child to speak in American Sign Language. They were passing on the torch of potential intelligence. How would he ever know if they could use all their potential?

Pasteur.

"Pasteur," he said out loud. "Jenner."

Vergil carefully prepared a syringe. Brows knitted together, he pushed the cannule through the cotton cap of the first tube and dipped it into the solution. He pulled back the plunger. The pastel fluid filled the barrel; five, ten, fifteen cc's.

He held the syringe before his eyes for several minutes, knowing he was contemplating something rash. *Until now,* he addressed his creations mentally, *you've had it real easy. Life of Riley. Sit in your serum and fart around and absorb all the hormones you need. Don't even have to work for a living. No severe test, no stress. No need to use what I gave you.*

So what was he going to do? Put them to work in their natural environment? By injecting them into his body, he could smuggle them out of Genetron, and recover enough of them later to start the experiment again.

"Hey, Vergil!" Ernesto Villar knocked on the doorframe and poked his head in. "We've got the rat artery movie. We're having a meeting in 233." He tapped his fingers on the frame and smiled brightly. "You're invited. We need our resident kluger."

Vergil lowered the syringe and looked off into nothing.

"Vergil?"

"I'll be there," he said tonelessly.

"Don't get all excited," Villar said peevishly. "We won't hold the premiere for long." He ducked out of the door. Vergil listened to his footsteps receding down the hall.

Rash, indeed. He reinserted the cannule through the cotton, squirted the serum back into the tube and dropped the syringe into a jar of alcohol. He replaced the tube in the rack and returned it to the Kelvinator. Before now, the spinner bottle and pallet of tubes had had no label but his name. He removed his name from the pallet and replaced it with, "Biochip protein samples; lab failures 21–32." On the spinner bottle he placed a label reading, "Rat anti-goat lab failures 13–14." No one would mess with an anonymous and unanalyzed group of lab failures. Failures were sacred.

He needed time to think.

Rothwild and ten of the key scientists on the MABs project had gathered around a large-screen projection TV in 233, an empty lab currently being used as a meeting room. Rothwild was a dapper red-haired fellow who acted as a controller and mediator between management and researchers. He stood beside the screen, resplendent in a cream-colored jacket and chocolate brown pants. Villar offered Vergil an avocado-green plastic chair and he sat at the rear of the room, legs crossed, hands behind his head.

Rothwild delivered the introduction. "This is the breakdown from Team Product E-64. You all contributed—" He glanced uncertainly at Vergil. "And now you can all share in the . . . uh, the triumph. I think we can safely call it that.

"E-64 is a prototype investigatory biochip, three hundred micrometers in diameter, protein on a silicon substrate, sensitive to forty-seven different blood fraction variables." He cleared his throat. They all knew that, but this was an occasion. "On May 10th, we inserted E-64 into a rat artery, closed the very small incision, and let it pass through the artery as far as it would go. The journey lasted five seconds. The rat was then sacrificed and the biochip recovered. Since that time, Terence's group has 'debriefed' the biochip and interpreted the results. By putting the results through a special vector imaging program, we've been able to produce a little movie."

He gestured to Ernesto, who pressed a button on the projector's video recorder. Computer graphics flashed by—Genetron's animated logo, stylized signatures from the imaging team, and then darkness. Ernesto switched off the room lights.

A pink circle appeared on the screen, expanded, and distorted into an irregular oval. More circles appeared within the first. "We've slowed the journey down six times," Rothwild explained. "And to simplify things, we've eliminated the readouts on chemical concentrations in the rat blood."

Vergil leaned forward in his chair, troubles momentarily forgotten. Streamers appeared and shot through the fluctuating tunnel of concentric circles.

"Blood flow through the artery," Ernesto chimed in.

The journey down the rat artery lasted thirty seconds. Vergil's arm-hair prickled. If his lymphocytes could see, this was what they would experience, traveling down a blood vessel . . . A long irregular tunnel, blood smoothly coursing, getting caught in little eddies, the artery constricting—smaller and smaller circles, jerks and nudges as the biochip bounced against the walls—and finally, the end of the journey, as the biochip wedged into a capillary.

The sequence ended with a flash of white.

The room filled with cheers.

"Now," Rothwild said, smiling and raising his hand to return order. "Any comments, before we show this to Harrison and Yng?"

Vergil bowed out of the celebration after one glass of champagne and returned to his lab, feeling more depressed than ever. Where was his spirit of cooperation? Did he actually believe he could tackle something as ambitious as his lymphocytes, all by himself? So far, he had—but at the expense of having the experiment discontinued, perhaps even destroyed.

He slid the notebooks into a cardboard box and sealed the box with tape. On Hazel's side of the lab, he found a masking tape label on a dewar jar—"Overton, do not remove"—and peeled it off. He applied the label to his box and put the box in a neutral territory beside the sink. He then set about washing the glassware and tidying his side of the lab.

When the time came for an inspection, he would be the meek supplicant; he would give Harrison the satisfaction of victory.

And then, surreptitiously—over the next couple of weeks—he would smuggle out the materials he needed. The lymphocytes would be removed last; they could be kept for some time at his apartment, in the refrigerator. He could steal supplies to keep them viable, but he wouldn't be able to do any more work on them.

He would decide later how he could best continue his experiment.

Harrison stood in the lab door.

"All clear," Vergil said, properly repentant.

3

They watched him closely for the next week; then, concerned with the final stages of MABs prototype testing, they called off their watchdogs. His behavior had been beyond reproach.

Now he set about the last steps in his voluntary departure from Genetron.

Vergil hadn't been the only one to step beyond the bounds of Genetron's ideological largesse. Management, again in the person of Gerald T. Harrison, had come down on Hazel just last month. Hazel had gone off on a sidetrack with her *E. coli* cultures, trying to prove that sex had originated as a result of the invasion of an autonomous DNA sequence—a chemical parasite called the F-factor—in early prokaryotic life forms. She had postulated that sex was not evolutionarily useful—at least not to women, who could, in theory, breed parthenogenetically—and that ultimately men were superfluous.

She had gathered enough evidence for Vergil, peeping into her notebooks, to agree with her conclusions. But Hazel's work did not meet the Genetron standards. It was revolutionary, socially controversial. Harrison had given the word; she had stopped that particular branch of research.

Genetron did not want publicity or even a tinge of controversy. Not yet. It needed a spotless reputation when it made its stock public and announced it was manufacturing functional MABs.

They had not been concerned with Hazel's papers, however. They had allowed her to keep them. That Harrison had retained his file bothered Vergil.

When he was certain their guard was down, he went into action. He requested access to the company computers (he had been put off restriction indefinitely); quite properly, he said he needed to check his figures on structures of denatured and unfolded proteins. Permission was granted, and he logged onto the system in the share lab one evening after eight.

Vergil had grown up a little too early to be classified as an eighties whizkid, but in the last seven years he had revised his credit records at three major firms and made an entry into the records of a famous university. That entry had practically guaranteed his getting the Genetron position. Vergil had never felt guilty about these intrusions and manipulations.

His credit was never going to be as bad as it had once been, and there was no sense in being punished for past indiscretions. He knew he was fully capable of doing Genetron's work—his fake university records were just a show for personnel directors who needed lights and music. Besides, Vergil had believed—until the past couple of weeks—that the world was his personal puzzle, and that any riddlings and unravelings he could perform, including computer hacking, were simply part of his nature.

He found it ridiculously easy to break the Rinaldi code used to conceal Genetron's confidential files. There were no mysteries for him in the Godel numbers and strings of seemingly random digits that came up on the screen. He slid into the numbers and information like a seal into water.

He found his file and switched a key equation for the code in that section only. Then he decided to play it safer—there was always the possibility, however remote, of someone being just as ingenious as he was. He deleted the file completely.

Next on his agenda was locating the medical records for Genetron employees. He altered his insurance designation and hid the alteration. Queries from outside sources would find him fully covered even after his termination, and there would never be any question about his not paying premiums.

He worried about such things. His health was never completely satisfactory.

He thought for a moment about other mischief that could be worked, and decided against it. He was not vindictive. He shut the terminal off and unplugged it.

Surprisingly little time—two days—passed before the deletion was noticed. Rothwild confronted him in the hall early one morning and told him his lab was off limits. Vergil protested mildly that he had a box of personal belongings he wanted to take with him.

"Fine, but that's it. No biologicals. I want to inspect everything."

Vergil calmly agreed. "What's wrong now?" he asked.

"Frankly, I don't know," Rothwild said. "And I don't care to know. I vouched for you. So did Thornton. You're a great disappointment to us all."

Vergil's mind raced. He had never removed the lymphocytes; they had seemed safe enough disguised in the lab refrigerator, and he had never expected the boom to be lowered so quickly. "I'm out?"

"You're out. And I'm afraid you're going to find it hard getting employment in any other private lab. Harrison is furious."

Hazel was already at work when they entered the lab. Vergil picked up the box in the neutral zone beneath the sink, covering the label with his hand. He hefted it and surreptitiously removed the tape, balling it up and dropping it into the trash basket. "One more thing," he said. "I have some lab failures laced with tracer that should be disposed of. Properly. Radionucleides."

"Oh, shit," Hazel said. "Where?"

"In the fridge. Not to worry—just carbon 14. May I?" He looked at Rothwild. Rothwild gestured for the box to be put on a counter so he could inspect it. "May I?" Vergil repeated. "I don't want to leave anything around that could be harmful."

Rothwild nodded reluctantly. Vergil went to the Kelvinator, dropping his lab coat on the counter. His hand brushed over a box of hypodermics, palming one.

The lymphocyte pallet was on the bottom shelf. Vergil kneeled and removed a tube. He quickly inserted the syringe and drew up twenty cc's of the serum. The syringe had never been used before and the cannule should therefore be reasonably sterile; he had no time for an alcohol swab, but he had to take that risk.

Before he inserted the needle under his skin, he wondered briefly what he was doing, and what he thought he could gain. There was very little chance the lymphocytes would survive. It was possible that his tampering had changed them sufficiently for them to either die in his bloodstream, unable to adapt, or do something uncharacteristic and be destroyed by his own immune system.

Either way, the lifespan of an active lymphocyte in the human body was a matter of weeks. Life was hard for the body's cops.

The needle went in. He felt a dull prick, a brief sting, and the cold fluid mixing with his blood. He withdrew the needle and lay the syringe in the bottom of the refrigerator. Pallet of tubes and spinner bottle in hand, he stood and shut the door. Rothwild watched nervously as Vergil put on rubber gloves and one by one poured the contents of the tubes into a beaker half-filled with ethanol. He then added the fluid in the spinner bottle. With a small grin, Vergil stoppered the beaker and sloshed its contents, then placed it into a protected waste box. He slid the box across the floor with his foot. "It's all yours," he said.

Rothwild had finished turning through the notebooks. "I'm not sure these shouldn't remain in our possession," he said. "You spent a lot of our time working on them."

Vergil's idiot grin didn't change. "I'll sue Genetron and spread dirt in every journal I can think of. Not good for your upcoming position in the market, no?"

Rothwild regarded him with half-lidded eyes, his neck and cheeks pinking slightly. "Get out of here," he said. "We'll send the rest of your stuff later."

Vergil picked up the box. The cold feeling in his forearm had passed now. Rothwild escorted him down the stairs and across the sidewalk to the gate. Walter accepted the badge, his face rigid, and Rothwild followed Vergil to the parking lot.

"Remember your contract," Rothwild said. "Just remember what you can and cannot say."

"I am allowed to say one thing, I believe," Vergil said, struggling to keep his words clear through his anger.

"What's that?" Rothwild asked.

"Fuck you. All of you."

Vergil drove by the Genetron sign and thought of all that had happened within those austere walls. He looked at the black cube beyond, barely visible through a copse of eucalyptus trees.

More than likely, the experiment was over. For a moment, he felt ill with tension and disgust. And then he thought of the billions of lymphocytes he had just destroyed. His nausea increased and he had to swallow hard to keep the taste of acid out of his throat.

"Fuck you," he murmured, "because everything I touch is fucked."

4

Humans were a randy bunch, Vergil decided as he perched on a stool and watched the cattle call. Mellow space music powered the slow, graceful gyrations on the dance floor and flashing amber lights emphasized the pulse of packed bodies, male and female. Over the bar, an amazing array of polished brass tubing hummed and spluttered delivering drinks—mostly vintage wines by the glass—and forty-seven different kinds of coffees. Coffee sales were up; the evening had blurred into early morning and soon Weary's would be turning off and shutting down.

The last-ditch efforts of the cattle call were becoming more obvious. Moves were being made with more desperation, less finesse; beside Vergil, a short fellow in a rumpled blue suit was plighting his one-night troth to a willowy black-haired girl with Asiatic features. Vergil felt aloof from it all. He hadn't made a move all evening, and he had been in Weary's since seven. No one had made a move on him, either.

He was not prize material. He shambled a bit when he walked— not that he had left the stool for any purpose but to go to the crowded restroom. He had spent so much time in labs the past few years that his skin was the unpopular shade of Snow White. He didn't look enthusiastic, and he wasn't willing to expend any amount of bullshit to attract attention.

Mercifully, the air conditioning in Weary's was good enough that his hay fever had subsided.

Mostly, he had spent the evening observing the incredible variety—and underlying sameness—of the tactics the male animal used on the female. He felt out of it, suspended in an objective and slightly lonely sphere he wasn't inclined to reach beyond. So why, he asked himself, had he come to Weary's in the first place? Why did he ever go there? He had never picked up a woman at Weary's—or any other singles bar—in his life.

"Hello."

Vergil jumped and turned, eyes wide.

"Excuse me. I didn't mean to startle you."

He shook his head. She was perhaps twenty-eight, golden-blonde, slender to the edge of skinny, with a pretty but not gorgeous face. Her eyes, large and clear and brown, were her best feature—except possibly for her legs, he amended, looking down on instinct.

"You don't come in here often," she said. She glanced back over her shoulder. "Or do you? I mean, I don't either. Maybe I wouldn't know."

He shook his head. "Not often. No need. My success rate hasn't been spectacular."

She turned back with a smile. "I know more about you than you think," she said. "I don't even need to read your palm. You're smart, first off."

"Yeah?" he said, feeling awkward.

"You're good with your hands." She touched his thumb where it rested on his knee. "You have very pretty hands. You could do a lot with hands like that. But they're not greasy, so you're not a mechanic. And you try to dress well, but . . ." She giggled a three-drink giggle and put her hand over her mouth. "I'm sorry. You do try."

He looked down at his black and green checked cotton shirt and black pants. The clothes were new. What could she complain about? Maybe she didn't like the Topsiders he was wearing. They were a little scuffed.

"You work . . . let's see." She paused, stroking her cheek. Her fingernails were masterpieces of the manicurist's art, thick and long and shiny bronze. "You're a techie."

"Pardon?"

"You work in one of the labs around here. Hair's too long to be Navy, and they don't come here much anyway. Not that I'd know. You work in a lab and you're . . . you're not happy. Why's that?"

"Because—" He stopped. Confessing he was out of a job might not be stategic. He had six months' unemployment coming; that and his savings could disguise his lack of gainful labor for a while. "How do you know I'm a techie?"

"I can tell. Your shirt pocket—" She slipped her finger into it and tugged gently. "Looks like it should hold a nerd pack of pencils. The kind you twist and the lead pokes out." She smiled deliciously and thrust the pink tip of her tongue out to demonstrate.

"Yeah?"

"Yeah. And you're wearing argyles. Only techies wear argyles now."

"I like 'em," Vergil said defensively.

"Oh, so do I. What I'm getting at is, I've never known a techie. I mean . . . intimately."

Oh Lord, Vergil thought. "What do you do?" he asked, immediately wishing he could suck the words back.

"And I'd like to, if you don't think that's being too forward," she said, ignoring his question. "Look, the bar's closing in a few minutes. I don't need any more to drink, and I don't much like the music. Do you?"

Her name was Candice Rhine. What she did was accept advertising for the *La Jolla Light*. She approved of his Volvo sportscar and she approved of his living quarters, a two-bedroom second-floor condominium four blocks from the beach in La Jolla. He had purchased it at a bargain price six years ago—just out of medical school—from a USCD professor who had departed to Ecuador shortly after to complete a study on South American Indians.

Candice entered the apartment as if she had lived there for years. She draped her suede jacket on the couch and her blouse on the dining table. Her bra she hung with a giggle on the chrome and glass light fixture over the table. Her breasts were small, amplified by a very narrow rib cage.

Vergil watched all this with awe.

"Come on, techie," Candice said, standing naked at the bedroom door. "I like the furs." He had a baby alpaca rug over his California king-sized bed. She posed with her finger tips delicately pressed near the top of the door jamb, one knee cocked wide, then rotated on one heel and sauntered into the darkness.

Vergil stood his ground until she turned the bedroom lamp on. "I knew it!" she squealed. "Look at all the books!"

In the darkness, Vergil thought all too clearly of the perils of sex. Candice slept soundly beside him, the sleep of three drinks and making love four times.

Four times.

He had never done so well. She had murmured, before sleep, that chemists did it in their tubes and doctors did it with patience, but only a techie would do it in geometric progression.

As for the perils . . . He had seen many times—most often in textbooks—the results of promiscuity in a well- and frequently-traveled world. If Candice was promiscuous (and Vergil couldn't help but believe only a promiscuous girl would be so forward with him) then there was no telling what sort of microorganisms were now setting up shop in his blood.

Still, he had to smile.

Four times.

Candice groaned in her sleep and Vergil jerked, startled. He would not sleep well, he knew that much. He wasn't used to having someone in his bed.

Four.

His brown-speckled teeth gleamed in the dark.

Candice was much less forward in the morning. She solemnly insisted on making breakfast. He had eggs and Beefstrips in his antique round-cornered refrigerator and she did an expert job on them, as if she had once been a short-order cook—or was that simply the way women did things? He had never caught the knack of frying eggs. They always came out with broken yokes and crackling seared edges.

She regarded him with her wide brown eyes from across the table. He was hungry and ate quickly. Not much on delicacy and manners, he thought. So what? What more could she expect from him—or he from her?

"I don't usually stay the night, you know," she said. "I call a lot of cabs at four in the morning when the guy's asleep. But you kept me busy until five and I just ... didn't want to. You wore me out."

He nodded and wiped up the last perfection of semisolid yoke with the last bite of toast. He didn't particularly care to know how many men she had been to bed with. Quite a few, by the sound of things.

Vergil had had three conquests in his entire life, only one moderately satisfactory. The first at seventeen—an incredible stroke of luck—and the third a year ago. The third had been the satisfactory one and had hurt him. That was the occasion that had forced him to accept his status as a hell of a mind but not much for looks.

"That sounds horrible, doesn't it?" she asked. "I mean, about the cabs and everything." She kept staring at him. "You made me come six times," she said.

"Good."

"How old are you?"

"Thirty-two," he said.

"You act like a teenager—in bed, I mean. Stamina."

He hadn't done nearly so well as a teenager.

"Did you enjoy it?"

He put his fork down and looked up, musing. He had enjoyed it too much. When would the next time be? "Yes, I did."

"You know why I picked you out of the crowd?" She had barely touched her single egg, and now chewed the end from her lone Beefstrip. Throughout the night, her nails had emerged unmarred. At least she hadn't scratched him. Would he have liked that?

"No," he said.

"Because I knew you were a techie. I've never screwed—I mean, made love with a techie before. Vergil. That's right, isn't it? Vergil Ian Ull-am."

"Oo-lam," he corrected.

"I would have started sooner if I'd known," she said. She smiled. Her teeth were white and even, if a touch large. Her imperfections endeared her to him even more.

"Thank you. I can't speak . . . or whatever for all of us. Them. Techies. Whoever."

"Well, I think you're very sweet," she said. The smile faded, replaced by serious speculation. "More than sweet. Honest to God, Vergil. You're the best fuck I ever had. Do you have to go to work today?"

"No," he said. "I work my own hours."

"Good. Done with your breakfast?"

Three more before noon. He couldn't believe it.

Candice was sore when she left. "I feel like I've just trained a year for the pentathlon," she said as she stood at the door, coat in hand. "Do you want me to come back tonight? I mean, to visit?" She looked anxious. "I couldn't make love any more. I think you've brought on my period early."

"Please," he said, reaching for her hand. "That would be nice." They shook hands rather formally and Candice walked out into the spring sunshine. Vergil stood at the door for a while, alternately smiling and shaking his head in disbelief.

5

Vergil's taste in food began to change a week into his relationship with Candice. Until then, he had stubbornly pursued sweets and starches, fatty meats and bread and butter. His favorite food was a garbage pizza; there was a parlor nearby that cheerfully loaded pineapple and prosciutto on top of the anchovies and olives.

Candice suggested he cut down his intake of grease and fat—she called it "that oily shit"—and increase his greens and grains. His body seemed to agree.

The amount of food he ate also declined. He reached satiety faster. His waistline diminished perceptibly. He felt restless around the apartment.

Along with his changing tastebuds came a change in his attitude toward love. Nothing unexpected there; Vergil was savvy enough about psychology to realize that all he really needed was a fulfilling relationship to correct his nervous misogyny. Candice provided that.

Some nights he spent exercising. His feet didn't hurt quite so much. Everything was turning around. The world was a better place. His back pains gradually faded, even from memory. They were not missed.

Vergil attributed much of this to Candice, just as adolescent rumor attributed the improvement of bad skin conditions to the loss of virginity.

Occasionally the relationship became stormy. Candice found him insufferable when he tried to explain his work. He approached the topic with barely concealed anger and seldom bothered to simplify technicalities. He almost confessed about injecting himself with the lymphocytes but stopped when it became obvious she was already thoroughly bored. "Just let me know when you find a cheap cure for herpes," she said. "We can make a bundle from the Christian Action League just to keep it off the market."

While he no longer worried about venereal disease—Candice had been up front about that and convinced him she was clean—he did break out in a rash one evening, a peculiar and irritating

31

series of white bumps across his stomach. They went away by morning and did not return.

Vergil lay in bed with the smooth white-sheeted form breathing softly next to him, fanny like a snow-covered hill, back unveiled as if she wore a seductive low-cut evening gown. They had finished making love three hours ago and he was still awake, thinking that he had made love to Candice more times in the past two weeks than he had with all other women in his life.

This caught his fancy. He had always been interested in statistics. In an experiment, figures charted success or failure, just as in a business. He was now beginning to feel that his "affair" (how strange that word was in his mind!) with Candice was moving over the line into success. Repeatability was the hallmark of a good experiment, and this experiment had—

And so on, endless night ruminations somewhat less productive than dreamless sleep.

Candice astonished him. Women had always astonished Vergil, who had had so little opportunity to know them; but he suspected Candice was more astonishing than the norm. He could not fathom her attitude. She seldom initiated lovemaking now, but participated with sufficient enthusiasm. He saw her as a cat searching for a new house, and once finding it, settling down to purr, with little care for the next day.

Neither Vergil's passion nor his life-plan allowed for that kind of sated indifference.

He was reluctant to think of Candice as being his intellectual inferior. She was reasonably witty at times, and observant, and fun to be around. But she wasn't concerned with the same things he was. Candice believed in the surface values of life—appearances, rituals, what other people were thinking and doing. Vergil cared little what other people thought, so long as they didn't actively interfere with his plans.

Candice accepted and experienced. Vergil sparked and observed.

He was deeply envious. He would have enjoyed a respite from the constant grinding of thoughts and plans and worries, the processing of information to glean some new insight. Being like Candice would be a vacation.

Candice, on the other hand, undoubtedly thought of him as a mover and shaker. She led her own life with few plans, without much thought, and with no scruples whatsoever . . . no bites of conscience, no second thoughts. When it had become clear that this mover and shaker was unemployed, and not likely to be employed again soon, her confidence had remained strangely unshaken. Perhaps, like a cat, she had little comprehension of these things.

So she slept, and he ruminated, going back and forth over what had happened at Genetron; chewing at the implications, the admittedly weird behavior of injecting his lymphocytes back into his bloodstream, his inability to focus on what he was going to do next.

Vergil stared up at the dark ceiling, then scrunched his eyes to observe the phosphene patterns. He reached up with both hands, brushing Candice's bottom, and pressed his index fingers against the outer orb of each of his eyelids to heighten the effect. Tonight, however, he could not entertain himself with psychedelic eyelid movies. Nothing came but warm darkness, punctuated by flashes as distant and vague as reports from another continent.

Beyond rumination, isolated from childhood tricks and still wide awake, Vergil settled into watchfulness, watching nothing, and thought with no object—

really trying to avoid

—waiting until morning.

trying to avoid

thoughts of all things lost

and all recently gained that could be

lost

he isn't ready

and still he moves and shakes

losing

On the Sunday morning of the third week:

Candice handed him a hot cup of coffee. He stared at it for a moment. Something was wrong with the cup and her hand. He fumbled for his glasses to put them on but they hurt his eyes worse. "Thanks," he mumbled, taking the cup and lurching up in bed against the pillow, spilling a bit of the hot brown liquid across the sheets.

"What are you going to do today?" she asked. (Look for work? implied, but Candice never stressed responsibility, and never asked questions about his means.)

"Look for work, I suppose," he said. He squinted through his glasses again, holding them by one flopping temple piece.

"I," she said, "am going to take ad copy down to the *Light* and shop at that little vegetable stand down the street. Then I am going to fix dinner by myself and eat it alone."

Vergil looked at her, puzzled.

"What's wrong?" she asked.

He put the glasses aside. "Why alone?"

"Because I think you're beginning to take me for granted. I don't like that. I can feel you accepting me."

"What's wrong with that?"

"Nothing," she said patiently. She had dressed and combed her hair, which now hung long and shining across her shoulders. "I just don't want to lose the spice."

"Spice?"

"Look, every relationship needs a scratch of the kitten now and then. I'm beginning to think of you as an available puppy-dog, and that's not good."

"No," said Vergil. He sounded distracted.

"Didn't sleep last night?" she asked.

"No," Vergil said. "Not much." He looked confused.

"So what else?"

"I'm seeing you just fine," he said.

"See? You're taking me for granted."

"No, I mean . . . without my glasses. I can see you just fine without my glasses."

"Well, good for you," Candice said with feline unconcern. "I'll call you tomorrow. Don't fret."

"Oh, no," Vergil said, squeezing his temples with his fingers.

She closed the door softly behind her.

He looked around the room.

Everything was in marvelous focus. He hadn't seen things so clearly since the measles had stricken his eyesight when he was seven.

It was the first improvement he was positively convinced he could not attribute to Candice.

"Spice," he said, blinking at the curtains.

6

Vergil had spent weeks, it seemed, in just such offices as this: pastel earth-colored walls, gray steel desk surmounted by neat stacks of papers and in-out baskets, man or woman politely asking psychologically telling questions. This time it was a woman, *zoftig* and well-dressed, with a friendly, patient face. Before her on the desk was his employment record and the results of a psych profile test. He had long since learned how to take such tests: When they ask for a sketch, avoid drawing eyes or sharp, wedge-shaped objects; draw items of food or pictures of pretty women; always state one's goals in sharp, practical terms, but with a touch of overreaching; exhibit imagination, but not wild imagination. She nodded over his papers and looked up at him.

"Your record is remarkable, Mr. Ulam."

"Vergil, please."

"Your academic background leaves a bit to be desired, but your work experience could more than make up for that. I suppose you know the questions we'll ask next."

He widened his eyes, all innocence.

"You're a bit vague about what you could do for us, Vergil. I'd like to hear a little more about how you'd fit in with Codon Research."

He glanced at his watch surreptitiously, not looking at the hour, but at the date. In a week there would be little or no hope of recovering his amplified lymphocytes. Really, this was his last chance.

"I'm qualified to perform all kinds of lab work, research or manufacturing. Codon Research has done very well with pharmaceuticals, and I'm interested in that, but I really believe I can help out with any biochip program you're developing."

The personnel manager's eyes narrowed by the merest millimeter. Bullseye, he thought. Codon Research *is* going to jump into biochips.

"We aren't working on biochips, Vergil. Still, your record in pharmaceutical-related work is impressive. You've done extensive culturing; looks to me like you'd be almost as valuable to a brewery

35

as to us." That was a watered-down version of an old joke among vat culturists. Vergil smiled.

"There is a problem, however," she continued. "Your security rating from one source is very high, but your rating from Genetron, your last employer, is abysmal."

"I've explained about the personality clash—"

"Yes, and we normally don't pursue these matters. Our company is different from other companies, after all, and if a potential employee's work record is otherwise good—as your appears to be—we allow for such clashes. But I sometimes have to work on instinct, Vergil. And something's not quite right here. You worked in Genetron's biochip program."

"Doing adjunct research."

"Yes. Are you offering us the expertise you acquired at Genetron?" That was code for *are you going to spill your former employer's secrets?*

"Yes, and no," he said. "First of all, I wasn't at the heart of the biochip program. I wasn't privy to the hard secrets. I can, however, offer you the results of my own research. So technically, yes, since Genetron had a work-for-hire clause, I'm going to spill some secrets if you hire me. But they'll be part and parcel of the work I did." He hoped that shot landed in some middle ground. There was an outright lie in it—he knew virtually everything there was to know about Genetron's biochips—but there was truth, also, since he felt the whole concept of biochips was obsolete, stillborn.

"Mm hmm." She flipped back through his papers. "I'm going to be straight with you, Vergil. Maybe straighter than you've been with me. You're a bit wizardly for us, and a loner, but we'd jump at the chance to hire you . . . if it weren't for one thing. I'm a friend of Mr. Rothwild at Genetron. A very good friend. And he's passed on some information to me that would otherwise be confidential. He didn't name names, and he couldn't possibly have known I would ever face you over this desk. But he told me someone at Genetron had broken a handful of NIH guidelines and recombined mammalian nuclear DNA. I strongly suspect you're that individual." She smiled pleasantly. "Are you?"

No one else had been fired or even let go at Genetron for over a year. He nodded.

"He was quite upset. He said you were brilliant, but that you'd be trouble for any company that employed you. And he said he threatened you with blacklisting. Now I know and he knows that such a threat doesn't really mean much with today's labor laws and the potential for litigation. But this time, just by accident,

Codon Research knows more about you than we should know. I'm being up front with you, because there shouldn't be any misunderstanding. I will deny saying any of these things if pressed. My real reason for not hiring you is your psychological profile. Your drawings are spaced too far apart and indicate an unwholesome predilection for self-isolation." She handed back his records. "Fair enough?"

Vergil nodded. He took his records and stood up. "You don't even know Rothwild," he said. "This has happened to me six times."

"Yes, well, Mr. Ulam, ours is a fledgling industry, barely fifteen years old. Companies still rely on each other when it comes to certain things. Cutthroat out front, and supportive behind the scenes. It's been interesting talking with you, Mr. Ulam. Good day."

He blinked in the sunshine outside the white concrete front of Codon Research. So much for recovery, he thought.

The whole experiment would soon fade away to nothing. Perhaps it was just as well.

7

He drove north through white-gold hills dotted with twisted oaks, past cerulean lakes deep and clear with the past winter's rains. The summer had been mild so far, and even inland, the temperature hadn't gone over ninety.

The Volvo hummed over the endless stretch of Highway 5 through fields given over to cotton, then through green nut groves. Vergil cut across 580 along the outskirts of Tracy, his mind almost blank, the driving a panacea against his worries. Forests of pylon-mounted propellers turned in harmony on both sides of the highway, each great swinging arm two thirds as wide as a football field.

He had never felt better in his life, and he was worried. He had not sneezed for two weeks, in the middle of a champion allergy season. The last time he had seen Candice, to tell her he was going to Livermore to visit his mother, she had commented on his skin color, which had changed from pallid to a healthy peach-pink, and his freedom from sniffles.

"You're looking better each time I see you, Vergil," she had said, smiling and kissing him. "Come back soon. I'll miss you. And maybe we'll find more spice."

Looking better, feeling better—and no excuse for it. He wasn't sentimental enough to believe that love cured all, even calling what he felt for Candice love. Was it?

Something else.

He didn't like thinking about it, so he drove. After ten hours, he felt vaguely disappointed as he turned onto South Vasco Road and motored south. He hung a right on East Avenue and drove into downtown Livermore, a small California burg with old stone and brick buildings, old wooden farmhouses now surrounded by suburbs, shopping centers not unlike those in every other town in California . . . and just outside of town, the Lawrence Livermore National Laboratory, where, among many other researches, nuclear weapons were designed.

He stopped at Guinevere's Pizza Parlor and forced himself to order a medium garbage pizza and a salad and Coke. As he sat down to wait in the pseudo-medieval dining area, he wondered idly whether the Livermore Labs had any facilities he could use. Who was the more Strangelovian—the weapons folks, or good ol' Vergil I. Ulam?

The pizza arrived and he looked down on the cheese and condiments and greasy sausage. "You used to like this stuff," he said under his breath. He picked at the pizza and finished the salad. That seemed to be enough. Leaving most of his meal on the table, he wiped his mouth, smiled at the young girl behind the cash register, and returned to his car.

Vergil did not look forward to visits with his mother. He needed them, in some uncertain and irritating way, but he did not enjoy them.

April Ulam lived in a well-maintained century-old two-story house just off First Street. The house was painted forest green and had a Mansard roof. Two little gardens fenced in with wrought iron flanked the steep front steps—one garden for flowers and herbs, the other for vegetables. The porch was screened-in, with a wood-frame screen door mounted on squeaking hinges and reined in by a complaining steel spring. Entrance to the house proper was through a heavy dark oak door with a beveled-glass window and lion-faced knocker.

None of these commodities were unexpected when attached to an old house in a small California town. But then his mother appeared, svelte and dressed in flowing lavender silks and high-heeled gold shoes, her raven black hair barely touched with gray at the temples, coming through the oak door and the screen door and stepping into the sunshine. She greeted Vergil with a reserved hug and led him through the parlor, thin cool fingers lightly gripping his hand.

In the living room, she sat on a gray velvet chaise longue, her gown flowing lightly over the sides. The living room suited the house, being furnished with items an elderly woman (*not* his mother) might have gathered over a long and moderately interesting life. Besides the chaise there was a blue flower-print overstuffed couch, a brass round table with Arabic proverbs stamped in concentric circles around abstract geometrics, Tiffany-style lamps in three corners and in the fourth, a decayed Chinese Kwan-Yin statue carved from a seven-foot teak log. His father—simply "Frank" in all conversations—had brought the statue back from Taiwan after a merchant marine tour; it had scared three-year-old Vergil half to death.

Frank had abandoned both of them in Texas when Vergil was
ten. They had then moved to California. His mother had not
remarried, saying that would cut down on her options. Vergil was
not even certain his mother and father had divorced. He remembered his father as dark, sharp-faced, sharp-voiced, not tolerant
and not intelligent, with a thundering laugh brought out for display
at moments of perverse anxiety. He could not imagine even now
his mother and father going to bed together, much less living
together eleven years. He had not missed Frank except in a theoretical way—missing *a* father, the imagined state of having a
father who could talk to him, help him with homework, be a touch
wiser when he was having trouble with being a child. He had
always missed having that sort of father.

"So you're not working," April said, surveying her son with
what passed for mild concern.

Vergil had not told his mother about his dismissal and didn't
even question how she knew. She had been much sharper than
her husband and still could match wits with her son, usually
overmatching in practical or worldly matters.

He nodded. "Five weeks now."

"Any prospects?"

"Not even looking."

"You were let go with prejudice," she said.

"Almost with extreme prejudice."

She smiled; now the verbal fencing could begin. Her son was
very clever, very amusing, whatever his other faults. She was not
sorry he had no job; that was simply the state of affairs, and he
would either sink, or swim. In the past, despite his difficulties,
her son had usually stayed on the surface, with much splashing
and poor form, but still, on the surface.

He hadn't asked for money from her since leaving home ten
years ago.

"So you come to see what your old mother's up to."

"What's my old mother up to?"

"Her neck, as usual," she said. "Six suitors in the past month.
It's a pain being old and not looking it, Verge."

Vergil chuckled and shook his head, as he knew she expected.
"Any prospects?"

She scoffed. "Never again. No man could replace Frank, thank
God."

"They fired me because I was doing experiments on my own,"
he said. She nodded and asked if he wanted tea or wine or a beer.
"A beer," he said.

She indicated the kitchen. "Fridge is unlocked."

He picked out a Dos Equis and wiped the condensation on his sleeve as he returned to the living room. He sat in a broad-backed armchair and took a long swallow.

"They didn't appreciate your brilliance?"

He shook his head. "Nobody understands me, Mother."

She stared off over his shoulder and sighed. "I never did. Do you expect to be employed again soon?"

"You already asked that."

"I thought maybe rephrasing would bring a better answer."

"Answer's the same if you ask in Swahili. I'm sick of working for somebody else."

"My unhappy misfit son."

"Mother," Vergil said, faintly irritated.

"What were you doing?"

He gave her a brief outline, of which she understood little but the most salient points. "You were setting up a deal behind their backs, then."

He nodded. "If I could have had a month more, and if Bernard had seen it—everything would have been just sweet." He was seldom evasive with his mother. She was virtually unshockable; tough to keep up with, and even tougher to fool.

"And you wouldn't be here now, visiting your old, feeble mater."

"Probably not," Vergil said, shrugging. "Also, there's a girl. I mean, a woman."

"If she lets you call her a girl, she isn't a woman."

"She's pretty independent." He talked for a while about Candice, about her brazen overtures at the beginning and her gradual domesticizing. "I'm getting used to having her around. I mean, we're not living together. We're on a sort of sabbatical right now, to see how things work out. I'm no prize in the domestic department." April nodded and asked him to get her a beer. He retrieved an unopened Anchor Steam.

"My fingernails aren't that tough," she said.

"Oh." He returned to the kitchen and uncapped it.

"Now. What did you expect a big brain surgeon like Bernard to do for you?"

"He's not just a brain surgeon. He's been interested in AI for years now."

"AI?"

"Artificial intelligence."

"Oh." She smiled radiant understanding. "You're unemployed," she said, "maybe in love, no prospects. Gladden your parent's heart some more. What else is going on?"

"I'm experimenting on myself, I think," he said.

April's eyes widened. "How?"

"Well, those cells I changed. I had to smuggle them out by injecting them into my body. And I haven't had access to a lab or doctor's office since. By now, I'll never recover them."

"Recover them?"

"Separate them from the others. There's billions of them, Mother."

"If they're your own cells, why should you worry?"

"Notice anything different?"

She squinted at him. "You're not so pale, and you've changed to contact lenses."

"I'm not wearing contacts."

"Then maybe you've changed your habits and aren't reading in the dark any more." She shook her head. "I never have understood your interest in all this nonsense."

Vergil stared at her, dumbfounded. "It's fascinating," he said. "And if you can't see how important it is, then—"

"Don't get snippy about my peculiar blindnesses. I admit them, but I don't go out of my way to change them. Not when I see the world in the shape it's in today, because of people with your intellectual inclinations. Why, every day, over at the Lab, they're coming up with more and more doomsday—"

"Don't judge most scientists by me, Mother. I'm not exactly typical. I'm a little more . . ." He couldn't find the word and grinned. She returned the grin with the slight smile he had never been able to decipher.

"Mad," she said.

"Unorthodox," Vergil corrected.

"I don't understand what you're getting at, Vergil. What kind of cells are these? Just parts of your blood you've been working on?"

"They can think, Mother."

Again, unshockable, she didn't react in any way he could perceive. "Together—I mean, all of them, or each one?"

"Each one. Though they tended to group together in the last experiments."

"Are they friendly?"

Vergil looked up at the ceiling in exasperation. "They're lymphocytes, Mother. They don't even live in the same world we do. They can't be friendly or unfriendly in the way we mean the words. Everything's chemicals for them."

"If they can think, then they feel something, at least if my life experience is any good. Unless they're like Frank. Of course, he didn't think much, so the comparison is not exact."

"I never had time to find out what they're like, or whether they can reason as much as . . . as their potential."

"What is their potential?"

"Are you sure you're understanding this?"

"Do I sound like I'm understanding?"

"Yes. That's why I'm doubtful. I don't know what their potential is. It's very large, though."

"Verge, there's always been method to your madness. What did you hope to gain by doing this?"

That stopped him. He despaired of ever communicating on that level—the level of achievement and goals—with his mother. She had never understood his need to accomplish. For her, goals were met by not ruffling the neighbors' feathers too often. "I don't know. Maybe nothing. Forget it."

"It's forgotten. Where shall we eat dinner tonight?"

"Let's eat Moroccan," Vergil said.

"Belly dancers it is."

Of all the things he didn't understand about April, the real topper was his childhood bedroom. Toys, bed and furniture, posters on the wall, his room had been preserved not as he had left it, but as it had been when he was twelve years old. The books he had read had been pulled out of boxes in the attic and lined up on the shelves of the single bookcase that had once sufficed to hold his library. Paperback and bookclub science fiction vied with comics and a small, important cluster of science and electronics books.

Movie posters—no doubt very valuable now—showed Robbie the Robot clutching a much amplified Anne Frances and stalking across a jagged planetscape, Christopher Lee snag-snarling with red eyes, Keir Dullea staring in wonder from his spacesuit helmet.

He had taken those posters down at age nineteen, folded them and stashed them in a drawer. April had put them back up after he left for college.

She had even resurrected his checked hunters-and-hounds bedspread. The bed itself was worn and familiar, seducing him back to a childhood he wasn't sure he had ever had, much less left behind.

He remembered his pre-adolescence as a time of considerable fear and worry. Fear that he was some kind of sex maniac, that he had been responsible for his father's exit, worry about measuring up in school. And along with the worry, exaltation. The light-headed and peculiar joy he had felt on half-twisting a strip of paper, pasting the ends together and manufacturing his first moebius strip; his ant farm and Heathkits; his discovery of ten years' worth of *Scientific Americans* in a trash can in the alley behind the house.

In the dark, just as he was on the edge of sleep, his back began to crawl. He scratched abstractedly, then sat up in bed with a whispered curse and curled the hem of his pajama top into a tight roll, drawing it up and down, back and forth with both hands to ease the itch.

He reached up to his face. It felt totally unfamiliar, somebody else's face—bumps and ridges, nose extended, lips protruding. But with his other hand, it felt normal. He rubbed the fingers of both hands together. The sensations weren't right. One hand was far more sensitive than usual, the other almost numb.

Breathing heavily, Vergil stumbled into the upstairs bathroom and switched on a light. His chest itched abominably. The spaces between his toes seemed alive with invisible ants. He hadn't felt so miserable since he had had chicken pox at eleven, a month before his father's departure. With the unspeculating concentration of misery, Vergil stripped off his pajamas and crawled into the shower, hoping for relief under cold water.

The water spluttered in a weak stream from the old plumbing and rippled across his head and neck, over his shoulders and back, rivulets snaking down his chest and legs. Both hands were exquisitely, painfully sensitive now, and the water seemed to come in needles, warming and then cooling, burning and then freezing. He held his arms out and the air itself felt bumpy.

He stood under the shower for fifteen minutes, sighing with relief as the irritation subsided, rubbing the offending areas of his skin with his wrists and the backs of his hands until they were angry red. His fingers and palms tingled and the tingling diminished to a low, blood pumping throb of returning normality.

He emerged and toweled off, then stood naked by the bathroom window, feeling the cool breeze and listening to crickets. "God damn," he said slowly and expressively. He turned and looked at himself in the bathroom mirror. His chest was splotchy and red from scratching and rubbing. He rotated and peered over his shoulder at his back.

From shoulder to shoulder, and criss-crossing down his spine, faint pale lines just beneath the surface of his skin drew a crazy and unwelcome road-map. As he watched, the lines slowly faded until he wondered whether they had been there at all.

Heart pounding heavily in his chest, Vergil sat on the lid of the toilet and stared at his feet, chin in both hands. Now he was really scared.

He laughed deep in the back of his throat.

"Put the little suckers to work, hm?" he asked himself in a whisper.

"Vergil, are you all right?" his mother asked from the other side of the bathroom door.

"I'm fine," he said. Better and better, every day.

"I will never understand men, as long as I live and breathe," his mother said, pouring herself another cup of thick black coffee. "Always tinkering, always getting into trouble."

"I'm not in trouble, Mother." He didn't sound convinced, even to himself.

"No?"

He shrugged. "I'm healthy, I can go for a few more months without work—and something's bound to turn up."

"You're not even looking."

That was true enough. "I'm getting over a depression." And that was an outright lie.

"Bull," April said. "You've never been depressed in your life. You don't even know what it means. You should be a woman for a few years and just see for yourself."

The morning sun illuminated the filmy curtains covering the kitchen window and filled the kitchen with subdued, cheerful warmth. "Sometimes you act like I'm a brick wall," Vergil said.

"Sometimes you are. Hell, Verge, you're my son. I gave you life—I think we can X out Frank's contribution—and I watched you grow older for twenty-two years steady. You never did grow up, and you never did get a full deck of sensibilities. You're a brilliant boy, but you're just not complete."

"And you," he said, grimacing, "are a deep well of support and understanding."

"Don't rile the old woman, Verge. I understand and sympathize as much as you deserve. You're in real trouble, aren't you? This experiment."

"I wish you wouldn't keep harping on that. I'm the scientist, and I'm the only one affected, and so far—" He closed his mouth with an audible snap and crossed his arms. It was all quite insane. The lymphocytes he had injected were beyond any doubt dead or decrepit by now. They had been altered in test-tube conditions, had probably acquired a whole new set of histocompatibility antigens, and had been attacked and devoured by their unaltered fellows weeks ago. Any other supposition was simply not supported by reason. Last night had simply been a complex allergic reaction. Why he and his mother, of all people, should be discussing the possibility—

"Verge?"

"It's been nice, April, but I think it's time for me to leave."

"How long do you have?"

He stood and stared at her, shocked. "I'm not dying, Mother."

"All his life, my son has been working for his supreme moment. Sounds to me like it's come, Verge."

"That's crazier than horseshit."

"I'll throw what you've told me right back at you, Son. I'm not a genius, but I'm not a brick wall, either. You tell me you've made intelligent germs, and I'll tell you right now ... Anyone who's ever sanitized a toilet or cleaned a diaper pail would cringe at the idea of germs that think. What happens when they fight back, Verge? Tell your old mother that."

There was no answer. He wasn't sure there was even a viable subject in their discussion; nothing made sense. But he could feel his stomach tensing.

He had performed this ritual before, getting into trouble and then coming to his mother, uneasy and uncertain, not sure precisely what sort of trouble he was in. With uncanny regularity, she had seemed to jump onto a higher plane of reasoning and identify his problems, laying them out for him so they became unavoidable. This was not a service that made him love her any more, but it did make her invaluable to him.

He stood and reached down to pat her hand. She turned it and gripped his hand in hers. "You're going now," she said.

"Yes."

"How long do we have, Vergil?"

"What?" He couldn't understand it, but his eyes suddenly filled with tears and he began to tremble.

"Come back to me, if you can," she said.

Terrified, he grabbed his suitcase—packed the night before—and ran down the steps to the Volvo, throwing open the trunk and tossing it in. He rounded the car and caught his knee on the rear bumper. Pain surged, then dropped off rapidly. He climbed into the bucket seat and started the engine.

His mother stood on the porch, silk gown flowing in the slight morning breeze, and Vergil waved at her as he pulled the car away. Normality. Wave at your mother. Drive away.

Drive away, knowing that your father never existed, and that your mother was a witch, and what did that make you?

He shook his head until his ears rang, somehow managing to keep the car going in a straight line down the street.

A white ridge lay across the back of his left hand, like a tiny thread glued to the skin with mucilage.

8

An uncharacteristic summer storm had left the sky ragged with clouds, the air cool, and the apartment's bedroom window flecked with drops of water. The surf could be heard from four blocks away, a dull rumble topped with hiss. Vergil sat before his computer, heel of one hand resting against the edge of the keyboard, finger poised. On the VDT was a twisting, evolving molecule of DNA surrounded by a haze of protein. Flickering separations of the double helix's phosphate-sugar backbones indicated high-speed intrusions by enzymes, spreading the molecule for transcription. Labeled columns of numbers marched along the bottom of the screen. He watched them without paying much attention.

He would have to talk with somebody soon—somebody besides his mother, and certainly besides Candice. She had moved in with him a week after he returned from his mother's house, apparently intent on domesticity, cleaning up the apartment and fixing his meals.

Sometimes they shopped together, and that was enjoyable. Candice enjoyed helping Vergil pick out better clothes, and he went along with her, even though the purchases drained his already low bank account.

When she asked about things she didn't like, his silences grew prolonged. She wondered why he insisted they make love in the dark.

She suggested they go to the beach, but Vergil demurred.

She worried about his spending time under the new lamps he had bought.

"Verge?" Candice stood in the bedroom doorway, wrapped in a terrycloth robe, embroidered with roses.

"Don't call me that. My mother calls me that."

"Sorry. We were going to ride up to the animal park. Remember?"

Vergil lifted his finger to his mouth and chewed on the nail. He didn't seem to hear.

"Vergil?"

"I'm not feeling too well."

"You never go out. That's why."

"Actually, I'm feeling fine," he said, turning in his chair. He looked at her but offered no further explanation.

"I don't understand."

He pointed to the screen. "You've never let me explain it to you."

"You get all crazy and I don't understand you," Candice said, her lip quivering.

"It's more than I ever thought possible."

"What, Vergil?"

"The concatenations. The combinations. The power."

"Please, make sense."

"I'm trapped. Seduced but hardly abandoned."

"I didn't just seduce you—"

"Not you, sweetums," he said abstractedly. "Not you."

Candice approached the desk slowly, as if the screen might bite. Her eyes were moist and she chewed her lower lip. "Honey."

He jotted down numbers from the bottom of the screen.

"Vergil."

"Hmm?"

"Did you do something at work, I mean, before you left, before we met?"

He swiveled his head around and looked at her blankly.

"Like with the computers? Did you get mad and screw up their computers?"

"No," he said, grinning. "I didn't screw them up. Screwed them *over,* maybe, but nothing they'll ever notice."

"Because I knew this guy once, he did something against the law and he started acting funny. He wouldn't go out, he wouldn't talk much, just like you."

"What did he do?" Vergil asked, still jotting numbers.

"He robbed a bank."

The pencil stopped. Their eyes met. Candice was crying.

"I loved him and I had to leave him when I found out," she said. "I just can't live with bad shit like that."

"Don't worry."

"I was all ready to leave you a few weeks ago," she said. "I thought maybe we'd done all we could together. But it's just crazy. I've never met anyone like you. You're crazy. Crazy smart, not crazy shit-headed like other guys. I've been thinking if we could just loosen up together, that it would be really wonderful. I'd listen to you when you explain things, maybe you could teach me about this biology and electronics stuff." She indicated the screen. "I'd try to listen. I really would."

Vergil's mouth hung open slightly. He drew it shut and looked at the screen, blinking rapidly.

"I fell in love with you. When you were gone to visit your mother. Isn't that weird?"

"Candice—"

"And if you've done something really awful, it's going to hurt *me* now, not just you." She backed away with her fist tucked under her chin, as if she were slowly hitting herself.

"I don't want to hurt anybody," Vergil said.

"I know. You're not mean."

"I'd explain everything to you, if I knew what was happening myself. But I don't. I haven't done anything they could send me to jail for. Nothing illegal." *Except tamper with the medical records*.

"You can't tell me something isn't bothering you. Why can't we just talk about it?" She pulled a folding chair from the closet and snicked it open a couple of yards from the desk, sitting on it with knees together and feet spread.

"I just said, I don't know what it is."

"Did you do something . . . to yourself? I mean, did you get some disease at the lab or something? I've heard that's possible, doctors and scientists get diseases they're working with."

"You and my mother," he said, shaking his head.

"We're worried. Will I ever meet your mother?"

"Probably not for some time," Vergil said.

"I'm sorry I . . ." She shook her head vigorously. "I just wanted to open up to you."

"That's all right," he said.

"Vergil."

"Yes?"

"Do you love me?"

"Yes," he said, and surprised himself by meaning it, though he did not look away from the screen.

"Why?"

"Because we're so much alike," he said. He was not at all sure how he meant that; perhaps both were destined to be failures, or at least never amount to much—to Vergil that was the same thing as failure.

"Come on."

"Really. Maybe you just don't see it."

"I'm not as smart as you, that's for sure."

"Sometimes being smart is a real pain," he said.

Is that what they're finding out, his little lymphocytes? The pain of being smart, of surviving?

"Can we go for a drive today, go someplace and have a picnic? There's cold chicken from last night."

He jotted down one last column of numbers and realized he now knew what he had wanted to know. The lymphocytes could indeed spread their biologic to other types of cells.

They could very easily do what it seemed they were doing to him.

"Yeah," he said. "A picnic would be great."

"And then, when we come back . . . With the lights on?"

"Why not?" She'd have to know sooner or later. And he could find some way of explaining the stripe patterns. The ridges had gone down since he had begun the lamp treatments; thank God for small favors.

"I love you," she said, still in the chair, still watching him.

He saved the computations and graphics and turned off the computer. "Thank you," he said softly.

PROPHASE

OCTOBER-DECEMBER

9

Irvine, California

It had been two years since Edward Milligan had last seen Vergil. Edward's memory hardly matched the tan, smiling and well-dressed gentleman standing before him. They had made a lunch appointment over the phone the day before, and now faced each other in the wide double doors of the employee's cafeteria of Irvine's new Mount Freedom Medical Center.

"Vergil?" Edward shook his hand and walked around him, a look of exaggerated wonder on his face. "Is it really you?"

"Good to see you again, Edward." He returned the handshake firmly. He had lost twenty to twenty-five pounds and what remained seemed better-proportioned. At medical school, Vergil had been the pudgy, shock-haired, snaggle-toothed kid who wired doorknobs, gave his dorm floormates punch that turned their piss blue, and never had a date except with Eileen Termagant, who had shared some of his physical characteristics.

"You look fantastic," Edward said. "Spend a summer in Cabo San Lucas?"

They stood in line at the counter and chose their food. "The tan," Vergil said, picking out a carton of chocolate milk, "is from spending three months under a sun lamp. My teeth were straightened just after I last saw you."

Edward looked closely, lifting Vergil's lip with one finger. "So they were. Still discolored, though."

"Yes," Vergil said, rubbing his lip and taking a deep breath. "Well. I'll explain the rest but we need a place to talk in private, or at least with nobody paying attention."

Edward steered him to the smoker's corner, where three diehard puffers were scattered among six tables. "Listen, I mean it," he said as they unloaded their trays. "You've changed. You're looking good."

"I've changed more than you know." Vergil's tone was motion-picture-ominous, and he delivered the line with a theatrical lift of his brows. "How's Gail?"

"Doing well. We've been married a year."

"Hey, congratulations." Vergil's gaze shifted down to his food—pineapple slice and cottage cheese, piece of banana cream pie. "Notice something else?" he asked, his voice cracking slightly.

Edward squinted in concentration. "Uh."

"Look closer."

"I'm not sure. Well, yes. You're not wearing glasses. Contacts?"

"No. I don't need them anymore."

"And you're a snappy dresser. Who's dressing you now? I hope she's as sexy as she is tasteful."

"Candice," he said, grinning the old familiar self-deprecating grin, but ending it with an uncharacteristic leer. "I've been fired from my job. Four months now. I'm living on savings."

"Hold it," Edward said. "That's a bit crowded. Why not do a linear breakdown? You got a job. Where?"

"I ended up at Genetron in Enzyme Valley."

"North Torrey Pines Road?"

"That's the place. Infamous. And you'll be hearing more very soon. They're putting out common stock any second now. It'll shoot off the board. They've broken through with MABs."

"Biochips?"

He nodded. "They have some that work."

"What?" Edward's brows lifted sharply.

"Microscopic logic circuits. You inject them into the human body, they set up shop where they're told and troubleshoot. With Dr. Michael Bernard's approval."

The angle of Edward's brows steepened. "Jesus, Vergil. Bernard's almost a saint. He's had his picture on the cover of *Mega* and *Rolling Stone* just the last month or two. Why are you telling me all this?"

"It's supposed to be secret—stock, breakthrough, everything. I have my contacts inside the place, though. Ever heard of Hazel Overton?"

Edward shook his head. "Should I?"

"Probably not. I thought she hated my guts. Turns out she had grudging respect for me. She gave me a call two months back and asked if I wanted to front a paper for her on F-factors in *E. coli* genomes." He looked around and lowered his voice. "But you do whatever the hell you want. I'm through with the bastards."

Edward whistled. "Make me rich, huh?"

"If that's what you want. Or you can spend some time listening to me before rushing off to your broker."

"Of course. So tell me more."

Vergil hadn't touched the cottage cheese or pie. He had, however, eaten the pineapple slice and drunk the chocolate milk. "I got in on the ground floor about five years ago. With my medical school background and computer experience, I was a shoo-in for Enzyme Valley. I went up and down North Torrey Pines Road with my resumes, and I was hired by Genetron."

"That simple?"

"No." Vergil picked at the cottage cheese with a fork, then laid the fork down. "I did some rearranging of the records. Credit records, school records, that sort of thing. Nobody's caught on yet. I came in as hot stuff, and I made my mark early with protein assemblies and the preliminary biochip research. Genetron has big money backers, and we were given as much as we needed. Four months and I was doing my own work, sharing a lab but allowed to do independent research. I made some breakthroughs." He tossed his hand nonchalantly. "Then I went off on tangents. I kept on doing my regular work, but after hours . . . The management found out, and fired me. I managed to . . . save part of my experiments. But I haven't exactly been cautious, or judicious. So now the experiment's going on outside the lab."

Edward had always regarded Vergil as ambitious and more than a trifle cracked. In their school years, Vergil's relations with authority figures had never been smooth. Edward had long ago concluded that science, for Vergil, was like an unattainable woman, who suddenly opens her arms to him before he's ready for mature love—leaving him afraid he'll forever blow the chance, lose the prize, screw up royally. Apparently, he had. "Outside the lab? I don't get you."

"I want you to examine me. Give me a thorough physical. Maybe a cancer diagnostic. Then I'll explain more."

"You want a ten thousand dollar exam?"

"Whatever you can do. Ultrasound, NMR, PET, thermogram, everything."

"I don't know if I can get access to all that equipment, Vergil. Natural-source PET full-scan has only been here a month or two. Hell, you couldn't pick a more expensive—"

"Then ultrasound and NMR. That's all you need."

"I'm an obstetrician, Vergil, not a glamour-boy lab tech. OB-GYN, butt of all jokes. If you're turning into a woman, maybe I can help you."

Vergil leaned forward, almost putting his elbow into the pie, but swinging wide at the last instant by scant millimeters. The old

Vergil would have hit it square. "Examine me closely, and you'll . . ." He narrowed his eyes and shook his head. "Just examine me."

"So I make an appointment for ultrasound and NMR. Who's going to pay?"

"I have medical. I messed with the personnel files at Genetron before I left. Anything up to a hundred thousand dollars and they'll never check, never suspect and it has to be absolutely confidential."

Edward shook his head. "You're asking for a lot, Vergil."

"Do you want to make medical history, or not?"

"Is this a joke?"

Vergil shook his head. "Not on you, roomie."

Edward made the arrangements that afternoon, filling in the forms himself. From what he understood of hospital paperwork, so long as everything was billed properly, most of the examination could take place without official notice. He didn't charge for his services. After all, Vergil had turned his piss blue. They were friends.

Edward stayed past his usual hours. He gave Gail a bare outline of what he was doing; she sighed the sigh of a doctor's wife and told him she'd leave a late snack on the table for when he came home.

Vergil returned at ten P.M. and met Edward at the appointed place, on the third floor of what the nurses called the Frankenstein Wing. Edward sat on an orange plastic chair reading a desk copy of *My Things* magazine. Vergil entered the small lobby, looking lost and worried. His skin was olive-colored under the fluorescent lighting.

Edward signaled the night supervisor that this was his patient and conducted Vergil to the examination area, hand on his elbow. Neither spoke much. Vergil stripped and Edward arranged him on the paper-covered padded table. "Your ankles are swollen," he said, feeling them. They were solid, not puffy. Healthy, but odd. "Hm." Edward said pointedly, glancing at Vergil. Vergil raised his eyebrows and cocked his head; his "you ain't seen nothing yet" look.

"Okay. I'm going to run several scans on you and combine the results in an imager. Ultrasound first." Edward ran paddles over Vergil's still form, hitting those areas difficult for the bigger unit to reach. He then swung the table around and inserted it into the enameled orifice of the ultrasound diagnostic unit—the hum-hole, so-called by the nurses. After twelve separate sweeps, head to toe, he removed the table. Vergil was sweating slightly, his eyes closed.

"Still claustrophobic?" Edward asked.

"Not so much."

"NMR is a little worse."

"Lead on, MacDuff."

The NMR full-scan unit was an imposing chrome and sky-blue mastaba-shaped box, occupying one small room with barely enough space to wheel in the table. "I'm not an expert on this one, so it may take a while," Edward said, helping Vergil into the cavity.

"High cost of medicine," Vergil muttered, closing his eyes as Edward swung down the glass hatch. The massive magnet circling the cavity buzzed faintly. Edward instructed the machine to send its data to the central imager in the next room and helped Vergil out.

"Holding up?" Edward asked.

"Courage," Vergil said, pronouncing it as in French.

In the next room, Edward arranged a large-screen VDT and ordered the integration and display of the data. In the half-darkness, the image took a few seconds to flow into recognizable shapes.

"Your skeleton first," Edward said. His eyes widened. The image then displayed Vergil's thoracic organs, musculature, and finally vascular system and skin.

"How long since the accident?" Edward asked, stepping closer to the screen. He couldn't quite conceal the quiver in his voice.

"I haven't been in an accident," Vergil said.

"Jesus, they beat you, to keep secrets?"

"You don't understand me, Edward. Look at the images again. That's not trauma."

"Look, there's thickening here," he indicated the ankles, "and your ribs—that crazy zig-zag interlocking. Broken somewhere, obviously. And—"

"Look at my spine," Vergil suggested. Edward slowly rotated the image on the screen.

Buckminster Fuller came to mind immediately. It was fantastic. Vergil's spine was a cage of triangular bones coming together in ways Edward could not even follow, much less comprehend. "Mind if I feel?"

Vergil shook his head. Edward reached through the slit in the robe and traced his fingers along the back. Vergil lifted his arms and looked off at the ceiling.

"I can't find it," Edward said. "It's smooth. There's something flexible; the harder I push, the tougher it becomes." He walked around in front of Vergil, chin in hand. "You don't have any nipples," he said. There were tiny pigment patches, but no nipple formations whatsoever.

"See?" Vergil said. "I'm being rebuilt from the inside out."

"Bullshit," Edward said. Vergil looked surprised.

"You can't deny your eyes," he said softly. "I'm not the same fellow I was four months ago."

"I don't know what you're talking about." Edward played around with the images, rotating them, going through the various sets of organs, playing the NMR movie back and forth.

"Have you ever seen anything like me? I mean, the new design."

"No," Edward said flatly. He walked away from the table and stood by the closed door, hands in his labcoat pocket. "What in hell have you done?"

Vergil told him. The story emerged in widening spirals of fact and event and Edward had to make his way through the circumlocutions as best he could.

"How," he asked, "do you convert DNA to read-write memory?"

"First you need to find a length of viral DNA that codes for topoisomerases and gyrases. You attach this segment to your target DNA and make it easier to lower the linking number—to negatively supercoil your target molecule. I used ethidium in some earlier experiments, but—"

"Simpler, please, I haven't had molecular biology in years."

"What you want is to add and subtract lengths of input DNA easily, and the feedback enzyme arrangement does this. When the feedback arrangement is in place, the molecule will open itself up for transcription much more easily, and more rapidly. Your program will be transcribed onto two strings of RNA. One of the RNA strings will go to a reader—a ribosome—for translation into a protein. Initially, the first RNA will carry a simple start-up code—"

Edward stood by the door and listened for half an hour. When Vergil showed no sign of slowing down, much less stopping, he raised his hand. "And how does all this lead to intelligence?"

Vergil frowned. "I'm still not certain. I just began finding replication of logic circuits easier and easier. Whole stretches of the genomes seemed to open themselves up to the process. There were even parts that I'll swear were already coded for specific logic assignments—but at the time, I thought they were just more introns, sequences not coding for proteins. You know, holdovers from old faulty transcriptions, not yet eliminated by evolution. I'm talking about the eukaryotes now. Prokaryotes don't have introns. But I've been thinking the last few months. Plenty of time to think, without work. Brooding."

He stopped and shook his head, folding and unfolding his hands, twisting his fingers together.

"And?"

"It's very strange, Edward. Since early med school we've been hearing about 'selfish genes,' and that individuals and populations have no function but to create more genes. Eggs make chickens to make more eggs. And people seemed to think that introns were just genes that have no purpose but to reproduce themselves within the cellular environment. Everyone jumped on the bandwagon, saying they were junk, useless. I didn't feel any qualms at all with my eukaryotes, working with introns. Hell, they were spare parts, genetic deserts. I could build whatever I wanted." Again he stopped, but Edward did not prompt. Vergil looked up at him, eyes moist. "I wasn't responsible. I was seduced."

"I'm not getting you, Vergil." Edward's voice sounded brittle, on the edge of anger. He was tired and old memories of Vergil's carelessness towards others were returning; he was exhausted, and Vergil was still droning on, saying nothing that really made sense.

Vergil slammed his fist on the edge of the table. "They made me do it! The goddamn genes!"

"Why, Vergil?"

"So they won't have to rely on us anymore. The ultimate selfish gene. All this time, I think the DNA was just leading up to what I've done. You know. Emergence. Coming out party. Tempting somebody, anybody, into giving it what it wanted."

"That's nuts, Vergil."

"You didn't work on it, you didn't feel what I felt. It should have taken a whole research team, maybe even a Manhattan Project, to do what I did. I'm bright but I'm not that bright. Things just fell into place. It was too easy."

Edward rubbed his eyes. "I'm going to take some blood and I'd like stool and urine."

"Why?"

"So I can find out what's happening to you."

"I've just told you."

"It's crazy."

"Edward, you can see the screen. I don't wear glasses, my back doesn't hurt, I haven't had an allergy attack in four months, and I haven't been sick. I used to get infections all the time in my sinuses because of the allergies. No colds, no infections, nothing. I've never felt better."

"So altered smart lymphocytes are inside you, finding things, changing them."

He nodded. "And by now, each cluster of cells is as smart as you or I."

"You didn't mention clusters."

"They used to cram together in the medium. Maybe a hundred or two hundred cells. I never could figure out why. Now it seems obvious. They cooperate."

Edward stared at him. "I'm very tired."

"The way I see it, I lost weight because they improved my metabolism. My bones are stronger, my spine has been rebuilt—"

"Your heart looks different."

"I didn't know about the heart." He examined the frame image from several inches. "Jesus. I mean, I haven't been able to keep track of anything since I left Genetron; I've been guessing and worrying. You don't know what a relief it is to tell someone who can understand."

"I don't understand."

"Edward, the evidence is overwhelming. I was thinking about the fat. They could increase my brown cells, fix up my metabolism. My eating habits have changed. But they haven't got around to my brain yet." He tapped his head. "They understand all the glandular stuff. Old-home week. But they don't have the *big* picture, if you see what I mean."

Edward felt Vergil's pulse and checked his reflexes. "I think we'd better get those samples and call it quits for the evening."

"And I didn't want them getting into my skin. That really scared me. Couple of nights, my skin started to crawl, and I decided to take some action. I bought a quartz lamp. I wanted to keep them under control, just in case. You know? What if they crossed the blood-brain barrier and found out about *me*—the brain's real function. I figured the reason they wanted to get into my skin was the simplicity of running circuits across the surface. Much easier than trying to maintain lines of communication through muscles and organs and the vascular system; much more direct. I alternate sunlamp with quartz lamp treatments now. Keeps them out of my skin, as far as I can tell. And now you know why I have a nice tan."

"Give you skin cancer, too," Edward said, falling into Vergil's terse manner of speech.

"I'm not worried. They'll take care of it. Like police."

"Okay," Edward said, holding up both hands in a gesture of resignation. "I've examined you. You've told me a story I cannot accept. What do you want me to do?"

"I'm not as nonchalant as I seem. I'm worried, Edward. I'd like to find a better way to control them before they find out about my brain. I mean, think of it. They're in the billions by now, more if they're converting other kinds of cells. Maybe trillions. Each cluster smart. I'm probably the smartest thing on the planet, and they haven't begun to get their act together. I don't want them to take over." He laughed unpleasantly. "Steal my soul, you know? So think of some treatment to block them. Maybe we can starve the little buggers. Just think on it. And give me a call."

He reached into his pants pocket and handed Edward a slip of paper with his address and phone number. Then he went to the keyboard and erased the image in the frame, dumping the memory of the examination. "Just you. Nobody else for now. And please . . . hurry."

It was one o'clock in the morning when Vergil walked out of the examination room. The samples had been taken. In the main lobby, Vergil shook hands with Edward. Vergil's palm was damp, nervous. "Be careful with the specimens," he said. "Don't ingest anything."

Edward watched Vergil cross the parking lot and get into his Volvo. Then he turned slowly and went back to the Frankenstein Wing. He poured a cc of Vergil's blood into an ampule, and several cc's of urine into another, inserting both into the hospital's tissue, specimen and serum analyzer. He would have the results in the morning, available on his office VDT. The stool sample would require manual work, but that could wait; right now he felt like one of the undead. It was two o'clock.

He pulled out a cot, shut off the lights and lay down without undressing. He hated sleeping in the hospital. When Gail woke up in the morning, she would find a message on the answerphone—a message, but no explanation. He wondered what he would tell her.

"I'll just say it was good ol' Vergil," he murmured.

10

Edward shaved with an old straight razor kept in his desk drawer for just such emergencies, examined himself in the mirror of the doctor's dressing room and rubbed his cheek critically. He had used the straight razor regularly in his student years, an affectation; since then the occasions had been seldom and his face showed it: three nicks patched with tissue paper and styptic pencil. He glanced at his watch. The batteries were running low and the display was dim. He shook it angrily and the display became crystal-clear: 6:30 A.M. Gail would be up and about, preparing for school.

He slipped two quarters into the pay phone in the doctor's lounge and fumbled with the pencils and pens in his coat pocket.

"Hello?"

"Gail, Edward. I love you and I'm sorry."

"A disembodied voice on the phone awaited me. It might have been my husband." She had a fine phone voice, one he had always admired. He had first asked her out, sight unseen, after hearing her on a phone at the house of a mutual friend.

"Yes, well—"

"Also, Vergil Ulam called a few minutes ago. He sounded anxious. I haven't talked to him in years."

"Did you tell him—"

"You were still at the hospital. Of course. Your shift is at eight today?"

"Same as yesterday. Two hours with premeds in the lab and six on call."

"Mrs. Burdett called, also. She swears little Tony or Antoinette is whistling. She can hear him/her."

"And your diagnosis?" Edward asked, grinning.

"Gas."

"High-pressure, I'd say," Edward added.

"Steam, must be," Gail said. They laughed and Edward felt the morning assume reality. Last night's mist of fantasy lifted and he was on the phone with his wife, making jokes about musical fetuses. That was normal. That was living.

64

"I'm going to take you out tonight," he said. "Another Heisenberg dinner."

"What's that?"

"Uncertainty," Edward said crisply. "We know where we are going, but not what we are going to eat. Or vice versa."

"Sounds wonderful. Which car?"

"The Quantum, of course."

"Oh, Lord. We just had the speedometer fixed."

"And the steering went out?"

"Shh! It's still working. We're cheating."

"Are you mad at me?"

Gail hmphed. "Vergil better see you during office hours today. Why is he seeing you, anyway? Sex-change?" The thought made her giggle and start to cough. He could picture her turning the phone away and waving at the air as if to clear it. "'Scuse. Really, Edward. Why?"

"Confidential, my love. I'm not sure I know, anyway. Maybe later."

"Got to go. Six?"

"Maybe five-thirty."

"I'll still be critiquing videos."

"I'll sweep you away."

"Delicious Edward."

He cupped the receiver and smooched indelicately before hanging up. Then, rubbing his cheek to ball up and remove the tissue paper, he walked to the elevator and rode up to the Frankenstein Wing.

The analyzer was still clinking merrily, running hundreds of samples bottle by bottle through the tests. Edward sat down to its terminal and called up Vergil's results. Columns and numbers appeared on the screen. The suggested diagnosis was unusually vague. Anomalies appeared in high-lighted red type.

24/c ser c/ count 10,000 lymphoc. / mm³
25/c ser c/count 14,500 lymphoc. / mm³
26/d check re/count 15,000 lymphoc. / mm³
DIAG (???) What are accompanying physical signs? If the spleen and lymph nodes show enlargement, then:
ReDIAG: Patient (name? file?) in late stages of severe infection.
Support: Histamine count, blood protein level (call), phagocyte count (call)

*DIAG (???) (Blood sample inconclusive): If anemia, pain
in joints, hemorrhage, fever:
ReDIAG: Incipient lymphocytic leukemia
Support: Not a good fit, no support but lymphocyte count.*

Edward asked for a hard copy of the analysis and the printer
quietly produced a tight-packed page of figures. He looked it over,
frowning deeply, folded it and stuck it in his coat pocket. The
urine test seemed normal enough; the blood was unlike any he
had ever seen before. He didn't need to test the stool to make up
his mind on a course of action: put the man in the hospital, under
observation. Edward dialed Vergil's number on the phone in his
office.

On the second ring, a noncommittal female voice answered,
"Ulam's house, Candice here."

"Could I speak to Vergil, please?"

"Whom may I say is calling?" Her tone was almost comically
formal.

"Edward. He knows me."

"Of course. You're the doctor. Fix him up. Fix up everybody."
A hand muffled the mouthpiece and she called out, somewhat
raucously, "Vergil!"

Vergil answered with a breathless "Edward! What's up?"

"Hello, Vergil. I have some results, not very conclusive. But
I want to talk with you, here, in the hospital."

"What do the results say?"

"That you are a very ill person."

"Nonsense."

"I'm just telling you what the machine says. High lymphocyte
count—"

"Of course, that fits perfectly—"

"And a very weird variety of proteins and other debris floating
around in your blood. Histamines. You look like a fellow dying
of severe infection."

There was silence on Vergil's end, then, "I'm not dying."

"I think you should come in, let others check you over. And
who was that on the phone—Candice? She—"

"No. Edward, I went to *you* for help. Nobody else. You know
how I feel about hospitals."

Edward laughed grimly. "Vergil, I'm not competent to figure
this out."

"I told you what it was. Now you have to help me control it."

"That's crazy, that's bullshit, Vergil!" Edward clamped his hand on his knee and pinched hard. "Sorry. I'm not taking this well. I hope you understand why."

"I hope you understand how *I'm* feeling, right now. I'm sort of high, Edward. And more than a little afraid. And proud. Does that make sense?"

"Vergil, I—"

"Come to the apartment. Let's talk and figure out what to do next."

"I'm on duty, Vergil."

"When can you come out?"

"I'm on for the next five days. This evening, maybe. After dinner."

"Just you, nobody else," Vergil said.

"Okay." He took down directions. It would take him about seventy minutes to get to La Jolla; he told Vergil he would be there by nine.

Gail was home before Edward, who offered to fix a quickie dinner for them. "Raincheck the night out?"

She took the news of his trip glumly and didn't say much as she helped chop vegetables for a salad. "I'd like to have you look at some of the videos," she said as they ate, giving him a sidewise glance. Her nursery class had been involved in video art projects for a week; she was proud of the results.

"Is there time?" he asked diplomatically. They had weathered some rocky times before getting married, almost splitting up. When new difficulties arose, they tended to be overly delicate now, tiptoeing around the main issues.

"Probably not," Gail admitted. She stabbed at a piece of raw zucchini. "What's wrong with Vergil this time?"

"This time?"

"Yeah. He's done this before. When he was working for Westinghouse and he got into that copyright mess."

"Freelancing for them."

"Yeah. What can you do for him now?"

"I'm not even sure what the problem is," Edward said, being more evasive than he wanted.

"Secret?"

"No. Maybe. But weird."

"Is he ill?"

Edward cocked his head and lifted a hand: Who knows?

"You're not going to tell me?"

"Not right now." Edward's smile, an attempt to placate, obviously only irritated her more. "He asked me not to."

"Could he get you in trouble?"

Edward hadn't thought about that. "I don't think so," he said.

"Coming back what time tonight?"

"As soon as I can," he said. He stroked her face with the tips of his fingers. "Don't be mad," he suggested softly.

"Oh, no," she said emphatically. "Never that."

Edward began the drive to La Jolla in an ambiguous mood; whenever he thought about Vergil's condition, it was as if he entered a different universe. The rules changed, and Edward was not sure he had even the inkling of an outcome.

He took the La Jolla Village Drive exit and wandered down Torrey Pines Road into the city. Modest and very expensive homes vied for space with three and four-story apartment buildings and condominiums along curving, sloping streets. Bicyclists and the perennial joggers wore brightly colored jumpsuits to ward off the cool night air; even at this hour of the night, La Jolla was active with strollers and exercisers.

He found a parking space with little difficulty and deftly pulled the Volkswagen in. Locking the door, he sniffed the sea air and wondered if he and Gail could afford to move. The rent would be very steep, the commute would be long. He decided he wasn't that concerned with status. Still, the neighborhood was nice— 410 Pearl Street, not the best the town had to offer, but more than he could afford, now at least. It was simply Vergil's way to fall into opportunities like the condominium. On the other hand, Edward decided as he buzzed at the ground level door, he wouldn't want Vergil's luck if it accompanied the rest of the package.

The elevator played bland music and displayed little hologram clips advertising condos for sale, various products and social activities for the upcoming week. On the third floor, Edward walked past imitation Louis 15th furniture and gold-marbled mirrors.

Vergil opened the door on the first ring and motioned him inside. He wore a checked robe with long sleeves and carpet slippers. His fingers twisted an unlit pipe in one hand as he walked into the living room and sat down, saying nothing.

"You have an infection," Edward reiterated, showing him the printout.

"Oh?" Vergil looked the paper over quickly, then set it down on the glass coffee table.

"That's what the machine says."

"Yes, well apparently it isn't prepared for such odd cases.'"

"Perhaps not, but I'd advise—"

"I know. Sorry to be rude, Edward, but what's a hospital going to do for me? I'd sooner take a computer into a shopful of cavemen and ask them to fix it. These figures . . . they undoubtedly show something, but we aren't able to decide what."

Edward removed his coat. "Listen. You have me worried now." Vergil's expression changed slowly to a kind of frantic beatitude. He squinted at the ceiling and pursed his lips.

"Where's Candice?"

"Out for the evening. We're not getting along too well right now."

"She knows?"

Vergil smirked. "How could she not know? She sees me naked every night." He turned away from Edward as he said that. He was lying.

"Are you stoned?"

He shook his head, then nodded once, very slow. "Listening," he said.

"To what?"

"I don't know. Sounds. Not sounds. Like music. The heart, all the blood vessels, the friction of the blood along the arteries, veins. Activity. Music in the blood." He regarded Edward plaintively. "What excuse did you give Gail?"

"None, really. Just that you were in trouble and I had to come see you."

"Can you stay?"

"No." He glanced around the apartment suspiciously, looking for ashtrays, packs of papers.

"I'm not stoned, Edward," Vergil said. "I may be wrong, but I think something big is happening. I think they're finding out who I am."

Edward sat down across from Vergil, staring at him intently. Vergil didn't seem to notice. Some inner process was absorbing him.

"Is there any coffee?" Edward asked. Vergil motioned to the kitchen. Edward filled a pot of water to boil and took a jar of instant from the fourth cabinet he looked into. Cup in hand, he returned to the seat. Vergil twisted his head back and forth, eyes wide open.

"You always knew what you wanted to be, didn't you?" he asked Edward.

"More or less."

"Smart moves. A gynecologist. Never false moves. I was different. I had goals, but no direction. Like a map without roads, just places to be. I didn't give a shit for anything or anybody but

myself. Even science. Just a means. I'm surprised I got so far."
He gripped his chair arms. "As for Mother . . ." The tension in his
hand was clear. "Witch. Witch and spook for parents. Changeling
child. Where small things make big changes."

"Something wrong?"

'They're talking to me, Edward." He shut his eyes.

"Jesus." There was nothing else he could think of to say. He
thought wildly of hoaxes and being made a fool of and Vergil's
unreliability in the past, but he could not get away from the hard
facts the diagnostic equipment had shown him.

For a quarter-hour Vergil seemed to be asleep. Edward checked
his pulse, which was strong and steady; felt his forehead—slightly
cool—and made himself more coffee. He was about to pick up
the phone, undecided whether to call a hospital or Gail, when
Vergil's eyelids flickered open and he shifted his gaze to meet
Edward's.

"Hard to understand exactly what time is like for them," he
said. "It's taken them maybe three, four days to figure out language, key human concepts. Can you imagine, Edward? They
didn't even *know*. They thought I was the universe. But now
they're on to it. On to me. Right now." He stood and walked
across the beige carpet to the curtained plate glass window, clum-
sily reaching behind the drapes to find the cord and pull it. A few
apartment and house lights descended to the abyss of the night
ocean. "They must have thousands of researchers hooked up to
my neurons. They're damned efficient, you know, not to have
screwed me up. So delicate in there. Making changes."

"The hospital," Edward said hoarsely. He cleared his throat.
"Please, Vergil. Now."

"What in hell can a hospital do? Did you figure out any way
to control the cells? I mean, they're my own. Hurt them, hurt
me."

"I've been thinking." Actually, the idea had just popped into
his head—a sure sign that he was starting to believe Vergil. "Actinomycin can bind to DNA and stop transcription. We could slow
them down that way—surely that would screw up this biologic
you've described."

"I'm allergic to actinomycin. It would kill me."

Edward looked down at his hands. That had been his best shot,
he was sure of it. "We could do some experiments, see how they
metabolize, differ from other cells. If we could isolate a nutrient
they require more of, we could starve them. Maybe even radiation
treatments—"

"Hurt them," Vergil said, turning toward Edward, "hurt me." He stood in the middle of the living room and held out his arms. The robe fell open and revealed Vergil's legs and torso. Shadow obscured any visible detail. "I'm not sure I want to be rid of them. They're not doing any harm."

Edward swallowed back his frustration and tried to control a flush of anger, only making it worse. "How do you know?"

Vergil shook his head and held up one finger. "They're trying to understand what space is. That's tough for them. They break distances down into concentrations of chemicals. For them, space is a range of taste intensities."

"Vergil—"

"Listen, think, Edward!" His tone was excited but even. "Something is happening inside me. They talk to each other with proteins and nucleic acids, through the fluids, through membranes. They tailor something—viruses, maybe—to carry long messages or personality traits or biologic. Plasmid-like structures. That makes sense. Those are some of the ways I programmed them. Maybe that's what your machine calls infection—all the new information in my blood. Chatter. Tastes of other individuals. Peers. Superiors. Subordinates."

"Vergil, I'm listening, but I—"

"This is my show, Edward. I'm their universe. They're amazed by the new scale." He sat down and was quiet again for a time. Edward squatted by his chair and pulled up the sleeve of Vergil's robe. His arm was criss-crossed with white lines.

"I'm calling an ambulance," Edward said, reaching for the table phone.

"No!" Vergil cried, sitting up. "I told you, I'm not sick, this is my show. What can they do for me? It would be a farce."

"Then what in hell am I doing here?" Edward asked, becoming angry. "I can't do anything. I'm one of the cavemen and you came to me—"

"You're a friend," Vergil said, fixing his eyes on him. Edward had the unnerving suspicion he was being watched by more than just Vergil. "I wanted you here to keep me company." He laughed. "But I'm not exactly alone, am I?"

"I have to call Gail," Edward said, dialing the number.

"Gail, yeah. But don't tell her anything."

"Oh, no. Absolutely."

11

By dawn, Vergil was walking around the apartment, fingering things, looking out windows, slowly and methodically making himself lunch. "You know, I can actually feel their thoughts," he said. Edward watched, exhausted and sick with tension, from an armchair in the living room. "I mean, their cytoplasm seems to have a will of its own. A kind of subconscious life, counter to the rationality they've acquired so recently. They hear the chemical 'noise' of molecules fitting and unfitting inside."

He stood in the middle of the living room, robe fallen open, eyes closed. He seemed to be taking brief naps. It was possible, Edward thought, that he was undergoing *petit mal* seizures. Who could predict what havoc the lymphocytes were wreaking in his brain?

Edward called Gail again from the kitchen phone. She was preparing for work. He asked her to phone the hospital and tell them he was too ill to come to work. "Cover up for you? This must be serious. What's wrong with Vergil? Can't he change his own diapers?"

Edward didn't say anything.

"Everything okay?" she asked, after a long pause.

Was it? Decidedly not. "Fine," he said.

"Culture!" Vergil said loudly, peering around the kitchen divider. Edward said good-by and quickly hung up. "They're always swimming in a bath of information. Contributing to it. It's a kind of gestalt thing, whatever. The hierarchy is absolute. They send tailored phages after cells that don't interact properly. Viruses specified to individuals or groups. No escape. One gets pierced by a virus, the cell blebs outward, it explodes and dissolves. But it's not just a dictatorship. I think they effectively have more freedom than we do. They vary so differently—I mean, from individual to individual, if there are individuals, they vary in different ways than we do. Does that make sense?"

"No," Edward said softly, rubbing his temples. "Vergil, you are pushing me close to the edge. I can't take this much longer.

72

I don't understand, I'm not sure I believe—"

"Not even now?"

"Okay, let's say you're giving me the right interpretation. Giving it to me straight and the whole thing's true. Have you bothered to figure out the consequences?"

Vergil regarded him warily. "My mother," he said.

"What about her?"

"Anyone who cleans a toilet."

"Please make sense." Desperation made Edward's voice almost whiny.

"I've never been very good at that," Vergil murmured. "Figuring out where things might lead."

"Aren't you afraid?"

"Terrified," Vergil said. His grin became maniacal. "Exhilarated." He kneeled beside Edward's chair. "At first, I wanted to control them. But they are more capable than I am. Who am I, a blundering fool, to try to frustrate them? They're up to something very important."

"What if they kill you?"

Vergil lay on the floor and spread out his arms and legs. "Dead dog," he said. Edward felt like kicking him. "Look, I don't want you to think I'm going around you, but yesterday I went to see Michael Bernard. He put me through his private clinic, took a whole range of specimens. Biopsies. You can't see where he took muscle tissue samples, skin samples, anything. It's all healed. He said it checks out. And he asked me not to tell anybody." His expression became dreamy again. "Cities of cells," he said. "Edward, they push pili-like tubes through the tissues, spread themselves, their information, convert other kinds of cells . . ."

"Stop it!" Edward shouted. His voice cracked. "What checks out?"

"As Bernard puts it, I have 'severely enlarged' lymphocytes. The other data isn't ready yet. I mean, it was only yesterday. So this isn't our common delusion."

"What does he plan to do?"

"He's going to convince Genetron to take me back. Reopen my lab."

"Is that what you want?"

"It's not just having the lab open again. Let me show you. Since I stopped the lamp treatments, my skin's been changing again." He pulled back the robe where he lay on the floor.

The skin all over Vergil's body was crisscrossed with white

lines. He turned over. Along his back, the lines were starting to form ridges.

"My God," Edward said.

"I'm not going to be much good anywhere else but the lab," Vergil said. "I won't be able to go out in public."

"You . . . you can talk to them, tell them to slow down." He was immediately aware how ridiculous that sounded.

"Yes, indeed I can, but that doesn't mean they listen."

"I thought you're their god."

"The ones hooked up to my neutrons aren't the big wheels. They're researchers, or at least serve the same function. They know I'm here, what I am, but that doesn't mean they've convinced the upper levels of the hierarchy."

"They're disputing?"

"Something like that." He pulled the robe back on and went to the window, peering through the curtains as if looking for someone. "I don't have anything left but them. They aren't afraid. Edward, I've never felt so close to anyone or anything before." Again, the beatific smile. "I'm responsible for them. Mother to them all. You know, until the last few days, I didn't even have a name for them. A mother should name her offspring, shouldn't she?"

Edward didn't answer.

"I looked all around—dictionaries, textbooks, everywhere. Then it just popped into my head. 'Noocytes.' From the Greek word for mind, 'noos.' Noocytes. Sounds kind of ominous, doesn't it? I told Bernard. He seemed to think it was a good name—"

Edward raised his arms in exasperation. "You don't know what they're going to do! You say they're like a civilization—"

"A thousand civilizations."

"Yes, and civilizations have been known to screw up before. Warfare, the environment—" He was grasping at straws, trying to restrain the panic that had been growing since he arrived. He wasn't competent to handle the enormity of what was happening. And neither was Vergil. Vergil was the last person Edward would have called insightful and wise with regard to large issues.

"But I'm the only one at risk," Vergil said.

"You don't know that. Jesus, Vergil, look what they're *doing* to you!"

"I accept it," he said stoically.

Edward shook his head, as much as admitting defeat. "Okay. Bernard gets Genetron to reopen the lab, you move in, become a guinea pig. What then?"

"They treat me right. I'm more than just good ol' Vergil I. Ulam right now. I'm a goddamned galaxy, a super-mother."

"Super-host, you mean."

Vergil conceded the point with a shrug.

Edward felt his throat constricting. "I can't help you," he said. "I can't talk to you, convince you, can't help you. You're as stubborn as ever." That sounded almost benign; how could "stubborn" describe an attitude like Vergil's? He tried to clarify what he meant but could only stammer. "I have to go," he finally managed to say. "I can't do you any good here."

Vergil nodded. "I suppose not. This can't be easy."

"No," Edward said, swallowing. Vergil stepped forward and seemed about to put his hands on Edward's shoulders. Edward backed away instinctively.

"I'd like at least your understanding," Vergil said, dropping his arms. "This is the greatest thing I've ever done." His face twisted into a grimace. "I'm not sure how much longer I can face it, face up to it I mean. I don't know whether they'll kill me or not. I think not. The strain, Edward."

Edward backed away toward the door and put his hand on the knob. Vergil's face, temporarily creased with an agony of worry, returned to beatitude. "Hey," he said. "Listen. They—"

Edward opened the door and stepped outside, closing it firmly behind him. He quickly walked to the elevator and punched the button for the ground floor.

He stood in the empty lobby for a few minutes, trying to control his erratic breathing. He glanced at his watch: nine in the morning.

Who *would* Vergil listen to?

Vergil had gone to Bernard; perhaps Bernard was now the pivot on which the whole situation turned. Vergil made it seem as if Bernard were not only convinced, but very interested. People of Bernard's stature didn't coax the Vergil Ulams of the world along unless they felt it was to their advantage. As Edward pushed through the double glass doors, he decided to play a hunch.

Vergil lay in the middle of the living room, arms and legs cruciform, and laughed. Then he sobered and asked himself what impression he had made on Edward, or on Bernard for that matter. Not important, he decided. Nothing was important but what was going on *inside,* the interior universe.

"I've always been a big fellow," Vergil murmured.

Everything

—Yes, I *am* everything now.

Explain

—What? I mean, explain what?

Simplicities

—Yes, I imagine it's tough waking up. Well, you deserve the difficulties. Damn very old DNA finally waking up.

SPOKEN with other.

—What?

WORDS communicate with *share body structure external* is this like *wholeness WITHIN* *totality* is EXTERNAL alike

—I'm not understanding, you're not clear.

Silence inside for how long? Difficult to tell the passage of time; hours and days in minutes and seconds. The noocytes had screwed up his brain clock. And what else?

YOU *interface* *stand BETWEEN* EXTERNAL and INTERNAL. Are they alike

—Inside and outside? Oh, no.

Are OUTSIDE *share body structure* alike

—You mean Edward, don't you? Yes indeed . . . share body structure alike.

EDWARD and other structure INTERNAL similar/same

—Oh yes, he's quite the same except for you. Only—yes, and is she better now? She wasn't well last night.

No answer to that question.

Query

—He doesn't have you. Nobody does. Is she all right? We're the only ones. I made you. Nobody else but us has you.

A deep and profound silence.

Edward drove to the La Jolla Museum of Modern Art and walked across the concrete to a payphone near a bronze drinking fountain. Fog drifted in from the ocean, obscuring the cream-plastered Spanish lines of the Church of St. James by the Sea and beading on the leaves of the trees. He inserted his credit card into the phone and asked information for the number of Genetron, Inc. The mechanical voice replied swiftly and he dialed through.

"Please page Dr. Michael Bernard," he told the receptionist.

"Who's calling, please?"

"This is his answering service. We have an emergency call and his beeper doesn't seem to be working."

A few anxious minutes later, Bernard came on the line. "Who the hell is this?" he asked quietly. "I don't have an answering service."

"My name is Edward Milligan. I'm a friend of Vergil Ulam's. I think we have some problems to discuss."

There was a long silence on the other end. "You're at Mount Freedom, aren't you, Dr. Milligan?"

"Yes."

"Staying down here?"

"Not really."

"I can't see you today. Would tomorrow morning be acceptable?"

Edward thought of driving up and back, of time lost and of Gail, worrying. It all seemed trivial. "Yes," he said.

"Nine o'clock, at Genetron. 60895 North Torrey Pines Road."

"Fine."

Edward walked back to his car in the morning grayness. As he opened the door and slid into the seat, he had a sudden thought. Candice hadn't come home last night.

She had been in the apartment that morning.

Vergil had been lying about her; he was sure of that much. So what role was she playing?

And where was she?

12

Gail found Edward lying on the couch, sleeping fitfully as a chill freak winter breeze whistled outside. She sat down beside him and stroked his arm until his eyes opened.

"Hi," she said.

"Hi to you." He blinked and looked around. "What time is it?"

"I just got home."

"Four-thirty. Christ. Have I been asleep?"

"I wasn't here," Gail said. "Have you?"

"I'm still tired."

"So what did Vergil do this time?"

Edward's face assumed a patent mask of equanimity. He caressed her chin with one finger—"Chin chucking," she called it, finding it faintly objectionable, as if she were a cat.

"Something's wrong," she said. "Are you going to tell me, or just keep acting like everything's normal?"

"I don't know what to tell you," Edward said.

"Oh, Lord," Gail sighed, standing. "You're going to divorce me for that Baker woman." Mrs. Baker weighed three hundred pounds and hadn't known she was pregnant until her fifth month.

"No," Edward said listlessly.

"Rapturous relief." Gail touched his forehead lightly. "You know this kind of introspection drives me crazy."

"Well, it's nothing I can talk about, so . . ." He took her hand in his and patted it.

"That's disgustingly patronizing," she said. "I'm going to make some tea. Want some?" He nodded and she went into the kitchen.

Why not just reveal all? he asked himself. An old friend was turning himself into a galaxy.

He cleared away the dining table instead.

That night, unable to sleep, Edward looked down on Gail from his sitting position, pillow against the wall, and tried to determine what he knew was real, and what wasn't.

I'm a doctor, he told himself. A technical, scientific profession. Supposed to be immune to things like future shock.

78

Vergil Ulam was turning into a galaxy.

How would it feel to be topped off with a trillion Chinese? He grinned in the dark, and almost cried at the same time. What Vergil had inside him was unimaginably stranger than Chinese. Stranger than anything Edward—or Vergil—could easily understand. Perhaps ever understand.

What kind of *psychology* or *personality* would a cell develop— or a cluster of cells, for that matter? He tried to recall all his schooling on cell environments in the human body. Blood, lymph, tissue, interstitial fluid, cerebrospinal fluid . . . He could not imagine an organism of human complexity in such surroundings not going crazy from boredom. The environment was simple, the demands relatively simple, and the levels of behavior were suited to cells, not people. On the other hand, stress might be the major factor—the environment was benign to familiar cells, hell on unfamiliar cells.

But he knew what was important, if not necessarily what was real: the bedroom, streetlights and tree shadows on the window curtains, Gail sleeping.

Very important. Gail, in bed, sleeping.

He thought of Vergil sterilizing the dishes of altered *E. coli*. The bottle of enhanced lymphocytes. Perversely, Krypton came to mind—Superman's home world, billions of geniuses destroyed in an all-encompassing calamity. Murder? Genocide?

There was no barrier between sleeping and waking. He was watching the window, and city lights glared through as the curtains opened. They could have been living in New York (Irvine nights were never that brightly illuminated) or Chicago; he had lived in Chicago for two years

and the window shattered, soundless, the glass peeling back and falling away. The city crawled in through the window, a great, spikey lighted-up prowler growling in a language he couldn't understand, made up of auto horns, crowd noises, construction bedlam. He tried to fight it off, but it got to Gail and turned into a shower of stars, sprinkling all over the bed, all over everything in the room.

He jerked awake to the sound of a gust of wind and the windows rattling. Best not to sleep, he decided, and stayed awake until it was time to dress with Gail. As she left for the school, he kissed her deeply, savoring the reality of her human, unviolated lips.

Then he made the long drive to North Torrey Pines Road, past the Salk Institute with its spare concrete architecture, past the dozens of new and resurrected research centers which made up Enzyme Valley, surrounded by eucalypti and the new hybrid fast-growing conifers whose ancestors had given the road its name.

The black sign with red Times Roman letters sat atop its mound of Korean grass. The buildings beyond followed the fashion of simple planar concrete surfaces, except for the ominous black cube of the defense contracts labs.

At the guardhouse, a thin, wiry man in dark blue stepped out of his cubicle and leaned down to the Volkswagen's window level. He stared at Edward with an air of aloofness. "Business, sir?"

"I'm here to see Dr. Bernard."

The guard asked for ID. Edward produced his wallet. The guard took it to his phone in the cubicle and spent some time discussing its contents. He returned it, still aloof, and said, "There ain't any visitor's parking. Take space 31 in the employee lot, that's around this curve and on the other side of the front office, west wing. Don't go anywhere but the front office."

"Of course not," Edward said testily. "Around this curve." He pointed. The guard nodded curtly and returned to the cubicle.

Edward walked down the flagstone path to the front office. Papyrus reeds grew next to concrete ponds filled with gold and silver carp. The glass doors opened at his approach, and he entered. The circular lobby held a single couch and table of technical journals and newspapers.

"May I help you?" the receptionist asked. She was slender, attractive, hair carefully arranged in the current artificial bun that Gail so fervently eschewed.

"Dr. Bernard, please."

"Dr. Bernard?" She looked puzzled. "We don't have—"

"Dr. Milligan?"

Edward turned to see Bernard entering the automatic doors. "Thank you, Janet," he said to the receptionist. She returned to her switchboard to route calls. "Please come with me, Dr. Milligan. We'll have a conference room all to ourselves." He led Edward through the rear door and down the concrete path flanking the west wing's ground floor.

Bernard wore a dapper gray suit that matched his graying hair; his profile was sharp and handsome. He closely resembled Leonard Bernstein; it was easy to see why the press had accorded him so much coverage. He was a pioneer—and photogenic, besides. "We keep very tight security here. It's the court decisions of the last ten years, you know. They've been absolutely insane. Losing patent rights because of simply mentioning work being done at a scientific conference. That sort of thing. What else can we expect when the judges are so ignorant of what's really happening?" The question seemed rhetorical. Edward nodded politely and obeyed Bernard's hand gesture to climb a flight of steel stairs to the second floor.

"You've seen Vergil recently?" Bernard asked as he unlocked room 245.

"Yesterday."

Bernard entered ahead of him and turned on the lights. The room was barely ten feet square, furnished with a round table and four chairs and a blackboard on one wall. Bernard closed the door. "Sit, please." Edward pulled out a chair and Bernard sat opposite him, putting his elbows on the table. "Ulam is brilliant. And I won't hesitate to say, courageous."

"He's my friend. I'm very worried about him."

Bernard held up one finger. "Courageous—and a bloody damned fool. What's happening to him should never have been allowed. He may have done it under duress, but that's no excuse. Still, what's done is done. You know everything, I take it."

"I know the basics," Edward said. "I'm still not clear on how he did it."

"Nor are we, Dr. Milligan. That's one of the reasons we're offering him a lab again. And a home, while we sort this out."

"He shouldn't be in public," Edward said.

"No, indeed. We're constructing an isolation lab right now. But we're a private company and our resources are limited."

"This should be reported to the NIH and the FDA."

Bernard sighed. "Yes. Well, we'd stand to lose everything if word leaked out right now. I'm not talking about business decisions—we'd stand to lose the whole biochips industry. The public outcry could be horrendous."

"Vergil is very sick. Physically, mentally. He may die."

"Somehow, I don't think he'll die," Bernard said. "But we're getting away from the focus."

"What is the focus?" Edward asked angrily. "I assume you're working hand-in-glove with Genetron now—you certainly talk like you are. What does Genetron stand to gain?"

Bernard leaned back in his chair. "I can think of a large number of uses for small, super-dense computer elements with a biological base. Can't you? Genetron has already made breakthroughs, but Vergil's work is something else again."

"What do you envision?"

Bernard's smile was sunny and certifiably false. "I'm not really at liberty to say. It'll be revolutionary. We'll have to study him in lab conditions. Animal experiments have to be conducted. We'll have to start from scratch, of course. Vergil's . . . um . . . colonies can't be transferred. They're based on his own cells. We have to develop organisms that won't trigger immune responses in other aminals."

"Like an infection?" Edward asked.

"I suppose there are similarities. But Vergil is not infected or ill in the normal uses of the words."

"My tests indicate he is," Edward said.

"I don't think the usual diagnostics are appropriate, do you?"

"I don't know."

"Listen," Bernard said, leaning forward. "I'd like you to come and work with us once Vergil's settled in. Your expertise might be useful to us."

Edward almost flinched at the openness of the offer. "How will you benefit from all this?" he asked. "I mean you, personally."

"Edward, I have always been at the forefront of my profession. I see no reason why I shouldn't be helping here. With my knowledge of brain and nerve functions, and the research I've been conducting in artificial intelligence and neurophysiology—"

"You could help Genetron hold off a government investigation," Edward said.

"That's being very blunt. Too blunt, and unfair." For a moment, Edward sensed uncertainty and even a touch of anxiety in Bernard.

"Maybe I am," Edward said. "And maybe that's not the worst thing that can happen."

"I don't get you," Bernard said.

"Bad dreams, Mr. Bernard."

Bernard's eyes narrowed and his brows lowered. Here was an uncharacterisic expression, not suitable for covers on *Time, Mega* or *Rolling Stone:* a puzzled and angry scowl. "Our time is too valuable to be wasted. I've made the offer in good faith."

"Of course," Edward said. "And of course, I'd like to visit the lab when Vergil's settled in. If I'm still welcome, bluntness and all."

"Of course," Bernard echoed, but his thoughts were almost nakedly apparent: Edward would never be playing on *his* team. They rose together and Bernard held out his hand. His palm was damp; he was as nervous as Edward.

"I assume you want this all in strict confidence," Edward said.

"I'm not sure we can require it of you. You're not under contract."

"No," Edward said.

Bernard regarded him for a long moment, then nodded. "I'll escort you out."

"There's one more thing," Edward said. "Do you know anything about a woman named Candice?"

"Vergil mentioned he had a girlfriend by that name."

"Had, or has?"

"Yes, I see what you mean," Bernard said. "She could be a security problem."

"No, that's *not* what I mean," Edward said emphatically. "Not at all what I mean."

13

Bernard went through the stapled papers carefully, hand on forehead, lifting the legal-sized pages and folding them back, his frown deepening.

What was going on in the black cube was enough to make his hair stand on end. The information was by no means complete, but his friends in Washington had done a remarkable job. The packet had arrived by special courier just half an hour after Edward Milligan left.

Their conversation had filled him with a biting, defensive shame. He saw a distant version of himself in the young doctor, and the comparison hurt. Had good old famous Michael Bernard been walking around in a fog of capitalistic seduction the last few months?

At first, Genetron's offer had seemed clean and sweet—minimal participation in the first few months, then status as a father-figure and pioneer, his image to be used to promote the company.

It had taken him entirely too long to realize how close he was to the trigger of the trap.

He looked up at the window and stood to raise the blinds. With a rustling snap, he had a clear view of the mound, the black cube, the wind-swept clouds beyond.

He could smell disaster. The black cube, ironically, would not be involved; but if Vergil Ulam had not triggered things, then the other side of Genetron would have done so eventually.

Ulam had been fired so precipitously, and blackballed so thoroughly, not because he had done sloppy research—but because he had followed so closely on the heels of the defense research division. He had succeeded where they had met frequent setbacks and failure. And even though they had studied his files for months (multiple copies had been made) they could not duplicate his results.

Harrison yesterday had murmured that Ulam's discoveries must have been largely accidental. It was obvious why he would say that now.

Ulam had come very close to taking his success and leaving Genetron, and the government, in the lurch. The Big Boys could not put up with that, and could not trust Ulam.

He was your basic crackpot. He could never have gotten a security clearance.

So they had tossed him out, and frozen him out.

And then he had come back to *haunt*. They could not refuse him now.

Bernard read the papers through once more and asked himself how he could back away from the mess with the minimum of damage.

Should he? If they were such fools, wouldn't his expertise be useful—or at least his clear thinking? He had no doubt he could think more clearly than Harrison and Yng.

But Genetron's interest in him was largely as a figurehead. How much influence could he have, even now?

He dropped the blinds and twisted the rod to close them. Then he picked up his phone and dialed Harrison's number.

"Yes?"

"Bernard."

"Certainly, Michael."

"I'm going to call Ulam now. We're going to bring him in now. Today. Get your whole team ready, and the defense research people, too."

"Michael, that's—"

"We can't just leave him out there."

Harrison paused. "Yes, I agree."

"Then get on it."

14

Edward ate lunch at a Jack-in-the-Box and sat in the glass-enclosed eating area after he was finished, arm on a window ledge, staring out at the passing traffic. Something wasn't right at Genetron. He could always rely on his strongest hunches; some part of his brain reserved for close observation and cataloging of minute details would sometimes put 2 and 2 together and get a disturbing 5, and lo and behold, one of the 2s would really be a 3; he just hadn't noticed it before.

Bernard and Harrison were hiding a very salient fact. Genetron was doing more than just helping an ex-employee with a work-related problem, more even than just preparing to take advantage of a breakthrough. But they couldn't act too quickly; that would arouse suspicion. And perhaps they weren't sure they had the wherewithal.

He scowled, trying to pry loose the chain of reasoning from the clay matrix where it had been pressed and examine it link by link. Security. Bernard had mentioned security in connection with Candice. They might just be concerned with company security, sharing the fear of industrial espionage that had turned every private research company along North Torrey Pines Road into a steel-shell turtle, closed to public scrutiny. But that couldn't be all.

They couldn't be as stupid and unseeing as Vergil; they had to know that what was happening to Vergil was far too important to be held close to the breast of a single business concern.

Therefore, they had contacted the government. Was that a justified assumption? (Perhaps it was something he should do, whether Genetron had or not.) And the government was acting as quickly as possible—that is, on a timescale of days or weeks—to make its decisions, prepare its plans, take action. In the meanwhile, Vergil was unattended. Genetron didn't dare do anything against his will; genetic research companies were already regarded with enough suspicion by the public, and a scandal could do much more than disrupt their stock plans.

Vergil was on his own. And Edward knew his old friend well enough to realize that meant no one was watching the store. Vergil was not a responsible person. But he was under self-imposed isolation, staying in the apartment (wasn't he?), suffering his mental transformation, locked in his psychosis-inducing ecstasy, filled with the results of his brilliance.

With a start, Edward realized he was the only person who could do something.

He was the last responsible individual.

It was time to return to Vergil's apartment and at least keep track of things until the Big Boys came on the scene.

As he drove, Edward thought about change. There was only so much change a single individual could stand. Innovation, even radical creation, was essential, but the results had to be applied cautiously, with careful forethought. Nothing forced, nothing imposed. That was the ideal. Everyone had the right to stay the same until they decided otherwise.

That was damned *naïve*.

What Vergil had done was the greatest thing in science since—

Since what? There were no comparisons. Vergil Ulam had become a god. Within his flesh he carried hundreds of billions of intelligent beings.

Edward couldn't handle the thought. "Neo-Luddite," he murmured to himself, a filthy accusation.

When he pressed the buzzer on the condo security panel, Vergil answered almost immediately. "Yeah," he said, sounding exhilarated, very up.

"Edward."

"Hey, Edward! Come on in. I'm taking a bath. Door's unlocked."

Edward entered Vergil's living room and walked down the hallway to the bathroom. Vergil was in the tub, up to his neck in pinkish water. He smiled vaguely at Edward and splashed his hands. "Looks like I slit my wrists, doesn't it?" he said, his voice a happy whisper. "Don't worry. Everything's fine now. Genetron's coming over to take me back. Bernard and Harrison and the lab guys, all in a van." His face was criss-crossed with pale ridges and his hands were covered with white bumps.

"I talked to Bernard this morning," Edward said, perplexed.

"Hey, they just called," Vergil said, pointing to his bathroom intercom and phone. "I've been in here for an hour, hour and a half. Soaking and thinking."

Edward sat on the toilet. The quartz lamp stood unplugged next to the linen cabinet.

"You're sure that's what you want," he said, his shoulders slumping.

"Yeah. I'm sure," Vergil said. "Reunion. Take back the prodigal son, not so prodigal? You know, I never understood what that prodigal bit meant. Does it mean 'prodigy'? I'm certainly that. I'm going back in style. Everything's style from here on."

The pinkish color in the water didn't look like soap. "Is that bubble bath?" Edward asked. Another thought came to him suddenly and left him weak.

"No," Vergil said. "It's coming from my skin. They're not telling me everything, but I think they're sending out scouts. Hey! Astronauts! Yeah." He looked at Edward with an expression that didn't quite cross over into concern; more like curiosity as to how he'd take it.

Edward's stomach muscles tightened as if waiting for a second punch. He had never seriously considered the possibility until now—not consciously—perhaps because he had been concentrating on accepting, and focusing on more immediate problems. "Is this the first time?"

"Yeah," Vergil said. He laughed. "I have half a mind to let the little buggers down the drain. Let them find out what the world's really about."

"They'd go everywhere," Edward said.

"Sure enough."

Edward nodded. Sure enough. "You never introduced me to Candice," he said. Vergil shook his head.

"Hey, that's right." Nothing more.

"How . . . how are you feeling?"

"I'm feeling pretty good right now. Must be billions of them." More splashing with his hands. "What do you think? Should I let the little buggers out?"

"I need something to drink," Edward said.

"Candice has some whiskey in the kitchen cabinet."

Edward knelt beside the tub. Vergil regarded him curiously. "What are we going to do?" Edward asked.

Vergil's expression changed with shocking abruptness from alert interest to a virtual mask of sorrow. "Jesus, Edward, my mother—you know, they're coming to take me back, but she said . . . I should call her. Talk to her." Tears fell across the ridges which pulled his cheeks out of shape. "She told me to come back to her. When . . . when it was time. Is it time, Edward?"

"Yes," Edward said, feeling suspended somewhere in a spark-filled cloud. "I think it must be." His fingers closed about the quartz lamp cord and he moved along its length to the plug.

Vergil had hot-wired door-knobs, turned his piss blue, played a thousand dumb practical jokes, and never grown up, never grown mature enough to understand how brilliant he was and how much he could affect the world.

Vergil reached for the bathtub drain lever. "You know, Edward, I—"

He never finished. Edward had inserted the plug into the wall socket. Now he picked up the lamp and upended it into the tub. He jumped away from the flash, the steam and the sparks. The bathroom light went out. Vergil screamed and thrashed and jerked and then everything was still, except for the low, steady sizzle and the smoke wafting from his hair. Light from the small ventilation window cut a shaft through the foul-smelling haze.

Edward lifted the toilet lid and vomited. Then he clenched his nose and stumbled into the living room. His legs went out from under him and he collapsed on the couch.

But there was no time. He stood up, swaying and nauseated again, and entered the kitchen. He found Candice's bottle of Jack Daniel's and returned to the bathroom. He unscrewed the cap and poured the contents of the bottle into the tub water, trying not to look at Vergil directly. But that wasn't enough. He would need bleach and ammonia and then he would have to leave.

He was about to call out and ask Vergil where the bleach and ammonia were, but he caught himself. Vergil was dead. Edward's stomach began to surge again and he leaned against the wall in the hallway, cheek pressed against the paint and plaster. When had things become less real?

When Vergil had entered the Mount Freedom Medical Center. This was another of Vergil's jokes. Ha. Turn your whole life deep midnight blue, Edward; never forget a friend.

He looked into the linen closet but saw only towels and sheets. In the bedroom, he opened Vergil's clothes closet and found only clothes. The bedroom had a master bathroom attached and he could see a small closet in there from where he stood by the corner of the unmade bed. Edward entered the master bath. At one end, opposite the closet, was a shower stall. A trickle of water came out from under the door. He tried the light switch but this whole section of the apartment was powerless; the only light came from the bedroom window. In the closet he found both bleach and a big half-gallon jug of ammonia.

He carried them down the hall and poured them one by one in the tub, avoiding Vergil's sightless pale eyes. Fumes hissed up and he closed the door behind him, coughing.

Someone softly called Vergil's name. Edward carried the empty bottles into the master bathroom, where the voice was louder. He stood in the doorway, one plastic jug brushing the frame, and cocked an ear, frowning.

"Hey, Vergil, that you?" the voice asked dryly. It came from the shower stall. Edward took a step forward, then paused. Enough, he thought. Reality had been twisted enough and he didn't really want to go any farther. He took another step, then another, and reached for the door of the shower stall.

The voice sounded like a woman, husky, strange, though not in distress.

He grasped the handle and tugged. With a hollow *click,* the door swung open. Eyes adjusting to the darkness, he peered into the shower.

"Jesus, Vergil, you've been neglecting me. We've *got* to get out of this hotel. It's dark and small and I don't like it."

He recognized the voice from the phone, though he could not possibly have recognized her by appearance, even had he seen a photograph.

"Candice?" he asked.

"Vergil? Let's go."

He fled.

15

The phone was ringing as Edward came home. He didn't answer. It could have been the hospital. It could have been Bernard—or the police. He envisioned having to explain everything to the police. Genetron would stonewall; Bernard would be unavailable.

Edward was exhausted, all his muscles knotted with tension and whatever name one could give to the feelings one has after—

Committing genocide?

That certainly didn't seem real. He could not believe he had just murdered a trillion intelligent beings. "Noocytes." Snuffed a galaxy. That was laughable. But he didn't laugh.

He could still see Candice, in the shower.

Work had proceeded on her much more rapidly. Her legs were gone; her torso had been reduced to an impressionistic spareness. She had lifted her face to him, covered with ridges as if made from a stack of cards.

He had left the building in time to see a white van speed around the curve and park in front, with Bernard's limousine not far behind. He had sat in his car and watched men in white isolation suits climb out of the van, which, he noted, was unmarked.

Then he had started his car, put it in gear, and driven away. Simple as that. Return to Irvine. Ignore the whole mess as long as he could, or he would very soon be as crazy as Candice.

Candice, who was being transformed over an open shower drain. Let the little buggers out, Vergil had said. Show them what the world's about.

It was not at all hard to believe that he had just killed one human being, a friend. The smoke, the melted lamp cover, the drooping electrical outlet and smoking cord.

Vergil.

He had dunked the lamp into the tub with Vergil.

Had he been thorough enough to kill all of them in the tub? Perhaps Bernard and his group would finish what he had started.

He didn't think so. Who could encompass it, understand it all? Certainly he couldn't; there had been horrors, fearsome things for the mind to acknowledge, to *see*, and he did not believe he could predict what was going to happen next, for he hardly knew what was happening now.

The dreams. Cities raping Gail. Galaxies sprinkling over them all. What anguish . . . and then again, what potential beauty—a new kind of life, symbiosis and transformations.

No. That was not a good thought. Change—too much change—and

so where did his objections begin, his objections to a new order, a new

trans

formation because he well knew that humans weren't enough that there had to be more Vergil had made more; in his clumsy unseeing way he had initiated the next stage.

No. Life goes on no period no end no change, no shocking things like Candice in the shower or Vergil dead in the tub Life is the right held by an individual to normality and normal progress normal aging who would take away that right who in their right minds would accept and what was it he was thinking was going to happen that he would have to accept?

He lay down on the couch and shielded his eyes with his forearm. He had never been so exhausted in his life—drained physically, emotionally, beyond rational thought. He was reluctant to sleep because he could feel the nightmares building up like thunderheads, waiting to shower refractions and echoes of what he had seen.

Edward pulled away his forearm and stared up at the ceiling. It was just barely possible that what had been started could be stopped. Perhaps he was the one who could trigger the chain of actions which could stop it. He could call the Centers for Disease Control (yes, but were they the ones he wanted to talk to?). Or perhaps the defense department? County health first, work through channels? Maybe even the VA hospital or Scripps Clinic in La Jolla.

He put his arm back over his eyes. There was no clear course of action.

Events had simply exceeded his capacity. He imagined that had happened often in human history; tidal waves of events overwhelming crucial individuals, sweeping them along. Making them wish there was a quiet place, perhaps a little Mexican village where nothing ever happened and where they could go and sleep just sleep.

"Edward?" Gail leaned over him, touching his forehead with cool fingers. "Every time I come home, here you are—sacked out. You don't look good. Feeling okay?"

"Yes." He sat on the edge of the couch. His body was hot and wooziness threatened his balance. "What have you planned for dinner?" His mouth wasn't working properly; the words sounded mushy. "I thought we'd go out."

"You have a fever," Gail said. "A very high fever. I'm getting the thermometer. Just stay there."

"No," he called after her weakly. He stood and stumbled into the bathroom to look in the mirror. She met him there and stuck the thermometer under his tongue. As always, he thought of biting it like Harpo Marx, eating it like a piece of candy. She peered over his shoulder into the mirror.

"What is it?" she asked.

There were lines under his collar, around his neck. White lines, like freeways.

"Damp palms," he said. "Vergil had damp palms." They had already been inside him for days. "So obvious."

"Edward, please, what is it?"

"I have to make a call," he said. Gail followed him into the bedroom and stood as he sat on the bed and punched the Genetron number. "Dr. Michael Bernard, please," he said. The receptionist told him, much too quickly, there was no such person at Genetron. "This is too important to fuck around with," he said coldly. "Tell Dr. Bernard this is Edward Milligan and it's urgent."

The receptionist put him on hold. Perhaps Bernard was still at Vergil's apartment, trying to sort out the pieces of the puzzle; perhaps they would simply send someone out to arrest him. It really didn't matter either way.

"Bernard here." The doctor's voice was flat and serpentine— much, Edward imagined, like he himself sounded.

"It's too late, Doctor. We shook Vergil's hand. Sweaty palms. Remember? And ask yourself whom we've touched since. We're the vectors now."

"I was at the apartment today, Milligan," Bernard said. "Did you kill Ulam?"

"Yes. He was going to release his ... microbes. Noocytes. Whatever they are, now."

"Did you find his girlfriend?"

"Yes."

"What did you do with her?"

"Do with her? Nothing. She was in the shower. But listen—"

"She was gone when we arrived, nothing but her clothes. Did you kill her, too?"

"Listen to me, Doctor. I have Vergil's microbes inside me. So do you."

There was silence on the other end, then a deep sigh. "Yes?"

"Have you worked out any way to control them, I mean, inside our bodies?"

"Yes." Then, more softly, "No. Not yet. Antimetabolites, controlled radiation therapy, actinomycin. We haven't tried everything, but . . . no."

"Then that's it, Dr. Bernard."

Another longer pause. "Hm."

"I'm going back to my wife now, to spend what little time we have."

"Yes," Bernard said. "Thank you for calling."

"I'm going to hang up now."

"Of course. Good-bye."

Edward hung up and put his arms around Gail.

"It's a disease, isn't it?" she said.

Edward nodded. "That's what Vergil made. A disease that thinks. I'm not sure there's any way to fight an intelligent plague."

16

Harrison leafed through the procedure manual, making notes methodically. Yng sat in a stressless leather chair in the corner, fingers of both hands forming a pyramid before his face, his long, lank black hair falling over his eyes and glasses. Bernard stood before the black formica-topped desk, impressed by the quality of the silence. Harrison leaned back from the desk and held up his notepad.

"First, we're not responsible. That's how I read it. Ulam did his research without our authorization—"

"But we didn't fire him when we learned of it," Yng countered. "That's going to be a bad point in court."

"We'll worry about all that later," Harrison said sharply. "What we *are* responsible for is reporting to the CDC. This isn't a vat spill or breach of lab containment, but—"

"None of us, not one of us, thought Ulam's cells could be viable outside the body," Yng said, twisting his hand into a jumble of fingers.

"It's very possible they weren't, at first," Bernard said, drawn into the discussion despite himself. "It's obvious there's been a lot of development since the original lymphocytes. Self-directed development."

"I still refuse to believe Ulam created intelligent cells," Harrison said. "Our own research in the cube has shown how difficult that would be. How did he determine their intelligence? How did he train them? No—something—"

Yng laughed. "Ulam's body was being transformed, redesigned . . . how can we doubt there was an intelligence behind the transformation?"

"Gentlemen," Bernard said softly. "That's all academic. Are we, or are we not going to alert Atlanta and Bethesda?"

"What in hell do we tell them?"

"That we are all in the early stages of a very dangerous infection," Bernard said, "generated in our laboratories by a researcher, now dead—"

"Murdered," Yng said, shaking his head in disbelief.

95

"And spreading at an alarming rate."

"Yes," Yng said, "but what can the CDC do about it? The contamination has spread, perhaps across the continent by now."

"No," Harrison said, "not quite that far. Vergil hasn't made contact with that many people. It could still be confined to Southern California."

"He made contact with *us*," Yng said ruefully. "It is your opinion we are contaminated?"

"Yes," Bernard said.

"Is there anything we can do, personally?"

He pretended to consider, then shook his head. "If you'll excuse me, there's work to do before we announce." He left the conference room and walked down the outside corridor to the stairs. Near the front of the west wing was a pay phone. Removing his credit card from his wallet, he inserted it into the slot and punched in the number of his Los Angeles office.

"This is Bernard," he said. "I'm going to take my limo to the San Diego airport shortly. Is George available?" The receptionist made several calls and placed George Dilman, his mechanic and sometimes-pilot, on the other end of the line. "George, sorry for such short notice, but it's something of an emergency. The jet should be ready in an hour and a half, fully fueled."

"Where this time?" Dilman asked, used to long flights on short notice.

"Europe. I'll let you know precisely in about half an hour, so you can file a flight plan."

"Not your usual, Doctor."

"Hour and a half, George."

"We'll be ready."

"I'm flying alone."

"Doctor, I'd rather—"

"Alone, George."

George sighed reluctantly. "All right."

He held down the receiver switch and then punched in a twenty-seven-digit number, beginning with his satellite code and ending with a secret scramble string. A woman answered in German.

"Doktor Heinz Paulsen-Fuchs, *bitte*."

She asked no questions. Whoever could get through on this line, the doctor would speak to. Paulsen-Fuchs answered several minutes later. Bernard glanced around uneasily, realizing he was taking some risk being observed in the open.

"Paul, this is Michael Bernard. I have a rather extreme favor to ask of you."

"Herr Doktor Bernard, always welcome, always welcome! What can I do for you?"

"Do you have a total isolation lab at the Wiesbaden facility you can clear within the day?"

"For what purpose? Excuse me, Michael, is it not a good time to ask?"

"No, not really."

"If there is a grave emergency, well, yes, I suppose."

"Good. I'll need that lab, and I'll need to use B.K. Pharmek's private strip. When I leave my plane, I must be placed in an isolation suit and a sealed biologicals transport truck immediately. Then my aircraft will be destroyed on the runway and the entire area sprayed with disinfectant foam. I will be your guest . . . if you can call it that . . . indefinitely. The lab should be equipped so that I can live there and do my work. I will require a computer terminal with full services."

"You are seldom a drunkard, Michael. And you have never been unstable, not in our time together. This sounds quite serious. Are we talking about a fire, Michael? A vat spill, perhaps?"

Bernard wondered how Paulsen-Fuchs had found out he was working with gene engineering. Or did he know? Was he just guessing? "A very extreme emergency, Herr Doktor. Can you oblige me?"

"Will all be explained?"

"Yes. And it will be to your advantage—and your nation's advantage—to know ahead of time."

"It does not sound trivial, Michael."

He felt an irrational singe of anger. "Compared to this, everything else is trivial, Paul."

"Then it will be done. We can expect you—?"

"Within twenty-four hours. Thank you, Paul."

He hung up and glanced at his watch. He doubted if anyone at Genetron understood the magnitude of what was about to happen. It was difficult for him to imagine. But one thing was clear. Within forty-eight hours of Harrison informing the CDC, the North American continent would be placed under virtual isolation—whether officials believed what was said, or not. The key words would be "plague" and "genetic engineering firm." The action would be completely justifiable, but he doubted if it would be sufficient. Then more drastic measures would be taken.

He did not want to be on the continent when that happened, but on the other hand, he did not want to be responsible for transmitting the contagion. So he would offer himself up as a specimen, to be kept at the finest pharmaceutical research firm in Europe.

Bernard's mind worked in such a way that he was never bothered by second guesses or extreme doubts—not in his work, at any rate. When in an emergency or tight situation, he always came up with one solution at a time—usually the correct one. The reserve solutions waited in the background of his thoughts, unconscious and unobtrusive, while he acted. So it had always been in the operating room, and so it was now. He did not regard this faculty without some chagrin. It made him seem like a bloody robot at times, self-confident beyond all reason. But it had been responsible for his success, his stature in neurophysiological research, and the respect he had been accorded by fellow professionals and public alike.

He returned to the conference room and picked up his briefcase. His limo, as always, would be waiting for him in the Genetron parking lot, the driver reading or playing chess on a pocket computer. "I'll be in my office if you need me," Bernard said to Harrison. Yng stood facing the blank white marker board, hands clasped behind his back.

"I've just called CDC," Harrison said. "They'll be getting back to us with instructions."

The word would soon go out to very hospital in the area. How soon before they closed the airports? How efficient were they? "Let me know, then," Bernard said. He walked out the door and wondered for a moment whether he needed to take anything else with him. He thought not. He had copies of Ulam's floppy diskettes in his briefcase. He had Ulam's organisms within his blood.

Surely that would be enough to keep him busy for a while.

People? Anyone he should warn?

Any of his three ex-wives? He didn't even know where they lived now. His accountant sent them their alimony checks. There was really no practical way—

Anybody he truly cared for, who truly cared for him?

He had last seen Paulette in March. The parting had been amicable. Everything had been amicable. They had orbited around each other like moon and planet, never really touching. Paulette had objected to being the moon, and quite rightly. She had done very well in her own career, chief cyto-technologist at Cetus Corporation in Palo Alto.

Now that he thought of it, she had probably been the one who had initially suggested his name to Harrison at Genetron. After they broke up. No doubt she had thought she was being very fair-minded and objective, helping all concerned.

He couldn't fault her for that. But there was nothing in him that urged a call to her, a warning.

It just wasn't practical.

His son he hadn't heard from in five years. He was in China someplace on a research grant.

He put the notion out of his head.

Perhaps I won't even need an isolation chamber, he thought. *I'm pretty damned isolated already.*

17

They nearly died. Within minutes, Edward was too weak to move. He watched as she called his parents, different hospitals, her school. She was frantic with fear that she might have infected her students. He imagined a ripple of news going out, being picked up. The panic. But Gail slowed, became dizzy, and lay down on the bed next to him.

She struggled and cursed, like a horse trying to right itself after breaking a leg, but the effort was useless.

With her last strength she came to him and they lay in each other's arms, drenched in sweat. Gail's eyes were closed, her face the color of talcum. She looked like a corpse in an embalming parlor. For a time Edward thought she was dead and sick as he was, he raged, hated, felt tremendous guilt for his weakness, his slowness to understand all the possibilities. Then he no longer cared. He was too weak to blink, so he closed his eyes and waited.

There was a rhythm in his arms, in his legs. With each pulse of blood, a kind of sound welled up within him as if an orchestra were performing thousands strong, but not in unison; playing whole seasons of symphonies at once. Music in the blood. The sensation became more coordinated; the wave-trains finally canceled into silence, then separated into harmonic beats.

The beats melted into the sound of his own heart.

Neither of them had any feel for the passage of time. It could have been days before he regained enough strength to go to the faucet in the bathroom. He drank until his stomach could hold no more and returned with a glass of water. Lifting her head with his arm, he brought the edge of the glass to Gail's mouth. She sipped at it. Her lips were cracked, her eyes bloodshot and ringed with yellowish crumbs, but there was some color in her skin. "When are we going to die?" she asked, her voice a feeble croak. "I want to hold you when we die."

Minutes later, he was strong enough to help her into the kitchen. He peeled an orange and shared it with her, feeling the pulse of the sugar and juice and acid down his throat. "Where is everybody?" she asked. "I called hospitals, friends. Where are they?"

The harmonic orchestral sensation returned, beats coordinating into recognizable fragments, the fragments coalescing, coming into a focus of meaning, and suddenly—

Is there DISCOMFORT?

—Yes.

He answered automatically and in kind, as if he had expected the exchange and was ready for a long conversation.

PATIENCE. There are difficulties.

—What? I don't understand—

Immune response. *Conflict*. Difficulties.

—Leave us, then! Go away!

Not possible. Too INTEGRATED.

They weren't recovering, not to the extent they were free of the infection. Any feeling of returning freedom was illusory. Very briefly, saying what his strength would allow, he tried to explain to Gail what he thought they were experiencing.

She propped herself up out of the chair and went to the window, where she stood on shaking legs, looking out at green commons, other rows of apartments. "What about other people?" she asked. "Have they got it, too? That's why they're not here?"

"I don't know. Probably soon."

"Are they . . . the disease. Is it talking to you?"

He nodded.

"Then I'm not crazy." She walked slowly across the living room. "I'm not going to be able to move much longer," she said. "How about you? Maybe we should try to escape."

He held her hand and shook his head. "They're inside, part of us by now. They are us. Where can we escape?"

"Then I'd like to be in bed with you, when we can't move any more. And I want your arms around me."

They lay back on the bed and held each other.

"Eddie . . ."

That was the last sound he heard. He tried to resist, but waves of peace rolled over him and he could only experience. He floated on a wide blue-violet sea. Above the sea, his body was mapped onto a seemingly limitless plane. The noocyte endeavors were charted there, and he had no problem understanding their progress. It was obvious that his body was more noocyte than Milligan now.

—What's going to happen to us?

No more MOTION.

—Are we dying?

Changing.

—And if we don't want to change?

No PAIN.

—And fear? You won't even allow us to be afraid?

The blue-violet sea and the chart faded into warm darkness.

He had plenty of time to think things through, but not nearly enough information. Was this what Vergil had experienced? No wonder he had seemed to be going crazy. Buried in some inner perspective, neither one place nor another. He felt an increase in warmth, a closeness and compelling presence.

>>Edward . . .

—Gail? I can hear you—no, not hear you—

>>Edward, I should be terrified. I want to be angry but I can't.

Not essential.

>>Go away! Edward, I want to fight back—

—Leave us, please, leave us!

PATIENCE. Difficulties.

They fell quiet and simply reveled in each other's company. What Edward sensed nearby was not the physical form of Gail; not even his own picture of her personality, but something more convincing, with all the grit and detail of reality, but not as he had ever experienced her before.

—How much time is passing?

>>I don't know. Ask *them*.

No answer.

>>Did they tell you?

—No. I don't think they know how to talk to us, really . . . not yet. Maybe this is all hallucination. Vergil hallucinated, and maybe I'm just imitating his fever dreams . . .

>>Tell me who's hallucinating whom. Wait. Something's coming. Can you see it?

—I can't *see* anything . . . but I feel it.

>>Describe it to me.

—I can't.

>>Look—it's doing something.

Reluctantly, >>It's beautiful.

—It's very . . . I don't think it's frightening. It's closer now.

No HARM. No PAIN. *Learn* here, *adapt*.

It was not a hallucination, but it could not be put into words. Edward did not struggle as it came upon him.

>>What is it?

—It's where we'll be for some time, I think.

>>Stay with me!

—Of course . . .

There was suddenly a great deal to do and prepare for.

Edward and Gail grew together on the bed, substance passing through clothes, skin joining where they embraced and lips where they touched.

18

Bernard was very proud of his Falcon 10. He had purchased it in Paris from a computer company president whose firm had gone bankrupt. He had cherished the sleek executive jet for three years, learning how to fly and getting his pilot's license within three months from "a sitting start," as his instructor had put it. He lovingly touched the edge of the black control panel with one finger, then smoothed his thumb across the panel's wood inlay facing. Peculiar, that out of so much left behind—and so much lost—an inert aircraft could mean something important to him. Freedom, accomplishment, prestige . . . Clearly, in the next few weeks, if he had that long, there would be many changes beyond the physical. He would have to come to grips with his fragility, his transience.

The plane had been refueled at La Guardia without his leaving the cockpit. He had radioed instructions, taxied up to the executive aircraft service bay, and shut the jets down. The attendants had performed their work quickly and he had filed a continuation flight plan with the tower. Not once did he have to touch human flesh or even breathe the same air as the ground crew.

In Reykjavik he had to leave the plane and attend to the fueling himself, but he wore a tightly wrapped muffler and made sure he touched nothing with his ungloved hands.

On his way to Germany, his mind seemed to clear—to become uncomfortably acute in his own self-analysis. He did not like any of the conclusions. He tried to blank them out, but there was little in the cockpit to completely absorb his attention, and the observations, the accusations, returned every few minutes until he put the plane on autopilot and gave them their due.

He would be dead very soon. It was, to be sure, a noble kind of self-sacrifice to donate himself to Pharmek, to the world that might not yet be contaminated. But it was far from making up for what he had allowed to happen.

How could he have known?

"Milligan knew," he said between clenched teeth. "Damn all

of them." Damn Vergil I. Ulam; but wasn't he similar to Vergil? No, he refused to admit that. Vergil had been brilliant (he saw the reddened, blistered body in the bathtub, *had been had been*) but irresponsible, blind to the precautions which should have been taken almost instinctively. Still, if Vergil had taken those precautions, he never would have been able to complete his work.

Nobody would have allowed it.

And Michael Bernard knew all too well the frustrations of being stopped dead in his tracks while following a promising path of research. He could have cured thousands of people of Parkinson's disease . . . if he had simply been allowed to collect brain tissue from aborted embryos. Instead, in their moral fervor, the people with and without faces who had contrived to stop him had also contrived to let thousands of people suffer and be degraded. How often had he wished that young Mary Shelley had never written her book, or at least had never chosen a *German* name for her scientist. All the concatenations of the early nineteenth and mid-twentieth century, coming together in people's minds—

Yes, yes, and hadn't he just cursed Ulam for *his* brilliance, and hadn't the same comparison crossed his mind?

Frankenstein's monster. Inescapable. Boringly obvious.

People were so afraid of the new, of change.

And now he was afraid, too, though admitting his fear was difficult. Best to be rational, to present himself for study, an unintentional human sacrifice like Dr. Louis Slotin, at Los Alamos in 1946. By accident, Slotin and seven others had been accidentally exposed to a sudden burst of ionizing radiation. Slotin had ordered the seven others not to move. He had then drawn circles around his feet and theirs, to give fellow scientists solid data about distances from the source and intensity of exposure on which to base their studies. Slotin had died nine days later. A second man died twenty years later of complications attributed to the radiation. Two others died of acute leukemia.

Human guinea pigs. Noble, self-possessed Slotin.

Had they wished, in those terrible moments, that no one had ever split the atom?

Pharmek had leased its own strip two kilometers from its countryside research facilities, outside Wiesbaden, to play host to businessmen and scientists, and also to expedite the receiving and processing of plant and soil samples from search teams around the world. Bernard circled over the divided fields and woods at ten thousand feet, the eastern sky touched with dawn.

He switched the secondary radio to the Pharmek automatic ILS system, and keyed the mike twice to activate the lights and glidepath. The strip appeared below him in the predawn grayness, wind direction indicated by an arrow of lights to one side.

Bernard followed the lights and glidepath and felt the wheels thump and squeal against the strip's concrete; a perfect landing, the last the sleek executive jet would ever make.

On the port side he could see a large white truck and personnel dressed in biohazard suits waiting for him to finish his taxi. They kept a brilliant spotlight trained on the aircraft. He waved out the window and motioned for them to stay where they were. Over the radio, he said, "I need an isolation suit ready for me about one hundred meters from the plane. And the truck will have to back off a hundred meters beyond that." A man standing on the truck cab listened to a companion inside and signaled thumbs-up. A limp isolation suit was arranged on the runway and the truck and personnel quickly increased their distance.

Bernard powered down the engines and cut the switches, leaving only the cabin lights and emergency fuel jettison system on. Jeppesen case under his arm, he stepped into the passenger cabin and took out a pressurized aluminum canister of disinfectant from the luggage compartment. With a deep breath, he slipped a rubber filter mask over his head and read the instructions on the side of the canister. The black conical nozzle had a flexible plastic hose with a brass fitting. The fitting slipped snugly into the top valve in the canister and snicked home.

Nozzle in one hand and canister in another, Bernard returned to the cockpit and sprayed the controls, seat, floor and ceiling until they dripped with the milky green, noxious fluid. He then re-entered the passenger cabin, applying the high-pressure stream to everything he had touched, and more besides. He unscrewed the nozzle when the can was empty and released the pressure valve, placing the canister in a leather-cushioned seat. With the twist of a lever, the hatch hissed open, descending to a few inches above the concrete.

He tapped his pants pocket with one hand to make sure the flare pistol was there, felt for the six extra shells, and climbed down the stairway to the concrete, setting the Jeppesen case on the runway about ten meters from the jet's bright red nose.

Step by step, he sabotaged his aircraft, first loosening and draining the hydraulics systems, then slashing the tires and letting out the air. With an ax he broke the windscreen on the starboard side of the cockpit, then the three passenger windows on the port side, clambering up on the wing to reach them.

He climbed up the stairs and entered the cockpit, reaching around the disinfectant-soaked seat to pull up the cover on the fuel jettison switch. With a hard click, the switch depressed under his finger and the valves opened. Bernard quickly left the plane, snatched the case and ran to where the gray and orange isolation suit lay on the strip.

The technicians and Pharmek personnel had made no attempt to interfere. Bernard removed the pistol and shells from his pocket, took off all his clothing and donned the pressurized suit. Balling up the clothing, he carried it to the pool of jet fuel under the Falcon. He returned and opened the case, removing his passport and dropping it into a plastic bag. Then he picked up the gun.

The shell slid smoothly into the barrel. He took careful aim—hoping the trajectory wouldn't be too curved—and fired a flare at his pride and joy.

The fuel blossomed in a mushroom of orange and roiling black. Silhouetted against the inferno, Bernard hefted his case and walked toward the truck.

A customs official was not likely to be present, but to be legal and aboveboard, he held the plastic-wrapped passport out and pointed at it. A man in a similar isolation suit took it from him.

"Nothing to declare," Bernard said. The man raised his hand to the suit's helmet in acknowledgment and stepped back. "Spray me down, please."

He pirouetted in the shower of disinfectant, lifting his arms. As he climbed the steps into the truck's isolation tank, he heard the faint hum of the air recirculator and saw the purple gleam of ultraviolet lights. The hatch swung shut behind him, paused, then sank into its seals with a distant sigh.

Heading toward Pharmek on a narrow two-lane road through grass pastures, Bernard peered through the thick side viewport at the landing strip. The fuselage of the jet had collapsed in a skeletal, blackened heap. Flames still leaped high into the summer dawn. The blaze seemed to be consuming everything.

19

Heinz Paulsen-Fuchs looked at the records of calls displayed on the screen of his phone. Already it was beginning. There had been inquiries from several agencies, including the *Bundesumwel-tamt*—House Environmental Oversight—and the *Bundesgesundheitsamt*, Federal Health. State officials in Frankfurt and Weisbaden were also concerned.

All flights to and from the United States had been canceled. He could expect officials on his doorstep within hours. Before they arrived, he had to hear Bernard's explanation.

Not for the first time in his life did he regret coming to the aid of a friend. It was not the least of his failings. One of the most important industrialists in post-war Germany, and he was still a sentimental soft-touch.

He donned a transparent raincoat over his trim gray wool suit and carefully placed a beret on his curly white hair. Then he waited by the front door for the rain-beaded Citröen.

"Good morning, Uwe," he greeted his chauffeur as the car door was opened for him. "I promised this for Richard." He leaned over the seat and handed Uwe three paperback mysteries. Richard was the chauffeur's twelve-year-old son, like Paulsen-Fuchs an avid mystery buff. "Drive even faster than usual."

"You will pardon me that I didn't meet you at the airstrip," Paulsen-Fuchs said. "I was here, preparing for your arrival—and then I was called away. There are already inquiries from my government. Something very serious is happening. You are aware of it?"

Bernard approached the thick, triple paned window separating the biological containment laboratory from the adjacent viewing chamber. He held up his hand, criss-crossed by white lines, and said, "I'm infected."

Paulsen-Fuchs' eyes narrowed and he held two fingers to his cheek. "You are apparently not alone, Michael. What is happening in America?"

"I haven't heard anything since I left."

"Your Centers for Disease Control in Atlanta have issued emergency instructions. All air flights intra- and international are cancelled. Rumors say some cities do not respond to communications—telephone or radio. There appears to be rapidly spreading chaos. Now, you come to us, burn your vehicle on our airstrip, make very certain that you are the only thing from your country to survive in ours—everything else is sterilized. What can we make from all this, Michael?"

"Paul, there are several things all countries must do immediately. You must quarantine recent travelers from the U.S., Mexico—possibly from all North America. I have no idea how far the contagion will spread, but it seems to be moving quickly."

"Yes, our government is working to do just this. But you know bureaucracy—"

"Go around the bureaucracy. Cut off all physical contact with North America."

"I cannot simply make them do that by suggesting—"

"Paul," Bernard said, holding up his hand again, "I have perhaps a week, less if what you say is accurate. Tell your government this is more than just a vat spill. I have all the important records in my flight case. I need to conference with your senior biologists as soon as I've had a couple of hours sleep. Before they talk to me, I want them to view the files I brought with me. I'll plug the disks into the terminal here. I can't say much more now; I'll fall over if I don't sleep soon."

"Very well, Michael." Paulsen-Fuchs regarded him sadly, deep lines of worry showing on his face. "Is it something we imagined could happen?"

Bernard thought for a moment. "No," he said. "I don't think so."

"All the worse, then," Paulsen-Fuchs said. "I will arrange things now. Transfer your data. Get sleep." Paulsen-Fuchs left and the light in the viewing chamber was turned off.

Bernard paced the three-by-three meters area of his new home. The lab had been built in the early eighties for genetic experiments which, at the time, were regarded as potentially dangerous. The entire inner chamber was suspended within a high-pressure tank; any ruptures in the chamber would result in atmosphere entering, not escaping. The pressurized tank could be sprayed with several kinds of disinfectant, and was surrounded by yet another tank, this one evacuated. All electrical conduits and mechanical systems which had to pass through the tanks were jacketed in sterilizing solutions. Air and waste materials leaving the lab were subjected to high-heat sterilization and cremation; any samples taken from the lab were processed in an adjacent chamber with the same safeguards. From now until the problem was solved, or he was dead, nothing from Bernard's body would be touched by another living thing outside the chamber.

The walls were neutral light gray; lighting was provided by fluorescents in vertical strips in the walls, and by three bright ceiling-mounted panels. Lights could be controlled from both inside and outside. The floor was featureless black tile. In the middle of the room—clearly visible from both of the opposed viewing chambers—was a standard business desk and secretary's chair, and on the desk, a high-resolution VDT. A utilitarian but comfortable-looking cot, without sheets or blanket, awaited him in one corner. A chest of drawers stood by the stainless steel pass-through hatch. On one wall, a large rectangular square marked a hatch for large equipment—waldoes, he suspected. The ensemble was completed by a lounge chair and a curtained commode-shower facility that looked like it had been removed in one piece from an airplane or recreational vehicle.

He picked up the pants and shirt laid out for him on the cot and felt the material between forefinger and thumb. There would be no accommodations for modesty or privacy from here on. He was no longer a private person. He would soon be wired, probed, inspected by doctors and generally treated like a laboratory animal.

Very well, he thought, lying back on the cot. I deserve it. I deserve whatever happens now. *Mea culpa.*

Bernard fell back on the cot and closed his eyes.

His pulse sang in his ears.

METAPHASE

NOVEMBER

20

Brooklyn Heights

"Mother? Howard?" Suzy McKenzie wrapped herself in the sky-blue flannel robe her boyfriend had given her the month before in celebration of her eighteenth birthday, and padded barefoot down the hall. Her eyes were bleary with sleep. "Ken?" She was usually the last to wake up. "Slow Suzy" she often called herself with a secret, knowing smile.

She didn't keep clocks in her room but the sun outside the window was high enough for it to be past ten o'clock. The bedroom doors were closed. "Mother?" She knocked on the door of her mother's room. No answer.

Surely one of her brothers would be up. "Kenneth? Howard?" She turned around in the middle of the hall, making the wood floor creak. Then she twisted the knob on her mother's door and pushed it open. "Mother?" The bed had not been made; the covers slumped around the bottom. Everybody must be downstairs. She washed her face in the bathroom, inspected the skin of her cheeks for more blemishes, was relieved to find none, and walked down the stairs into the foyer. She couldn't hear a sound.

"Hey," she called out from the living room, confused and unhappy. "Nobody woke me up. I'll be late for work." She was in her third week of waitressing at a neighborhood deli. She enjoyed the work—it was much more interesting and *real* than working at the Salvation Army thrift store—and it helped her mother financially. Her mother had lost her job three months before and lived on the irregular checks from Suzy's father, plus their rapidly diminishing savings. She looked at the Benrus ship's clock on the table and shook her head. Ten thirty; she was *really* late. But that didn't worry her as much as where everybody had gone. They fought a lot, sure, but they were a close family—except for her father, whom she hardly missed any more, not much anyway—and everybody wouldn't just go away and not tell her, not even wake me up.

She pushed the swinging door to the kitchen and stepped half-

way through. What she saw didn't register at first: three shapes
out of place, three bodies, one in a dress on the floor, slumped
up against the sink, one in jeans with no shirt in a chair at the
kitchen table, the third half-in, half-out of the pantry. No muss,
no fuss, just three bodies she couldn't immediately recognize.

She was quite calm at first. She wished she hadn't opened the
door just then; perhaps if she had opened it a few moments earlier,
or later, everything would have been normal. Somehow it would
have been a different door—the door to *her* world—and life would
have gone on with just the minor lapse of no one awakening her.
Instead, she hadn't been warned, and that wasn't fair, really. She
had opened the door at just the wrong time, and it was too late
to close it.

The body against the sink wore her mother's dress. The face,
arms, legs, and hands were covered with raised white stripes.
Suzy entered the kitchen two small steps, her breath coming short
and uneven. The door slipped out of her fingers and swung shut.
She took a step back, then one sideways, a small dance of terror
and indecision. She would have to call the police, of course.
Maybe an ambulance. But first she would have to find out what
happened and all her instincts told her just to get out of the kitchen,
out of the house.

Howard, twenty, regularly wore jeans without a shirt around
the house. He liked to go bare-chested to show off his well-
muscled, if not brawny frame. Now his chest was a reddish brown
color, like an Indian's, and ridged like a potato chip or an old-
fashioned washboard. His face was calm, eyes closed, mouth shut.
He was still breathing.

Kenneth—it had to be Kenneth—looked more like a pile of
dough in clothes than her eldest brother.

Whatever had happened was completely incomprehensible. She
wondered if it was something everybody else knew about, but had
forgotten to tell her.

No, that didn't make sense. People were seldom cruel to her,
and her mother and brothers were never cruel. The best thing to
do was back out the door and call the police, or somebody; somebody who would know what to do.

She looked at the list of numbers pinned above the old black
phone in the foyer, then tried to dial the emergency number. She
kept fumbling, her finger jerking from the hole in the dial. Tears
were in her eyes when she finally managed to complete the three
digits.

The phone rang for several minutes without answer. Finally a recording came on: "All our lines are busy. Please do not hang up or you will lose your priority." Then more ringing. After another five minutes, she hung up, sobbing, and dialed for the operator. No answer there, either. Then she thought of the conversation they had had the night before, about some sort of bug in California. It had been on the radio. Everybody getting sick and troops being called in. Only then, remembering this, did Suzy McKenzie go out the front door and stand on the steps, screaming for help.

The street was deserted. Parked cars lined both sides—inexplicably, for parking was forbidden between eight in the morning and six at night every day but Thursday and Friday, and this was Tuesday, and the enforcement was strict. Nobody was driving. She couldn't see anybody in a car or walking or sitting in a window. She ran up one side of the street, weeping and shouting first in supplication, then in anger, then terror, then again begging for help.

She stopped screaming when she saw a postman lying on the front walk of a brownstone between two parallel wrought-iron fences. He lay on his back, eyes shut, and he looked just like Mother and Howard. To Suzy, postmen were sacred beings, always reliable. She used her fingers to push the terror out of her face and scrunched her eyes shut in concentration. "That bug's gotten everywhere," she told herself. "Somebody has to know what to do."

She returned to her house and picked up the phone again. She began dialing all the numbers she knew. Some went through; others created only silence or strange computer noises. None of the phones that rang were answered. She redialed the number of her boyfriend, Cary Smyslov, and listened to it ring eight, nine, ten times before hanging up. She paused, considered for a moment, and dialed the number of her aunt in Vermont.

The phone was answered on the third ring. "Hello?" The voice was weak and tremulous, but it was definitely her aunt.

"Aunt Dawn, this is Suzy in Brooklyn. I'm in big trouble here—"

"Suzy." It seemed to take time for the name to sink in.

"Yes, you know, Suzy. Suzy McKenzie."

"Honey, I'm not hearing too well now." Aunt Dawn was thirty-one years old, no decrepit old woman, but she didn't sound at all well.

"Mom's sick, maybe she's dead. I don't know, and Kenneth and Howard, and nobody's around, or everybody's sick, I don't know—"

"I'm kind of under the weather, myself," Aunt Dawn said.
"Got these bumps. Your uncle's gone, or maybe he's out in
the garage. Anyway he hasn't been in here for..." She paused.
"Since last night. He went out talking to himself. Not back yet.
Honey—"

"What is going on?" Suzy asked, her voice cracking.

"Honey, I don't know, but I can't talk anymore, I think I'm
going crazy. Good-bye, Suzy." And then, incredibly, she hung up.
Suzy tried ringing again, but there was no answer and finally, on
the third attempt, not even a ringing sound.

She was about to open the phone book and begin dialing at
random, but she thought better of it and returned to the kitchen.
She might be able to do something—keep them cool, or warm,
or bring whatever medicine was in the house.

Her mother looked thinner. The ridges seemed to have collapsed
on her face and arms. Suzy reached out to touch her mother's
face, hesitated, then forced herself. The skin was warm and dry,
not feverish, normal enough for its appearance. Her mother's eyes
opened.

"Oh, Mother," Suzy sobbed. "What's happening?"

"Well," her mother said, tongue licking at her lips, "it's quite
beautiful, actually. You're all right, aren't you? Oh, Suzy." And
then she shut her eyes and said no more. Suzy turned to Howard
sitting in the chair. She touched him on the arm and jumped back
as the skin seemed to deflate. Only then did she notice the network
of root-like tubes extending from the cuffs of his jeans, vanishing
into the crevice between the floor and the wall.

More roots stretched from Kenneth's paste-colored arms into
the pantry. And behind her mother, reaching over her skirt and
into the cabinet beneath the sink, was a single thick pipe of pale
flesh. Suzy thought wildly for a moment of horror movies and
makeup and maybe they were shooting a movie and hadn't told
her. She bent closer to peer behind her mother. She was no expert,
but the pipe of flesh wasn't makeup. She could see blood pulsing
in it.

Suzy climbed slowly back up the stairs to her bedroom. She
sat on the bed, braiding and unbraiding her long blond hair with
her fingers, then lay back and stared at the very old silvery linoleum
on the ceiling. "Jesus, please come and help me, because I need
you now," she said. "Jesus, please come and help me, because I
need you now."

And so on, into the afternoon, when thirst drove her to the
bathroom for a drink. Around her gulps of water, she repeated

her prayer, until the monotony and futility silenced her. She stood by the banister, still in her sky-blue robe, and began to make plans. She wasn't sick—not yet—and she certainly wasn't dead.

So there had to be something to do, someplace to go.

And still, in the back of her mind, she hoped that perhaps in the way she opened a door, or on some path she might follow through the streets, she could find her way back to the old world. She didn't think it was likely, but anything was worth the chance.

There were some tough decisions to be made. What good was all her education and special training if she couldn't think for herself and make tough decisions? She did not want to go into the kitchen any more than she had to, but food was in the kitchen. She could try entering other houses, or even the grocery store at the end of the block, but she suspected there would be other bodies there.

At least these bodies—alive or dead—were her relatives.

She entered the kitchen with her head held high. Gradually, as she went from cabinet to cabinet and then to the refrigerator, her eyes lowered. The bodies had collapsed even further; Kenneth seemed little more than a filament-covered white patch in wrinkled clothes. The fleshy roots into the pantry had gone straight for the plumbing, climbing up into the small sink and into the water tap, as well as down the drain. At any minute she expected something to reach out and grab her—or for Howard or her mother to turn into lurching zombies—and she gritted her teeth until her jaws ached, but none of them moved. They no longer looked like they could move.

She emerged with a box full of the canned goods she thought she would need for the next few days—and the can opener, which she had almost forgotten.

It was dusk by the time she thought to turn on the radio. They hadn't had a television since the last set broke beyond repair; its hulk sat in the foyer under the stairs, gathering dust behind boxes of old magazines. She pulled out the multiband portable her mother kept for emergencies and methodically searched the dials. She had once play-acted at being a ham radio operator, but of course the portable couldn't send anything.

Not a single station played on AM or FM. She picked up signals on the short wave bands—some very clear—but none in English.

The room was rapidly darkening now. She agonized before trying to switch on the lights. If everybody was sick, would there still *be* lights?

When the shadows had filled the living room and there was no avoiding the dilemma—either sit in the dark, or find out whether she would *have* to sit in the dark—she reached up to the big reading lamp beside the couch and turned the switch quickly.

The light came on, strong and steady.

This broke a very weak dam in her, and she began to mourn. She rocked back and forth on her curled-up legs on the couch and keened like someone demented, her face wet, hands braiding and unbraiding her hair and using it to dry her face until it hung in damp strips down to her collarbone. With the single light casting a golden crescent over her face, she wept until her throat ached and she could barely keep her eyes open.

Without eating, she went upstairs, switching on all the lights— each steady glow a miracle—and crawled into her bed, where she could not sleep, imagining she heard someone coming up the stairs, or walking down the hall toward her door.

The night lasted an eternity, and in that time Suzy became a little more mature, or a little crazier, she couldn't decide which. Some things no longer mattered much. She was quite willing, for example, to forego her past life and find a new way to live. She made this concession in the hopes that whatever was in charge would simply allow the lights to keep burning.

By dawn she was a physical wreck—exhausted, hungry but unwilling to eat, her whole body tense and wrung out from terror and watchfulness. She drank from the bathroom tap again . . . and suddenly thought of the roots leading into the plumbing. Wretching, Suzy sat down on the toilet and watched the water pour clean and clear from the tap. Thirst finally compelled her to take the chance and drink more, but she vowed to lay in a supply of bottled water.

She prepared a cold meal of green beans and corned beef hash in the living room, and was hungry enough to throw in a can of plums in heavy syrup for good measure. The cans stood in a row on the battered coffee table. She sipped the last of the plum syrup; nothing had ever tasted so good.

She returned to her bedroom and lay down, and this time slept for five hours, until awakened by a noise. Something heavy had fallen within the house. Cautiously, she descended the stairs and looked around the foyer and living room.

"Not the kitchen," she said, and knew immediately that was where the sound had come from. She opened the swinging door slowly. Her mother's clothes—but not her mother—lay in a pile before the sink. Suzy entered and looked at where Kenneth had been in the pantry. Clothes, but nothing else. She turned.

Howard's jeans hung from the seat of the stool, which had toppled to one side. A glistening pale brown sheet hung down along the whole wall, neatly edged into the cornices, protruding slightly where it covered a framed print.

She took the mop from the opposite corner, behind the refrigerator, and stepped forward with the handle pointing at the sheet. I'm being incredibly brave, she thought. She poked the sheet gently at first, then drove the broom clear through it into the lath and plaster beyond. The sheet quivered but did not otherwise react. "You!" she screamed. She swung the handle back and forth over the sheet, shredding it from corner to corner. "You!"

When most of the shreds had fallen to the floor and the wall was covered with holes, she dropped the broom and fled the kitchen.

It was one o'clock in the afternoon, the ship's clock said. She regained her breath and then went around the house, turning off the lights. The miraculous energy might last longer if she didn't use it up immediately.

Suzy then took an address book from beneath the phone in the foyer and made a list of her supplies, and what she would need. There were at least five more hours of daylight, or light enough to see by. She put on her coat and left the snow porch door open behind her.

Down the street, lined with the same parked cars, to the corner, to the grocery, without purse or money, wearing her coat over her pajamas and sky-blue robe; out into the upside-down outside world to see what there was to see. She even felt vaguely cheerful. The wind was blowing fall-cool and a few leaves rattled along the pavement from the trees spaced every few houses. Vines crawled along the wrought-iron fencing between the steps, and flowerpots sat on ledges before the first floor windows.

Mithridates' grocery was closed, iron bars across the front doors. She peered through the bars on the windows, wondering if there was any way to get in, and thought of the service entrance on the other side. The door there hung slightly ajar, a great heavy black metal-sheathed thing she had to heave with all her might to push open farther. She felt it catch and let it go, watching it for an instant to make sure it would stay open. In the service corridor, she stepped over another pile of clothes, topped by a grocer's apron, and pushed through double swinging doors into the deserted grocery.

Methodically, Suzy went to the front of the store and pulled out a rickety shopping cart. A computer cash register ticket clung

to the bottom of the basket with a leaf of very old lettuce. She
wobbled the cart down the aisles, picking out what she hoped was
a sensible array of foods. Her usual eating habits were not the
best. Even so, she had a better figure than most of the health food
and diet fanatics she knew—something in which she took solemn
pride.

Canned hams, stew beef in tins, canned chicken, fresh vegetables and fruit (soon to be scarce, she imagined), canned fruit,
as many bottles of spring or mineral water as she could fit into a
liquor box and wedge into the cart's lower rack, bread and some
slightly stale breakfast rolls, two gallon jugs of milk from the still-
cold dairy case. A bottle of aspirin and some shampoo, though
she wondered how long the water would come out of the shower
tap. Vitamins, a big jar. She tried to find something in the drug
shelves which might fight off what had happened to her family—
and the mailman and the grocer, and perhaps everybody else.
Carefully she read and re-read bottles and instructions on boxes,
but nothing seemed appropriate.

Then she pushed the cart up to the cash register, blinked at the
aisle and the locked door beyond, and swung her load around.
Nobody to pay. She hadn't brought money anyway. She was halfway toward the back when another thought occurred to her, and
she returned to the register.

Where rumor had said it would be, on a shelf above the bag
storage bin, was a large heavy black pistol with a long barrel. She
fiddled with it, carefully pointing it away from her, until she found
a way to roll out a cylinder. The gun was loaded with six big
bullets.

Suzy didn't like holding the gun. Her father owned guns and
the few times she visited, he always warned her to stay away from
them, not even touch them. But guns were for protection, not
play, and she didn't want to play with it, that was for sure. Anyway,
she doubted there was anything she could shoot effectively.

"But you never know," she said. She put the gun in a brown
bag and placed it in the upper basket of the cart, then wheeled
the cart down the service corridor, over the grocer's empty clothes
and onto the sidewalk.

She stored the food in the foyer and stood with the milk jugs
one in each hand, trying to decide whether she wanted to put them
in the refrigerator. "They won't last long if I don't," she told
herself, assuming a very practical tone. "Oh, God," she said,
shuddering violently. She put down the jugs and wrapped her arms
around herself. When she closed her eyes, she saw every kitchen

in every home in Brooklyn, filled with empty clothes or dissolving bodies. She leaned against the stair railing and dropped her head into her arms. "Suzy, Suzy," she whispered. She took a deep breath, straightened, and picked up the jugs. "Here I go," she said with forced brightness.

The brown sheet had vanished, leaving only the holes in the wall. She opened the refrigerator and wedged the milk jugs into the lower shelf, then inspected what food was available for supper.

The clothes didn't look right, just lying there. She took the broom and stirred her mother's dress to see if anything was hidden beneath the folds; nothing was. With forefinger and thumb, she lifted the dress. Slip and panties fell out, and from the edge of the panties peeped a tampon, white and pristine. Something glinted near the collar and she bent to see. Little lumps of grey and gold metal, irregularly shaped.

The answer came to her too quickly, thought out with a panicky kind of brilliance she wasn't used to.

Fillings. Tooth fillings and gold crowns.

She picked up the clothes and dumped them in the hamper in the service porch. So much for that, she thought. Good-bye Mother and Kenneth and Howard.

Then she swept the floor, pushing the fillings and dust (no dead cockroaches, which was unusual) into a dustpan and dropping them into the trash beside the refrigerator.

"I am the only one," she said when she was finished. "I am the only one left in Brooklyn. I didn't get sick." She stood by the table with an apple in her hand, chewing thoughtfully. "Why?" she asked.

"Because," she answered, twirling around the kitchen floor, eye going quickly to haunted corners. "Because I am so beautiful, and the devil wants me for his wife."

21

"In the past four days," Paulsen-Fuchs said, "contact with most of the North American continent has been cut off. The etiology of the disease is not known precisely, but it is apparently passed through every vector known to epidemiologists, and then some. Mr. Bernard's materials indicate that the components of the disease are themselves intelligent and capable of directed action."

The visitors in the viewing chamber—Pharmek executives and representatives from four European countries—sat in their folding chairs, faces impassive. Paulsen-Fuchs stood with his back to the three-layer window, facing the officials from France and Denmark. He turned and indicated Bernard, who sat at the desk, tapping its surface lightly with a hand heavily marked by white ridges.

"At great risk, and some foolhardiness, Mr. Bernard has come to West Germany to provide a subject for our experiments. As you can see, our facilities here are well-equipped to keep Mr. Bernard safely isolated, and there is no need for removal to another laboratory or hospital. Such a transfer could, in fact, be very dangerous. We are quite willing to follow outside suggestions on the scientific approach, however.

"Frankly we don't yet know what sort of experiments to conduct. Tissue samples from Mr. Bernard indicate that the disease—if we should actually call it that—is spreading rapidly throughout his body, yet in no way impairs his functions. In fact, he claims that with the exception of certain peculiar symptoms, to be discussed later, he has never felt better in his life. And it is apparent that his anatomy is being altered substantially."

"Why hasn't Mr. Bernard been transformed completely?" asked the representative from Denmark, a young-looking plump man in a black suit, his hair like close-cropped fur. "Our few communications with the United States show that transformation and dissolution takes place within a week of infection."

"I don't know," Bernard said. "My circumstances are not the same as victims in a natural environment. Perhaps the organisms in my body are aware that it would do them no good to complete the transformation."

The dismay on their faces showed they were still not used to the concept of noocytes. Or perhaps they simply did not believe.

Paulsen-Fuchs continued the discussion, but Bernard closed his eyes and tried to shut the visitors out. It was worse than he had imagined; in just four days, he had been subjected—politely enough, and with great concern—to fourteen such meetings, to a battery of tests conducted through the sliding panel, to questions about every aspect of his life, past, present, private and public. He was the center of a secondary shock wave spreading around the world—the wave of reaction to what had happened in North America.

He had gotten out just in time. The etiology of the plague had altered drastically and now followed several patterns, or perhaps no pattern at all; it was possible the organisms reacted to their environment and altered their methods accordingly. Thus, large cities tended to be silenced immediately, most or all of their citizens being infected and transformed within forty-eight hours. Outlying towns and rural areas, perhaps because of a lack of common sewage and water systems, were affected less rapidly. Spread of the plague to these areas appeared to proceed through animal and insect vectors as well as direct human contact.

Infrared pictures taken by Landsats and spy satellites, processed and interpreted by countries like Japan and Great Britain, showed incipient changes even in the forests and waterways of North America.

Already, he felt like Michael Bernard no longer existed. He had been swallowed up in something larger and far more impressive, and now he was on display in a museum, tagged and curiously enough, able to talk back. Ex-neurosurgeon, male, once well-known and wealthy, not very active of late, caught in social whirl and with scads of money to spend from lecture tours, book royalties, appearances in motion pictures . . .

It seemed quite possible that Michael Bernard hadn't existed for six years, having vanished sometime after he last applied scalpel to flesh, drill to skull.

He opened his eyes and saw the men and one woman in the chambers.

"Dr. Bernard." The woman was trying to attract his attention, apparently for the third or fourth time.

"Yes?"

"Is it true that you are at least in part to blame for this disaster?"

"No, not directly."

"Indirectly?"

"There was no way I could have foreseen the consequences of other peoples' actions. I am not psychic."

The woman's face was visibly flushed, even behind the three layers of glass. "I have—or had—a daughter and a sister in the United States. I am from France, yes, but I was born in California. What has happened to them? Do you know?"

"No, madame, I do not."

The woman shrugged Paulsen-Fuchs' hands away and shouted, "Will it never end? Disaster and death, scientists—responsible, you are all responsible! Will it—" And she was hustled from the viewing chamber. Paulsen-Fuchs raised his hands and shook his head. The two chambers quickly emptied and he was left alone.

And since he was nothing, nobody, that meant that when he was alone, there was nothing there at all.

Nothing but the microbes, the noocytes, with their incredible potential, biding their time . . . unrealized.

Waiting to make him more than he had ever been.

22

The lights went out on the fourth day—in the morning, just after she awoke. She put on her designer jeans (from the Salvation Army thrift store) and her best bra and a sweater, took out her windbreaker from the closet behind the stairs, and stepped out into the daylight. No longer blessed, she thought. No longer desirable to the devil or anybody. "My luck's running out," she said aloud.

But she had food, and the water was still running. She considered her situation for a moment and decided she wasn't that badly off. "Sorry, God," she said, squinting at the sky.

Across the street, the houses were completely draped with mottled brown and white sheets that glistened like skin or leather in the sun. The trees and iron railings were hung with tatters of the same stuff. The houses on her side were starting to be overgrown, too.

It was time to move on. She wouldn't be spared for long.

She packed food into boxes and stacked the boxes in the basket. The gas was still on; she cooked herself a fine breakfast with the last of the eggs and bacon, toasted bread over the fire as her mother had once taught her, spread it with the last of the butter and slathered it with jam. She finished four slices and went upstairs to pack a small overnight bag. Travel light, she thought. Heavy winter jacket and clothes, gun, boots. Wool socks from her brothers' drawers. Gloves. Frontier time, pioneer time.

"I might be the last woman on Earth," she mused. "I'll have to be practical."

The last thing into the cart, waiting at the foot of the stairs on the sidewalk, was the radio. She only played it a few minutes each night, and she had scrounged a boxful of batteries from Mithridates'. It should be useful for some time.

From the radio, she had learned that people were very worried, not just about Brooklyn, but about the entire United States, all the way to the borders, and Mexico and Canada beyond. Short wave news broadcasts from England talked about the silence, the "plague," about air travelers being quarantined, and submarines and aircraft patrolling up and down the coast. No aircraft had as yet penetrated to the interior of North America, a very distinguished-sounding British commentator said, but secret satellite photographs, it was rumored, showed a nation paralyzed, perhaps dead.

Not me, Suzy thought. Paralyzed meant not moving. "I'll move. Come look at me with your submarines and planes. I'll be moving and I'll be wherever I am."

It was late afternoon as Suzy pushed the cart along Adams. Fog obscured the distant towers of Manhattan, allowing only pale silhouettes of the World Trade Center to rise above gray and white opacity. She had never seen fog so dense on the river.

Looking back over her shoulder, she saw great kitelike sails of brown and tan loft up in the wind over Cadman Plaza. Williamsburgh Savings Bank was sheathed along its 500-foot height with brown, no white this time, like a skyscraper wrapped for mailing. She crossed Tillary, heading for access to the bridge, when she thought how much she looked like a bag lady.

She had always been afraid of becoming a bag lady. She knew sometimes people with problems like hers couldn't find places to live, so they lived on the streets.

She wasn't afraid of that now. Everything was different. And the thought tickled her sense of humor. A bag lady in a city covered with brown paper bags. It was very funny but she was too tired to laugh.

Any kind of company would have been welcome—bag lady, cat, bird. But nothing moved except the brown sheets.

She pushed the cart up Flatbush, stopping to sit on a bus bench and rest, getting up and moving on. She took Kenneth's heavy jacket from the cart and slipped it over her shoulders; evening was closing and the air was becoming quite chilly. "I'm going to sing now," she told herself. Her head was full of lots of rhythms and rock beats, but she couldn't find a tune. Pulling the cart up the steps to the bridge walkway, one step at a time, the cart lurching and the understrings scraping, a tune finally popped into her head, and she began humming the Beatles' "Michelle," recorded before she was born. "Michelle, ma belle," was the only part of the lyric she remembered, and she sang that out between pulls and gasps.

Fog enveloped the East River and spilled across the expressway. The bridge rose above the fog, a highway over the clouds. Alone, Suzy pushed her cart along the middle walkway, hearing the wind and a weird, low humming sound she realized must be the bridge cables vibrating.

With no traffic on the bridge, she heard all kinds of noises she never would have heard before; great metallic moans, low and subdued but very impressive; the distant singing of the river; the deep silence beyond. No horns, no cars, no subway rumbles. No people talking, jostling. She might as well have been in the middle of a wilderness.

"A pioneer," she reminded herself. Darkness lay everywhere but over New Jersey, where the sun made its final testimony with a ribbon of yellow-green light. The walkway was pitch black. She stopped pushing the cart and huddled next to it, wrapping her coat tighter, then getting up to put on boots and wool socks. For several hours she sat in a stupor beside the cart, one foot wedged against a wheel to keep it from rolling.

Below the bridge, the sound of the river changed. Her neck hair stood on end, though she had no real reason to be spooked. Still, she could feel something going on, something different. Overhead, the stars gleamed still and clear, and the Milky Way blazed unobscured by city lights and dirty air.

She stood and stretched, yawning, feeling scared and lonely and exalted all at once. She climbed up and over the walkway railing, onto the southbound lanes of the bridge, and walked to the edge. Gripping the railing with gloved, cold-numbed fingers, she looked across the East River, toward South Street, then swept her gaze over the no-longer dark to the outlines of the ferry terminals.

It was still a long time to dawn, but wherever the river touched there was light, and wherever the river flowed there was a green and blue brilliance. The water was filled with eyes and pinwheels and ferris wheels and slow, stately bursts like fireworks, all speckled against a steady cobalt glow. She might have been looking down on a million cities at night, twisted and spun around each other.

The river was alive, from shore to shore and past Governors Island, where the Upper Bay became a Milky Way in reverse. The river glowed and moved and every part of it had a purpose; Suzy knew this.

She knew that she was like an ant on the street of a big city now. She was the uncomprehending, the limited, the transient and fragile. The river was even more complex and beautiful than the early evening skyline of Manhattan.

"I'm never going to understand this," she said. She shook her head and looked up at the dark skyscrapers.

One of them was not completely dark. In the top floors of the south tower of the World Trade Center, a greenish light flickered. "Hey," she said, marveling more at that light than everything else.

She pushed away from the railing and returned to her cart on the walkway. All very pretty, she told herself, but the important thing was to keep from freezing, and then to move when the dawn was bright enough to see by. She huddled next to the cart.

"I'll go see what's in the building," she said. "Maybe it's somebody like me, somebody smarter who knows about electricity. Tomorrow morning I'll go see."

Asleep or awake, shivering or still, she fancied she could hear something beyond hearing: the sound of the change, the plague and the river and the drifting sheets, like a big church choir with all its members' mouths wide open, singing silence.

23

Paulsen-Fuchs pulled up a chair in the viewing chamber with a distant scrape of metal and sat on it. Bernard watched him drowsily from the bed. "So early in the morning," he said.

"It is afternoon. Your time sense is slipping."

"I'm in a cave, or might as well be. No visitors today?"

Paulsen-Fuchs shook his head, but did not volunteer an explanation.

"News?"

"The Russians have pulled out of the Geneva U.N. Obviously they see no advantage to a United Nations when they are the sole nuclear superpower on the Earth. But before they left, they tried to get the security council to declare the United States a nation without leadership and hazardous to the rest of the world."

"What are they aiming for?"

"I believe they are aiming for some consensus on a nuclear strike."

"Good God," Bernard said. He sat up on the edge of the cot and held the back of his hands up before his eyes. The ridges had receded slightly; the quartz lamps treatments were making at least cosmetic improvements. "Did they mention Mexico and Canada?"

"Just the United States. They wish to kick the corpse."

"So what is everybody else saying, or doing?"

"The U.S. forces in Europe are organizing an interim government. They have declared a touring U.S. Senator from California in line of succession for the Presidency. Your Air Force officers at the base here are putting up some resistance. They believe the United States government should be military for the time being. Diplomatic offices are being rearranged into governmental centers. The Russians are asking American ships and submarines to put into special quarantine stations in Cuba and along the Russian coast in the northern Pacific and the Sea of Japan."

"Are they doing it?"

"No reply. I think not, however." He smiled.

"Any more on the bird-fish kills?"

"Yes. In England they are killing all migratory birds, whether they come from North America or not. Some groups want to kill all birds. There is much savagery, and not just against animals, Michael. Americans everywhere are being subjected to great indignities, even if they have lived in Europe for decades. Some religious groups believe Christ has established a base in America and is about to march on Europe to bring the Millennium. But you'll have your news over the terminal this morning, as usual. You can read about it all there."

"It's better if it comes from a friend."

"Yes," Paulsen-Fuchs said. "But even a friend's words cannot improve the news as it is today."

"Would a nuclear strike solve the problem? I'm no expert on epidemiology—could America actually be sterilized?"

"Highly unlikely, and the Russians are well aware of that. We know something about the accuracy of their warheads, failure rates, and so on. They could at best manage to burn out perhaps half of North America sufficiently to destroy all life forms. That would be next to useless. And the radiation hazard, not to mention the meteorological changes and the hazard of biologicals in the dust clouds, would be enormous. But—" He shrugged. "They are Russians. You do not remember them in Berlin. I do. I was just a boy, but I remember them—strong, sentimental, cruel, crafty and stupid at once."

Bernard restrained himself from commenting on Germany's behavior in Russia. "So what's holding them back?"

"NATO. France, surprisingly. The strong objections of most of the non-aligned countries, especially Central and South America. Now enough talk of that. I need a report."

"Ay, ay," Bernard said, saluting. "I feel fine, though a touch groggy. I'm considering going crazy and making a great deal of noise. I feel like I'm in prison."

"Understandable."

"Any women volunteers yet?"

"No," Paulsen-Fuchs said, shaking his head. Perfectly seriously, he added, "I do not understand it. Always they have said fame is the best aphrodisiac."

"Just as well, I suppose. If it's any consolation, I haven't noticed any changes in my anatomy since the day before yesterday." That was when the lines in his skin began to recede.

"You have decided to continue the lamp treatments?"

Bernard nodded. "Gives me something to do."

"We are still considering anti-metabolites and DNA polymerase inhibitors. The infected animals are showing no symptoms—apparently your noocytes are not pleased with animals. Not here, at least. All sorts of theories. Are you experiencing headaches, muscle aches, anything of that nature, even though they may be normal for you?"

"I've never felt better in my life. I sleep like a baby, food tastes wonderful, no aches or pains. An occasional itch in my skin. Oh . . . and sometimes I itch inside, in my abdomen, but I'm not sure where. Not very irritating."

"A picture of health," Paulsen-Fuchs said, finishing the short report on his clipboard. "Do you mind if we check your honesty?"

"Not much choice, is there?"

They gave him a complete medical twice a day, as regularly as his unpredictable sleep periods allowed. He submitted to them with a grim kind of patience; the novelty of an examination conducted by waldoes had long since worn off.

The large panel hummed open and a tray containing glassware and tools slid forward. Then four long metal and plastic arms unfolded, their grasping parts flexing experimentally. A woman standing in a booth behind the arms peered at Bernard through a double glass window. A television camera on the elbow of one of the arms spun around, its red light glowing. "Good afternoon, Dr. Bernard," the woman said pleasantly. She was young, sternly attractive, with red-brown hair tied back in a stylishly compact bun.

"I love you, Dr. Schatz," he said, lying on the low table which rolled out below the waldoes and the tray.

"Just for you, and just for today, I am Frieda. We love you, also, Doctor," Schatz said. "And if I were you, I wouldn't love me at all."

"I'm starting to like this, Frieda."

"Hmph." Schatz used the fine-maneuver waldo to pick up a vacuum ampule from the tray. With uncanny expertise she guided the needle into a vein and withdrew ten cc's of blood. He noticed with some interest that the blood was purple-pink.

"Be careful they don't bite back," he warned her.

"We are *very* careful, Doctor," she said. Bernard sensed tension behind her banter. There could be a number of things they weren't telling him about his condition. But why hide anything? He already considered himself a doomed man.

"You're not telling it to me straight, Frieda," he said as she applied a skin culture tape to his back. The waldo removed the tape with a sticky rip and dropped it into a jar. Another arm quickly stoppered the jar and sealed it in a small bath of molten wax.

"Oh, I think we are," she replied softly, concentrating on the remotes. "What questions do you have?"

"Are there any cells left in my body that haven't been converted?"

"Not all are noocytes, Dr. Bernard, but most have been altered in some way, yes."

"What do you do with them after you've analyzed them?"

"By that time, they are all dead, Doctor. Do not worry. We are very thorough."

"I'm not worried, Frieda."

"That is good. Now turn over, please."

"Not the urethra again."

"I am told this was once a very expensive indulgence among wealthy young gentlemen in the Weimar Republic. A rare experience in the brothels of Berlin."

"Frieda, I am constantly amazed."

"Yes. Now please turn over, Doctor."

He turned over and closed his eyes.

24

Candles lined the long ground-floor lobby window facing the plaza. Suzy stood back and surveyed her handiwork. The day before, she had pulled her way through a wind-shredded stretch of brown sheet and found a candle shop. Using another cart stolen from an Armenian grocery on South Street, she had heisted a load of votive candles and taken them back to the World Trade Center, where she had established her camp in the ground floor of the north tower. She had seen the green light at the top of that building.

With all the candles, maybe the submarines or airplanes would find her. And there was another impulse, too, one so silly she giggled thinking about it. She was determined to answer the river. She stuck the candles onto the window ledge, lighted them one by one, and watched their warm glows become lost in the vaster darkness all around.

Now she arranged them in spirals along the floor, going back to space them out as her supply diminished. She lighted the candles and walked from flame to flame across the broad carpet, smiling at the light, feeling vaguely guilty about the dripping wax.

She ate a package of M&Ms and read by the light of five bunched candles a copy of *Ladies Home Journal* stolen from a concourse newsstand. She was pretty good at reading—slow, but she knew many of the words. The magazine pages with their abundance of ads and tiny columns of words about clothes and cooking and family problems were welcome doses of anesthetic.

Lying on her back on the carpet with the food cart and the empty candle cart nearby, she wondered if she would ever be married—if there would be anybody to marry—and ever have a house where she could apply some of the hints she now pored over. "Probably not," she told herself. "I'm a spinster for sure now." She had never dated extensively, had never gone all the way with Cary, and had graduated from special classes in high school with the reputation of being nice . . . and *dull*. Some people like her were kind of wild, making up for not being too bright by doing lots of daring things.

"Well, I'm still here," she said to the high dark ceiling, "and I'm still dull."

She carried the magazine down the stairs back to the stand, candle in one hand, and picked out a *Cosmopolitan* to read next. Back on the lobby level, she fell asleep briefly, woke up with a start when the magazine fell across her stomach, and walked around from candle to candle, snuffing them out in case she wanted to use them again tomorrow night. Then she lay down on her side on the carpet, using Kenneth's coat for a pillow, one candle still burning, and thought of the massive building above her. She couldn't remember whether the twin towers were still the tallest in the world. She thought not. Each was like an ocean liner upended and stuck into the sky—taller than any ocean liner, actually; so the tourist brochure said.

It would be fun to explore all the shops on the concourse, but even half-asleep, Suzy knew what she would have to do, eventually. She would have to climb the stairs to the top, wherever the stairs were, find out what made the light, and look out across New York—she could see all of the city and much of the state from that vantage. She could see what had happened, and what was happening. The radio might receive more stations that high up. Besides, there was a restaurant on top, and that meant more food. And a bar. She suddenly wanted to get very drunk, something she had tried only twice before in her life.

It wouldn't be easy. Climbing the stairs could take a day or longer, she knew.

She started up out of light sleep. Something had made a noise nearby, a squeaky, sliding scrape. Dawn was gray and dim outside. There was a motion in the plaza—things rolling, like dust-kittens under a bed, like tumbleweeds. She blinked and rubbed her eyes and got to her knees, squinting to see more clearly.

Feathery cartwheels blew in with the wind, sometimes spinning and falling over, crossing the five acres of the plaza, their wind-vane spokes flapping at the edges. They were gray and white and brown. The fallen ones disassembled on the concrete and flattened out, adhering to the pavement and lifting foot-high fronds. They were pouring into the plaza now, more as day brightened, running into the glass and smearing, spreading outward.

"No more going outside," she told herself. "Uh-*uh*."

She ate a granola bar and turned on the radio, hoping to still be able to receive the British station she had heard the day before. With a little tuning, the speaker produced a weak voice, cross-thatched with interference, like a man speaking through felt.

"... to say that the world economy will suffer is certainly an understatement. Who knows how much of the world's resources—both in raw materials and manufactured goods, not to mention, financial records and capital—lies inaccessible in North America now? I realize most people worry more about their immediate survival, and wonder when the plague will cross the ocean, or whether it is already with us, biding its time—" Static overwhelmed the signal for several minutes. Suzy sat with crossed legs next to the radio, waiting patiently. She didn't understand much, but the voice was comforting. "—yet my concern, as an economist, must be with what happens after the crisis passes. If it passes. Well, I'm an optimist. God in all His wisdom has some reason for this. Yes. So there has been no communication from the whole of North America, with the exception of the famous meteorological station on Afognak Island. The financiers are dead, then. The United States has always been the great bastion of private capital. Russia is now the dominant nation on the globe, militarily and perhaps financially. What can we expect?"

Suzy turned the radio off. Blather. She needed to know what it was that happened to her home.

"Why?" she asked out loud. She watched the wheels tumbling through the plaza, their remains beginning to obscure the concrete. "Why not just kill myself and end it all?" She tossed her arms out with self-conscious melodrama, then began to laugh. She laughed until it hurt and became frightened when she realized she couldn't stop. Hands over her mouth, she ran to a water fountain and gulped the clear, steady stream down.

What really scared her, Suzy realized, was the thought of climbing the tower. Would she need keys? Would she get halfway and find she couldn't go any farther?

"I'll be brave," she said around a bite of the granola bar. "There's nothing else I can be."

25

Livermore, California

It had been a normal and a good life, selling parts and junk out
of his back yard, going to auctions and picking up odds and ends,
raising his son and being proud of his wife, who taught school.
He had taken great pleasure in his major acquisitions: a load of
tile, all different kinds, to fix up the bathroom and kitchen in the
huge old white house; an old British jeep; fifteen different cars
and trucks, all blue; a ton and a half of old office furniture,
including an antique wooden file cabinet which proved to be worth
more than he had paid for the whole load.

The weirdest thing he had ever done (since getting married)
was shave the thinning hair on his crown to expedite going bald.
He had hated the in-between state. Ruth had cried when she saw
him. That had been two months ago and the thinning hair had
come back, as unruly and distasteful as ever.

John Olafsen had made a good living back when life had been
normal. He had kept Ruth and seven-year-old Loren in good clothes
and well fed. The house had been in his family for ninety years,
since it had been new. They had wanted for little.

He pulled away the scratched black enamel binoculars and
wiped fatigue and sweat from his eyes with a red bandana. Then
he continued his peering. He was surveying the broad spread of
Lawrence Livermore National Laboratories, and the Sandia Labs
across the road. The smell of dried grass and dust made him want
to blow his nose, leave, pack up . . . and go nowhere because that
was exactly the only place he had left to go. It was five thirty and
dusk was coming on. "Wave your flag, Jerry," he murmured, "you
sonofabitch."

Jerry was his twin brother, five minutes younger, twice as
reckless. Jerry had flown crop dusters in the Salinas Valley. How
John had escaped, neither of them knew, but it was obvious Jerry
was too full of DDT and EDB and what have you. He just plain
didn't taste good to whatever had eaten the town of Livermore.

And Ruth, and Loren.

Jerry was down between the big modern squarish buildings and the old bungalows and barracks, scouting the thirty-foot-high mounds that now rose wherever there was empty space on the LLNL grounds. He carried another red bandana on a stick. Neither brother was ever without a bandana. Each Christmas, they had bought each other new ones, wrapping them up in red foil with big red ribbons.

"Wave," John growled. He shifted the binoculars and saw the red bandana circling rapidly on the stick: once clockwise, once counterclockwise, then three times clockwise. That meant John should come down and see what there was to see. Nothing dangerous . . . as far as Jerry could tell.

He hefted his two hundred and fifty pounds up and brushed down the knees of his ragged black Levis. Curling red hair and beard glowing against the eastern grayness, he climbed out of the drainage ditch and squeezed through the barbed wire fence, the chickenwire fence, and the no-longer-electrified inner perimeter fence.

Then he ran and slid down the twenty-foot grade and hopped another culvert before slowing to a casual walk. He lit up a cigarette and broke the match before tossing it into the dirt. Fifteen or twenty cars were still parked in a lot next to the old Yin-Yang fusion project buildings. An especially impressive mound, about sixty feet in diameter, rose from the earth near the lot. Jerry stood on top of the mound. He had come across a pick somewhere and was dangling it head-down by the handle, a big grin on his beardless face.

"No more joggers," he said as John climbed the mound to join him. They called some of the peculiar things they had seen in Livermore joggers. The name seemed appropriate, since the things almost always ran; not once had they seen one standing still.

"Gladdens my heart," John said. "What's your plan?"

"Dig my way to China," Jerry said, tapping the mound. "Ain't you curious?"

"There's curious, and curious," John said. "What if these mounds are something the lab people put in . . . you know, defense, or maybe an experiment out of hand?"

"I'd say an experiment's already got out of hand."

"I still don't think it came from here."

"Shit." Jerry plunked the head of the pick on the mound, cracking the already fissured dirt and dried grass. "Why not, and where in hell else?"

"Other places got labs."

"Sure, and maybe it's aliens."

John shrugged. They'd probably never know. "Dig, then."

Jerry brought the pick up and expertly swung it down. The point broke through the dirt like a pin through an eggshell and the handle almost jerked from his hands. "Hollow," he grunted, pulling it loose with some effort. He knelt down and peered into the pick hole. "Can't see." He got to his feet and swung the pick again.

"Hit 'em," John said, licking his lips. "Let me hit 'em."

"We don't know anything's down there," Jerry said, snatching the pick handle away from his brother's broad, thick, outstretched hand.

John nodded reluctantly and put the hand in his jeans pocket. He looked off at the setting sun and shook his head. "There's nothing we can do to them," he said. "There's just us."

Jerry swung three times in quick succession and a hole a yard wide caved in. The brothers jumped back, then retreated several more steps for caution's sake. The rest of the mound held. Jerry got on his hands and knees and crawled up to the hole. "Still can't see," he said. "Go get the flashlight."

It was getting dark when John returned with a heavy-duty waterproof lantern from their truck. Jerry sat by the hole, smoking a cigarette and tapping the ashes into it. "Brought a rope, too," John said, dropping the coil next to his brother's knee.

"What's the town look like?" Jerry asked.

"From what I could see, same as before, only more so."

"Be anything left tomorrow?"

John shrugged. "Whatever it turns into, I suppose."

"Okay. It's dark down there, night makes no difference. You hold on, I'll go on down with the light—"

"No way," John said. "I'm not staying up here without a light."

"Then you go down."

John thought about that. "Hell, no. We'll tie the rope to a car and both go down."

"Fine," Jerry said. He ran with the rope to the nearest car, tied it to a bumper, and paid it out on the way back. About thirty feet of rope remained when he reached the top of the mound. "Me first," he said.

"Dur rigor, as the Frogs say."

Jerry lowered himself into the hole. "Light."

John gave him the light. Jerry's head dropped below the rim. "It's reflecting," he said. The beam shot back up into the moist evening air and caught John's face as he peered after. When enough space presented itself, he took hold of the taut rope and followed his twin.

Their mother had told them stories, passed on from a Danish-speaking grandmother, about such mounds full of elf gold, dead bodies, weird blue fire and "skirlin' and singin'."

He never would have admitted it, but what he truly expected to find was Morlocks.

Both twins were sweating by the time they set foot on the bottom of the hollow mound. The air was much warmer and more humid than outside. The lantern beam cut through a thick, sweet-tasting fog. Their boots sunk into a resilient dark purple surface that squeaked when they moved. "Gaw-aw-od-damn," they said simultaneously.

"What the fuck are we going to do, now that we're here?" John asked plaintively.

"We're going to find Ruth and Loren, and maybe Tricia." Tricia had been Jerry's girlfriend for the past six years. He had not seen her dissolve, but it was easy to assume that was what had happened to her.

"They're gone," John said, his voice low and hidden in the back of his throat.

"Hell they are. They just been disassembled and brought down here."

"Where in hell do you get that idea?"

Jerry shook his head. "It's either that or, like you say, they're gone. Do they feel like they're gone?"

John thought a moment. "No," he admitted. Both of them had known the feeling of having someone emotionally close to them die, and knowing it without even being told. "But maybe I'm just foolin' myself."

"Bullshit," Jerry said. "I *know* they're not dead. And if they're not dead, then nobody else is, either. Because you saw—"

"I saw," John butted in. He had seen the clothing filled with dissolving flesh. He had not known what to do. It had been late morning and Ruth and Loren had come down with what seemed like some kind of bug the night before. White stripes on their hands, their faces. He had told them they would all go into the doctor in the morning.

The time between seeing the clothes and when Jerry arrived was still blank. He had screamed, or done something to hurt his throat so he could hardly talk. "Then why weren't we taken, too?"

Jerry patted his belly, as prominent as John's. "Too big a bite," he said. He swirled at the fog with his hand. The beam wouldn't go more than a few feet in any direction. "Jesus, I'm scared," he said.

"Gladdens my heart," John said.

"Well, you're the one suggested we go down here," Jerry said. John didn't object to the reversal of truth. "So now you tell us which way to go."

"Straight ahead," John said. "And watch out for Morlocks."

"Yeah. Jesus. Morlocks."

They walked slowly across the spongy purple floor. Several moist and unhappy minutes passed before the beam showed a surface ahead. Glistening, irregular pipes, mottled gray and brown, Vaseline-shiny, covered a wall, pulsing rhythmically. To the left, the pipes bent around a curve and vanished into a dark tunnel. "I don't believe this," Jerry said.

"Well?" John pointed to the tunnel.

Jerry nodded. "We know what the worst is already," he said.

"You fucking hope we do," John growled.

"You first." Jerry pointed.

"Love you, too."

"Go!"

They entered the tunnel.

26

Paulsen-Fuchs told Uwe to pause at the top of the hill. The camps of protestors around Pharmek's compound had doubled in size in just a week. There were now about a hundred thousand, a sea of tents and flags and banners, most on the eastern side of the compound, near the main gates. There didn't seem to be any particular organization to their protest, which worried him. They were not political—just a cross-section of the German people, driven to distraction by disasters they could not comprehend. They came to Pharmek because of Bernard, not yet knowing what they wanted to do. But that would change. Someone would take charge, give them a direction.

Some of the more ignorant of the public were demanding Bernard's destruction and the sterilization of the containment chamber, but that wasn't likely. Most European governments acknowledged that research on Bernard could be the only way to study the plague and find out how to control it.

Still, Europe was in the grip of panic. A great many travelers—tourists, businessmen, even military personnel—had returned to Europe from North America before the quarantine. Not all of them had been rounded up. Some had been found undergoing transformation in hotels, apartments, houses. Almost invariably the victims were killed by local authorities, the buildings carefully incinerated and sewage and water systems liberally dosed with sterilizing agents.

Nobody knew whether such measures were effective.

Many people, around the world, were convinced it was just a matter of time.

With the news he had received that morning, he halfway hoped they might be right. Plague might be preferable to suicide. "North gate," Paulsen-Fuchs said, getting back into the car.

The equipment had finally been delivered and now crowded half the containment chamber. Bernard rearranged the cot and desk and stood back, looking at the compact laboratory with satisfaction. Now at least he would have something to do. He could poke and prod *himself*.

Weeks had passed and he had still not undergone the final transformation. No one outside could tell him why; nor could he explain to himself why he had not yet communicated with the noocytes, as Vergil had. Or thought he had.

Perhaps Vergil had simply gone insane. Communication might not be possible.

He needed far more equipment than could be crammed into the chamber, but most of the chemical analysis he was planning could be done outside and the information fed into his terminal.

He felt something like the old Michael Bernard now. He was on a trail. He would find out or help the others discover how the cells communicated, what chemical language they used. And if they would not speak with him directly, he would then find a way to speak to *them*. Perhaps control them. Pharmek had all the necessary expertise and equipment, everything Ulam had had and more; if necessary, they could duplicate the experiments and start from scratch.

Bernard doubted that would be allowed to happen. From conversations with Paulsen-Fuchs and other Pharmek personnel, he had the impression there was quite a storm raging around him now.

After running a brief inventory on the equipment, he began refreshing his memory on procedures by reading the manuals. A few hours later he tired of that and made an entry in his computer notebook, knowing that it was not private, that it would be read now or later by Pharmek and government personnel—psychologists perhaps, the doctors certainly. Everything about him was important now.

> There is no biological reason I am aware of why the Earth has not already succumbed. The plague is versatile, can transform any living thing. But Europe remains free—except for scattered incidents and I doubt it is because of their extreme measures. Perhaps the answer to why I am atypical of recent victims—why I am undergoing changes more like Vergil Ulam's—will explain this other mystery, as well. Tomorrow I will have the experts take blood and tissue samples from me, but not all of the sample will be removed from the chamber. I will work on some of them myself, particularly blood and lymph.

He hesitated, fingers over the keyboard, and was about to continue when Paulsen-Fuchs buzzed for his attention from the viewing chamber.

"Good afternoon," Bernard said, spinning his chair around. As usual now, he was naked. A camera in the upper right hand corner of the viewing chamber window continually fed his body contours and characteristics into the computers for analysis.

"Not a good afternoon, Michael," Paulsen-Fuchs said. His long face was even longer and more haggard than usual. "As if we do not have problems enough, now we face the possibility of war."

Bernard stepped close to the window and watched the executive shake out a British newspaper. The headlines sent a queasy thrill down his spine.

RUSS NUKE PANAMA

"When?" he asked.

"Yesterday afternoon. The Cubans reported a radioactive cloud advancing across the Atlantic. NATO military satellites confirmed the hot-spot. I suppose the military knew ahead of time—they must have their seismographs or whatever—but the press only found out this morning. The Russians used nine or ten one-megaton bombs, probably submarine-launched. The whole canal area is . . ." He shook his head, "Nothing from the Russians. Half the people in Germany expect we will be invaded within the week. The other half are drunk."

"Any word on the continent?" That was how they had come to refer to North America in the last two days: *the* continent, the *real* center of the action.

"Nothing," Paulsen-Fuchs said, slamming the paper on the viewing chamber table.

"Do you—the Europeans—expect the Russians to invade North America?"

"Yes. Any day now. Eminent domain, or whatever you English-speakers call it. Right of salvage." He began to chuckle. "I am not their lawyer, but they will think of the correct words, and justify themselves in Geneva, if they haven't bombed Geneva by then, too." He stood with his hands spread on the table, around the paper. "No one is prepared to discuss what will happen to them if they do invade. The U.S. government in exile postures and threatens with its European-based troops and navy, but Russia does not take them seriously. Before your call last month, I had planned to go on my first vacation in seven years. Obviously, I cannot go on vacation," he said. "Michael, you have brought something into my life that may kill me. Pardon my self-centered moment."

"Understood," Bernard said quietly.

"Old saying in Germany," Paulsen-Fuchs said, staring at him. "'It is the bullet you don't hear that gets you.' Does that have meaning for you?"

He nodded.

"Then work, Michael. Work very hard, before we are all dead by our own hand."

27

At the security desk Suzy found a long, powerful flashlight—very fancy, black like binoculars with a beam that could be spread wide or focused in by turning a knob—and set about exploring the concourse and lower-level walkway between the two towers. She spent some time trying on clothes in a boutique, but she couldn't see herself very well in the flashlight beam and that quickly palled. Besides, it was spooky. She made a half-hearted effort to see if others like herself had entered the building, and even ventured briefly into the Cortlandt Street subway station. When she was satisfied that the lower floors were empty—except for the ubiquitous piles of clothes—she returned to her Candlelight Room, as she had dubbed it, and planned her ascent.

She had found a chart of the north tower and now traced her finger along the plan of the lobby and lower floors. Flipping back each sheet of the thick manual, she realized that the building did not have long stairwells, but stairs at different places on each floor.

That would make her climb even more difficult. She found the door that led to the first stairway on the chart and walked to it. It was locked. Doubling back to the security desk, she nudged a pile of uniform with her foot and revealed a massive ring of keys on a retractable cord. She pulled the belt from the loops, noticing a bra in the clothing, and removed the keys. "Excuse me," she whispered, rearranging the clothes into an approximation of their former state. "I'm just going to borrow them. I'll be right back." She caught herself and bit the fleshy part of her thumb until she left vivid tooth marks. Nobody there, she told herself. Nobody anywhere. Just me, now.

It took her a few minutes of slowly reading the labels on the keys to find the one that opened the door to the stairwell. Beyond the door, the stairs were utilitarian concrete and steel. On the next floor they opened onto a hallway. She peered around the corner and down a white corridor leading past doors to various offices, some marked and some merely numbered. A quick look into several of the offices told her little.

"Okay," she told herself. "It's nothing but a hike, a long hike. I'll need food and water." She looked down at her loafers and sighed. They'd have to do, unless she decided to borrow a pair of empty shoes from—

She didn't relish that idea. In the ground floor lobby, she took a plastic shopping bag from behind the newsstand and filled it with lightweight foods from her cart. Water was more difficult; the plastic jugs were too bulky to hang comfortably from her belt, but she decided there was little alternative. And if she found water still available on the upper floor—there *had* to be water-coolers— she could always leave the jugs behind.

She began her climb at eight thirty in the morning. It was best, she thought, to climb steadily ten floors and then rest, or explore and see what was visible from that level. That way, she might reach the top by the end of the day.

Humming "Michelle," she went from flight to flight, hands gripping the steel rails, passing through door after door. She tried to establish a rhythm. Kenneth and Howard had taken her hiking in Maine once and she had learned that every hiker had a certain rhythm. Following that rhythm made the trail a lot easier; breaking the rhythm to follow someone else made it much more difficult.

"Nobody to follow," she told herself on the fourth level. She tried singing "Michelle" again, but the rhythm didn't match her steps, so she whistled a march by John Williams. On the ninth level she began to feel winded. "One more." And on the tenth, she squatted with her back against the wall of the elevator lobby, staring at the doors. "Maybe this wasn't a good idea." But she was stubborn—her mother had always said so, somewhat proudly—and she would persist. "Nothing else to do," she said, her voice hollow in the deserted lobby.

When her breathing eased, she stood and arranged the bottle of water and the sack of food. Then she crossed to the next door and opened it. Up another flight. Another lobby, more hallways, more offices. She decided to investigate one of the restrooms.

"Check for water," she said. She looked between the Men's and Women's and giggled, then chose the Men's. Shining the flashlight over the mirrors and fixtures, she gave into curiosity and walked the length of the lavatory. She had never before seen the tall white porcelain fixtures lining the wall. She had even forgotten what they were called. She looked under the stalls and froze, fear tangling and twisting with perverse laughter inside.

A pile of clothes lined the floor in one of the stalls. "Got sucked right down the toilet," she murmured, straightening and wiping tears from her eyes. "Poor guy. Goddammit." She dabbed at her eyes with her rolled-up sleeves and twisted the hot-water knob on the sink. A trickle of water came out. More came when she turned the cold knob, but it didn't look promising.

She left the lavatory and sauntered down a hallway. Behind a big double wood door with Japanese-sounding names on it was a waiting room, plush velvet couches and glass tables with a big desk near the back wall. There was no receptionist behind the desk, and no pile of clothes, either. Nothing for her there.

From the waiting room, she looked down on the plaza. The concrete was completely covered with brown now. "Climb," she told herself. Stairway to heaven. Die at the top and be closer. But climb.

28

"It's like crawling down a throat," John said.

"Jesus, you're morbid."

"It is, though, ain't it?"

"Yeah," Jerry said. He grunted and stooped lower. "We're behaving like idiots. Why *this* mound, and why now?"

"You picked it out."

"And I don't know why. Maybe no reason at all."

"Good as any, I suppose."

The tunnel walls were changing as they walked farther along. Big fleshy pipes gave way to fine, glistening net, like spray-painted tripe. John poked his face and the light up close to the surface and saw each little dimple in the net filled with tiny disks and cubes and balls, stacked atop each other in a jumble. The floor was narrowing, the spongy purple rising up in ridges, the ridges running parallel with the tunnel. "Drainage," Jerry said, pointing.

They passed the light back and forth to share its comfort, sometimes shining it at each other's faces, or inspecting their skin and clothing to see that nothing was clinging to them.

The tunnel widened abruptly and the thick sweet fog drifted around them. "We've walked far enough to be under another mound," Jerry said. He stopped and pulled his boot from something sticky. "There's stuff all over the floor."

John trained the light on Jerry's boot. Brownish-red goo covered the sole. "Doesn't look too deep," he said.

"Not yet, anyway." The fog smelled faintly like fertilizer, or like the sea. Alive. It circulated in thin, high veils, as if caught between curtains of air.

"Which way now? We don't want to just walk in circles," Jerry said.

"You're the leader," John said. "Don't ask me for initiative."

"Smells like someone left seaweed in a candy store," Jerry said. "Makes you gag."

"Mushrooms," John said, pointing the light down. White capped objects about two inches wide lay all around their feet, popping beneath them as they walked. He aimed the light higher and saw vertical and horizontal lines through the fog ahead.

"Shelving," Jerry said. "Shelves with things growing on them." The shelves were less than a quarter-inch thick, supported by irregularly spaced brackets, all made from a hard white substance that glistened in the beam. On the shelves were stacks of what looked like burned paper—wet burned paper.

"Yucch," Jerry commented, feeling one of the stacks with a curled finger.

"Wouldn't touch anything if I was you," John said.

"Hell, you *are* me, brother. Minor differences."

"I'm still not touching anything."

"Yeah. Probably a smart idea."

They proceeded along the length of the shelving and came to a wall covered with pipes. The pipes grew out onto the shelves and diverged into smaller clusters, leading to the glistening brown stacks. "What is this stuff, plastic or what?" Jerry asked, feeling one of the shelf braces.

"Doesn't look like plastic," John said. "Looks more like clean white bone." They stared at each other.

"I hope not," Jerry said, turning away. Walking through the fog and swirling air to the other end of the shelving, they found a foamlike white matrix, resembling a rubbery honeycomb, pocked with open bubbles filled to the rim with purple syrup. Some of the bubbles dripped purple onto the floor, where each drop hissed and smoked on impact.

John held back an urge to gag and mumbled something about having to get out.

"Sure," Jerry said, bending down to peer at the bubbles. "Look at this, first."

John reluctantly bent, hands on knees, and looked at the bubble his brother had indicated.

"Look at all those little wires," Jerry said. "Little beads traveling on wires, above the purple. Red beads. Looks like blood, don't it?"

John nodded. He dug into his jeans pocket and pulled out a Swiss army knife he had found under the torn-up seats of the British jeep. He used his fingernails to withdraw a small magnifying glass from the knife handle. "Shine the light on it." With the beam filling the bubble, he peered through the glass at the purple liquid and the tiny wires with red drops.

The closer he looked, the more detailed it became. Nothing he could identify, but the purple fluid's surface was composed of thousands of pyramids. The white material resembled foam plastic or cork.

He gritted his teeth. "Very pretty," he said. He took hold of the edge of a bubble and tore it away. The liquid splashed at his feet and the fog thickened. "They're not here."

"Why'd you do that?" Jerry asked.

John slugged the soft honeycomb and pulled his hand away glistening with purple. "Because they're not here."

"Who?"

"Ruth and Loren. They're just gone."

"Hold on—" Jerry admonished, but John swung with both hands now, tearing the lattice of bubbles apart. They could hardly see each other for the sweet, cloying fog. Jerry grabbed his brother's shoulder and tried to pull him back. "Stop it, stop it, John, goddammit!"

"They took 'em!" John screamed. His throat spasmed and he clutched it with one hand, still gripping and tearing and punching with the other. "They're not in here, Jerry!"

They rolled in the goo until Jerry pinned both his brother's arms. The light fell with its beam tilting upward behind them. John shook his head, sweat flying, and began a long, silent sob, eyes scrunched shut, mouth stretched wide. Jerry hugged his brother tightly and looked over his shoulder at the beam-lit, swirling fog. "Shh," he said over and over. They were covered with the smelly brown muck. "Shh."

"I been holdin' it in," John said after sucking a deep, tremulous breath. "Jerry, let me go. I been holdin' it in too long. Let's get out of here. Nobody's here. There's nobody down here."

"Yeah," Jerry said. "Not here. Maybe somewhere, but not here."

"I can *feel* them, Jerry."

"I know. But not here."

"Then where *the hell*—"

"Shhhh." They lay in the muck, listening to the soft hiss of the fog and the curtains of air. Jerry could feel his eyes opening as wide as a cat's in the dark. "Sh. There's something—"

"Oh, Christ," John said, struggling from his brother's arms. They stood, dripping muck, facing the direction of the lantern's beam. The fog roiled and puffed in the light.

"It's a jogger," Jerry said as a silhouette took shape.

"It's too big," John said.

The object was at least ten feet across, flattened, fringe hanging from its side, appearing brownish in the uncertain light.

"It doesn't have legs," Jerry said, awed. "It's just floating there."

John stepped forward. "Goddamn Martians," he said quietly. He raised his fist. "I'll break—"

And there was a moment of forgetfulness.

Morning light tinted the east aquamarine. The town, covered with brown and white sheets, resembled something that more properly belonged underwater, a low, flat section of ocean bed.

They stood in the drainage ditch beyond the fences, looking toward the town.

"I can't move much," Jerry said.

"I can't either."

"I think it stung us."

"I didn't feel anything."

John moved his arm experimentally. "I think I saw them."

"Saw who?"

"I'm pretty confused, Jerry."

"Me too."

The sun was well into the sky before they were able to walk. Over the town, transparent hemispheres drifted between the outlines of the buildings, occasionally shooting down thin pencils of light. "Looks like jellyfish," Jerry commented as they wobbled toward the road and the truck.

"I think I saw Loren and Ruth. I'm not sure," John said. They approached the truck slowly, stiffly, and sat in the front seat, closing the doors behind. "Let's go."

"Where?"

"I saw them down where we were. But they weren't there. That doesn't make sense."

"No, I mean, where do we go now?"

"Out of town. Somewhere else."

"They're everywhere, John. Radios say that."

"Goddamn Martians."

Jerry sighed. "Martians would have zapped us, John."

"Fuck 'em. Let's go away."

"Whatever they are," Jerry said, "I'm pretty sure they're from right around here." He pointed emphatically toward the ground. "Right from inside the fence."

"Drive," John said. Jerry started the engine, put the truck in gear and roared them off down the dirt road. They spun out on East Avenue, narrowly missed a deserted car at the next intersec-

tion, and squealed onto South Vasco road, heading for the highway.
"How much gas we got?"

"I filled 'er up in town yesterday. Before the sheets got the
pumps."

"You know," John said, bending to pick up an oil rag from the
floor and wiping his hands, "I don't think we're smart enough to
figure out anything. We just don't have any idea."

"No good ideas, maybe." Jerry squinted. Someone stood by
the road a mile ahead, waving vigorously. John followed his brother's puzzled stare.

"We're not alone," he said.

Jerry slowed the truck. "It's a woman." They stopped forty or
fifty yards from where she stood on the road shoulder. Jerry leaned
out the driver's side window to see her more clearly. "Not a young
woman," he said, disappointed.

She was in her fifties, hair jet black and flowing, and she wore
a peach-colored silk gown that flagged behind her as she ran. The
brothers looked at each other and shook their heads, unsure what
to think or do.

She approached the passenger side, out of breath and laughing.
"Thank God," she said. "Or whomever. I thought I was the only
one left in the whole town."

"Guess not," Jerry said. John opened the door and she stepped
up into the cab. He moved over for her and she sat, releasing a
deep breath and laughing again. She turned her head and regarded
him sharply. "You fellows aren't hoodlums, are you?"

"Don't believe so," Jerry said, eyes trained on the road. "Where
you from?"

"Back in town. My house is gone, and the neighborhood's all
wrapped up like a Christmas package. I thought I was the only
one in the world left alive."

"Haven't been listening to the radio, then," John said.

"No. Don't like electronic things. But I know what's going on
anyway."

"Yeah?" Jerry asked, moving the truck back onto the road.

"Yes indeed. My son. He's responsible for this. I had no idea
what form it would take, but there's no doubt in my mind. And
I warned him, too."

The twins glanced at each other again. The woman tossed her
hair and deftly slipped a flexible band around it.

"Yes, I know," she said, chuckling. "Crazy as a bedbug. Crazier
than all that back in town. But I can tell you where we should be
going."

"Where?" Jerry asked.

"South," she said firmly. "To where my son was working." She smoothed her gown down over her knees. "My name, by the way, is Ulam, April Ulam."

"John," John said, awkwardly extending his right hand and gripping hers. "This is my brother, Jerry."

"Ah, yes," April said. "Twins. Makes sense, I suppose."

Jerry started laughing. Tears came into his eyes and he wiped them with a muck-stained hand. "South, lady?" he said.

"Definitely."

29

Electronic Journal of Michael Bernard

January 15: Today, they began speaking with me. Halting at first, then with greater confidence as the day progressed.

How do I describe the experience of their "voices"? Having finally crossed the blood-brain barrier, and explored the (to them) enormous frontier of my brain, and having discovered a pattern in the activities of this new world—the pattern being me—and realizing that the information from their distant past, months ago, was accurate, that a macroscopic world does exist—

Having learned this much, they have now had to learn what it is to be human. For only then could they communicate with this God in the Machine. Appointing tens of millions of "scholars" to work on this project, in perhaps only the last three days, they have indeed cracked the case, and now chatter with me no more strangely than if they were (for example) aboriginal Australians.

I sit in my desk chair, and when the appointed time comes, we converse. Some of it is in English (I think—the conversation may occur in pre-literate portions of the brain, and be translated by my own mind into English afterward), some of it visual, some of it in other senses—mostly taste, a sense which seems particularly attractive to them.

I cannot really comprehend the size of the population within me. They come in many classes: the original noocytes and their derivatives, those converted immediately after the invasion, the categories of mobile cells, many of them apparently new to the body, newly designed, with new functions; the fixed cells, perhaps not individuals in a mental sense having no mobility and being assigned fixed, if complex, functions; the as-yet unaltered cells (nearly all the cells in my brain and nervous system fall into this category); and others I am not yet clear on.

Together, they number in the tens of trillions.

At a crude guess, perhaps two trillion fully developed, intelligent individuals exist within me.

If I multiply this crude number times the number of people in North America—half a billion, another rough guess—then I end up with a billion trillon, or on the order of 10^{20}. That is the number of intelligent beings on the face of the Earth at this moment—neglecting, of course, the entirely negligible human population.

Bernard pushed his chair back from the desk after saving the entry in memory. There was too much to record, too much detail; he despaired of ever being able to explain the sensations to the researchers outside. After weeks of frustration, of cabin fever, and then trying to break the chemical language within his blood, there was suddenly a feast of information so huge he couldn't begin to absorb it. All he had to do was ask, and a thousand or a million intelligent beings would organize to analyze his question and return detailed, rapid answers.

"What am I to you?" would bring in reply:

Father/Mother/Universe
World-Challenge
Source of all
Ancient, slow
mountain-galaxy

And he could spend hours replaying the sensual complexes which accompanied the words: the taste of his own blood serum, the fixed tissues of his body, the joy at nutrition being diffused, the necessity of cleansing, protecting.

In the quiet of night, lying on his cot with only infra-red scanners trained on him and the ubiquitous sensors taped to his body, he swam in and out of his own dreams and the cautious, almost reverent inquiries and replies of the noocytes. Now and then, he would awaken as if alerted by some mental guard dog that a new territory was being probed.

Even in the day, his sense of time became distorted. The minutes spent conversing with the cells felt like hours, and he would return to the world of the containment chamber with a disconcerting lack of conviction about its reality.

The visits by Paulsen-Fuchs and others seemed to come at longer intervals, though in fact the visits were made at the same established times each day.

At three P.M., Paulsen-Fuchs arrived with his elaborations of the news reports Bernard had read or seen earlier that morning. The news was invariably bad and getting worse. The Soviet Union, like an untamed horse set loose, had now left Europe panicked and bristling with helpless rage. It had then retreated into sullen silence, which reassured no one. Bernard thought briefly of these problems, then asked Paulsen-Fuchs what progress there was on controlling the intelligent cells.

"None. They are obviously in control of all the immune system; other than having an increased metabolic rate, they are very thoroughly camouflaged. We believe they can now neutralize any anti-metabolite before it begins to work; they are already alert to inhibitors like actinomycin. In short, we cannot damage them without damaging you."

Bernard nodded. Oddly, that didn't concern him now.

"And you are, now, communicating with them," Paulsen-Fuchs said.

"Yes."

Paulsen-Fuchs sighed and turned away from the triple glass. "Are you still a human, Michael?"

"Of course I am," he said. But then it occurred to him that he was not, that he had not been *just* a human for more than a month. "I'm still me, Paul."

"Why have we had to snoop to find this fact out?"

"I wouldn't call it snooping. I assumed my entries were being intercepted and read."

"Michael, why haven't you told *me?* I am foolishly hurt. I assumed I was an important person in your world."

Bernard shook his head and chuckled. "You are indeed, Paul. You're my host. And as soon as I figured out precisely what to say, in speech, you would have been told. Will be told. The dialogue between the noocytes and myself is just beginning. I can't be sure we don't still have fundamental misunderstandings."

Paulsen-Fuchs stepped toward the viewing chamber hatchway. "Tell me when you are ready. It could be very important," he said wearily.

"Certainly."

Paulsen-Fuchs left the chamber.

That was almost cold, Bernard thought. I was behaving like someone suspended from society. And Paul is a friend.

Yet what could he do?

Perhaps his humanity *was* coming to an end.

30

On the sixtieth floor, Suzy realized she would not be able to climb any higher that day. She sat in an executive chair behind a sprawling executive desk (she had pushed the executive's gray suit and fine silk shirt and alligator shoes into a corner) and looked through the window at the city some six hundred feet below. The walls were covered with real wood paneling and signed Norman Rockwell prints in buffed bronze frames. She ate a cracker with jam and peanut butter from her plastic shopping bag and sipped on a bottle of Calistoga mineral water from the executive's well-stocked bar.

A brass telescope mounted in the windows gave her great views of her home neighborhood, now thickly shrouded with the leathery brown stuff, and whatever else she wanted to look at to the south and the west. The river around Governors Island no longer looked like water. It looked muddy and frozen, and peculiar solidified waves spread out in circles to meet other waves from Ellis Island and Liberty Island. It looked more like raked sand than water, but she knew it couldn't have turned into sand.

"You must have been very rich, made a lot of money," she said to the gray suit and silk shirt and shoes. "I mean, this is nice and fancy. I'd thank you if I could." She finished her bottle and dropped it into a wooden trash basket under the desk.

The chair was comfortable enough to sleep in, but she hoped to find a bed. She had seen rich executives on the old television with private bedrooms in their office suites. This office certainly looked fancy enough. She was too tired to search for a bedroom right now, however.

The sun descended over New Jersey as she massaged her cramped legs.

Most of the city, what she could see of it, was covered with brown and black blankets. There was no better description. Someone had come along and wrapped surplus army blankets all the way to the tenth or twentieth floors of all the buildings in Manhattan. Occasionally she saw vast sheets of the material rise up

157

and sail away, just as they had in Brooklyn, but there was less of that activity now.

"Good-bye, sun," she said. The tiny red arc dipped and vanished, and for the first time in her life she saw, in the last second of refracted light, a brief flash of green. She had been told about that in high school, and the teacher had said it was very rare (and hadn't bothered to explain what caused it) and now she grinned with pleasure. She had actually seen it.

"I'm just privileged, that's all," she said. An idea began to form. She wasn't sure whether it was one of her weird touches of insight, or whether it was just some daydream. She was being watched. The brown was watching her, and the river. The piles of clothes. Whatever the people had turned into was watching her. It wasn't an unpleasant sort of watching, because she knew she pleased them. She wouldn't be changed as long as she kept on doing what she was doing.

"Well, gotta search for my bed now," she said, pushing up from the chair. "Nice office," she said to the gray suit.

Beyond the secretary's desk in the outer office was a small unmarked door. She tried it and found a closet full of forms and papers stacked on shelves, with supplies lower down and an odd little box with a glowing red light. Something was still feeding the box electricity. Maybe it was a burglar alarm, she thought, working off batteries. Maybe it was a smoke detector. She closed the door and went the opposite direction. Around the corner from the big office was another door, this one marked with a brass plaque saying PRIVATE. She nodded and tried the knob. It was locked, but she was already an expert pilferer of keys. She picked out a likely candidate from a desk drawer and inserted it. The second choice worked. She turned the knob and opened the door.

The room was dark. She flicked the flashlight switch. The wide beam swept a comfortable-looking bed, nightstand, a table with small computer in one corner, and—

Suzy screamed. She heard a thump and out of the corner of her eye saw a small thing move under the desk, and other things under the bed. She lifted the light. A pipe rose beside the bed. On top of the pipe was a round object with many flat triangular sides and strings hanging from each side. It swayed and tried to avoid the light. Something small and dark scampered past her feet and she jumped back, pointing the light at her shoes.

It might have been a rat, but it was too large and not shaped right, and too small for a cat. It had many large eyes or shiny parts on a round head but it had only three legs, covered with red fur. It ran into the big office. She quickly shut the door on the bedroom and backed away, hand clamped over her mouth.

The hell with the top floor. She didn't care any more.

The hallway outside the secretary's office was clear. She picked up the radio from the secretary's desk, the bottle of water and her bag of food and quickly arranged them, looping her belt through the bottle's handle and hanging the bag over her shoulder and behind her back. "Jesus, Jesus," she whispered. She ran down the hallway, bottle thumping against her butt, and opened the door to the stairwell. "Down," she murmured. "Down, down, down!" She would try to leave the building. If there were things on the upper floor, she had no other choice. Her loafers thumped rapidly on the stairs. The bag of food bounced and suddenly ruptured, scattering crackers and small jars and bits of jerky down the stairs. Jars broke and an unopened can of plums descended one stair at a time, rolling and clumping, rolling and clumping.

She hesitated, reached to pick up the plums, and then looked at the wall. Slowly, eyes wide, she peered around the railing. Filaments of white covered the door and a sheet of dark brown was torturously creeping up the side wall.

"No!" she screamed. "Goddammit, no! You fuckers, you leave me alone, you let me go down!" She tossed her head and pounded on the railing until her fists were bruised. Tears flew from her eyes. "You leave me alone!" Still, the sheets advanced.

Up again. Whatever was higher up, she had to go. She could fight it off with a broom, but she couldn't wade through it—that would be too much, and she really would go crazy.

She picked up what food she could and stuffed it into her pockets. There had to be food in the restaurant.

"I'm not going to think about it," she told herself over and over again, not in reference to eating, which was of small concern to her now. She wasn't going to think about what she would do *after* she made it to the top.

The sea of brown, leathery blanket-material was obviously intent on covering the whole city, even to the upper floors of the World Trade Center.

And that would leave very little room for Suzy McKenzie.

31

April Ulam shielded her eyes to look into the sunrise. The windmills of Tracy were silhouetted against the yellow sky, propellors still turning, feeding power to the deserted gas station where the twins had refueled the truck. She glanced at John and nodded as if in agreement; yes, indeed, another day. Then she walked back into the small grocery store to supervise Jerry's search for provisions.

She was a lot tougher than she looked, John decided. Crazy or not, she had the brothers in a spell. They had spent the night in the station, exhausted, after traveling less than twenty miles out of Livermore. They had finally decided to take the central valley route. This had been suggested by April; it was best, she thought, to avoid what had once been populated areas. "Judging from what happened in Livermore," she had said, "we don't want to get bogged down in San Jose or anyplace else."

The way they were going, they would inevitably have to drive through Los Angeles, or find some way to skirt around it, but John hadn't mentioned that.

She gave them direction, at least. There was no sense criticizing because without her they would still be in Livermore, going mad one way or another—probably violently. John walked around the truck, hands in his pockets, looking at the dirt.

They were all going to die.

He didn't mind. He had become very, very tired last night—tired in a way sleep could never cure. He could tell Jerry was feeling the same way. Let the mad woman lead them around by the nose. Who cared?

Los Angeles might be interesting. He doubted they would ever get to La Jolla.

Jerry and April came out of the store with shopping bags in both arms. They propped the bags in the back of the truck and Jerry took out a worn map from the truck's glove compartment.

"580 south to 5," he said. April agreed. John took the wheel and they rumbled down the freeway.

For the most part, the highway was free of cars. But at wide intervals they passed deserted (or at least empty) vehicles—trucks, cars, even an Air Force bus—along the roadside. They didn't stop to investigate.

The asphalt was clean and the drive was fast. The hills around the San Luis and Los Banos reservoirs should have been green with winter rains, but they were a matte gray, as if coated with primer before application of a new color. The reservoirs themselves were glossy green and still as glass. Nowhere was bird or insect visible. April regarded all this with fated pride; *my son did this,* she seemed to be thinking, and while a frown crossed her face as they passed the reservoirs, on the whole she did not seem to disapprove.

Jerry was both intrigued and thoroughly spooked by her, but he wasn't about to say anything. Still, John could sense his unease.

The fields to each side of 5 were covered with mossy brown sheets that glistened in the sun like plastic. "All those trees and vegetables," April said, shaking her head. "What do you think happened to the crops?"

"I don't know, Ma'am," Jerry said. "I just spray 'em, I don't judge 'em."

"Not just people. Takes over *everything.*" She smiled and shook her head. "Poor Vergil. Had no idea."

They made a pitstop at a Carl's Junior just off the highway. The franchise's doors were open, and there were a few piles of clothes behind the service counter, but the building was undisturbed and unconverted. In the restroom, as they pissed in parallel, John said, "I believe her."

"Why?"

"Because she's so sure."

"Hell of a reason."

"And she ain't lying."

"Hell no. She's looney tunes."

"I don't think so."

Jerry zipped up and said, "She's a witch, John."

John didn't disagree.

The monotonous brown-covered farmlands gradually changed color and character as they approached the Lost Hills turnoff. More bare earth appeared, dusty and dead-looking. Little spouts of air swept the land in the distance like maids cleaning up after a wild party. "Where *did* all the crops go?" April wondered.

Jerry shook his head. Don't know. Don't want to know.

John squinted into the dusty haze ahead and tapped the truck's brake pedal, down-shifting expertly. Then he slammed the brakes hard and the truck spun out, tires squealing. Jerry cursed and April grimly hung on to the edge of the window.

The truck came to a halt reversed on the roadway. John turned them around and grabbed the gearshift back into neutral.

They stared. No words were necessary—or even possible.

A hill was crossing the highway. Slow, ponderous, perhaps a hundred feet high, the mass of shiny brown and primer gray moved through the wind-churned dust barely a quarter mile ahead.

"How many of those are there, do you think?" April asked pertly, breaking the silence.

"Can't say," John demurred.

"Must be one of them Lost Hills they were announcing," Jerry said without a hint of levity.

"Maybe that's where all the crops went," April speculated. The brothers did not care to discuss the point. John waited until the hill had passed, and a half hour later, as it slid over the fields toward the west, started the truck again and put it back in gear. They slowly crossed the mangled asphalt. The air smelled of crushed plants and dust.

"Martians," John said. That was his last protest to April's claim of knowing what had really happened. He said very little after that, until they started the climb up the Grapevine, past the un-converted trees and buildings of Fort Tejon and the vague outlines of tiny Gorman. As they neared the ridge, he stared at Jerry with wide eyes, pupils dilated, and said, "City of Angels, coming up."

It was five o'clock, early evening and getting dark.

The air over Los Angeles was as purple as raw meat.

32

At noon, Bernard's lunch was delivered through the small hatch—a bowl of fruit and a roast beef sandwich with a glass of sparkling water. He ate slowly, reflectively, occasionally glancing at the VDT. It displayed the lab's recent results in analyzing some of his serum proteins.

The screen's alphanumerics were mint green. Red lines were taking shape under the numbers, which scrolled up as new series were added.

Bernard, what is this?

—Not to worry, he answered the internal query. If I don't do research, I malfunction.

Their level of communication had improved enormously in just a couple of days.

?You are analyzing something to do with our communication. There is no need. You already communicate through the proper channels, through us.

—Yes, indeed. But will you tell me all I need to know?

We tell you what we are assigned to tell you.

—You've riddled me, so allow me to riddle you. I have to feel I'm not powerless, that I'm doing something useful.

With great difficulty, we have been trying to comprehend *encode* your situation. To VISUALIZE. You are in an enclosed SPACE. This SPACE is of *concentration* you regard as SMALL.

—But adequate, now that I have you fellows to chat with.

You are restrained. You cannot *diffuse* through the limits of the enclosed SPACE. Is this restraint by your choice?

—I'm not being punished, if that's what you're worried about.

We do not *encode* comprehend PUNISHED. You are well. Your body functions are in order. Your EMOTION is not extreme.

—Why should I be upset? I've lost. It's all over but the (ahem) loud encoding.

We WISH you were more aware of the physiology of your brain. We could tell you much more about your state. As it

163

is, we have extreme difficulty finding WORDS to describe the location of our teams. But to return to the prior question. Why do you WISH to process other forms of communication?

—I'm not blocking my thoughts, am I? (Am I?) You should be able to figure out what I'm doing on your own. (How could I block my thoughts to you?)

You realize our inadequacy. You are so new to us. We regard you with . . .

—Yes?

Those who have been assigned to replicate this state to *******This is unclear.

—I'll say.

We regard you as if you were capable of mild *dissociation* reproof for minimal performance of assigned processing.

—You regard me as what?

We regard you as a *supreme command cluster*.

—What is that? And that brings up a whole host of questions I would like to ask.

We have been authorized to answer those questions.

(Jesus! They knew the gist of the questions even before he had formed them in his mind.)

—I'd like to speak to an individual.

INDIVIDUAL?

—Not just the team or research group. One of you, acting alone.

We have studied INDIVIDUAL in your conception. We do not fit the word.

—There are no individuals?

Not precisely. Information is shared between clusters of *******

—Not clear.

Perhaps this is what you mean by INDIVIDUAL. Not the same as a single mentality. You are aware that cells cluster for basic structuring; each cluster is the smallest INDIVIDUAL. These clusters rarely separate for long into single cells. Information is passed between clusters sharing in assigned tasks, including instruction and memory. Mentality is thus divided between clusters performing a function. Important memory may be *diffused* through all clusters. What you think of as INDIVIDUAL may be spread throughout the *totality*.

—But you're not all of one mentality, a group mind, collective consciousness.

No, as much as we can analyse those concepts.

—You can argue with each other.

There can be differences of approach, yes.

—So what is a command cluster?

Key cluster placed along travel *juncture*, lymph and blood vessels, to monitor performance of traveling clusters, servant cells, *tailored* cells. You are like the mightiest of cell command clusters, yet you are ENCLOSED and have not yet chosen to exert your power to *lyse*. Why do you not exert control?

Eyes closed he pondered that question for a long while—perhaps a second or more—and replied.

—You are becoming acquainted with mystery.

Are you attempting to challenge by these researches into our communication?

—No.

There is a *disjunction* here.

—I'm getting tired now. Please leave me alone for a while.

Understood.

He rubbed his eyes and picked up a piece of fruit. He suddenly felt exhausted.

"Michael?"

Paulsen-Fuchs stood in the reception area. "Hello, Paul," Bernard said. "I've just been having the weirdest conversation."

"Yes?"

"I think they're treating me like some sort of minor deity."

"Oh, dear," Paulsen-Fuchs said.

"And I probably only have a couple of weeks left."

"You said that when you arrived—only then, you said a week."

"I can feel the changes now. It's slow, but it's still going to happen."

They stared at each other through the three-layer glass. Paulsen-Fuchs tried to speak several times, but nothing came out. He lifted his hands helplessly.

"Yeah," Bernard said, sighing.

33

*North America, Satellite Transmission
from High-Altitude Reconnaissance RB-1H;
Voice of Lloyd Upton, Correspondent EBN*

Yes, in place—leads separate and patched—we're all a bit nervous here, don't mind the teeth chattering. Taping now? And the direct feed . . . yes, Arnold? 1,2,3. Lloyd Upchuck here, yes, that's how I feel . . . Okay. Colin, that bottle. The orange suit won't upset the viddy? It upsets me. Let's begin.

Hello, I'm Lloyd Upton from the British branch of the European Broadcasting Network. I'm now at twenty thousand meters over the heartland of the United States of America, in the rear compartment of an American B-1 bomber modified for high-altitude reconnaissance, an RB-1H. With me are correspondents from four major continental networks, from European branches of two United States news organizations, and the BBC. We are the first civilian journalists to fly over the United States since the beginning of the most hideous plague in world history. We are accompanied by two civilian scientists whom we will interview on the return leg of our flight, which has thus far averaged twice the speed of sound, that is Mach 2.

In just eight weeks, two short months, the entire North American continent has undergone a virtually indescribable transformation. All familiar landmarks—entire cities—have vanished beneath, or perhaps been transformed into, a landscape of biological nightmare. Our aircraft has followed a zig-zag course from New York to Atlantic City, then over to Washington, DC, through Virginia, Kentucky, and Ohio, and soon we will be dipping down to one thousand meters to pass over Chicago, Illinois and the Great Lakes. At that point, we will double back and fly along the Eastern seaboard to Florida, and over the Gulf of Mexico we will be refueled from aircraft flying out of Guantanamo Naval Base in

Cuba, which, miraculously, has escaped the major effects of the plague.

We can imagine the grief of Americans stranded in England, Europe and Asia, as well as other parts of the globe. I greatly fear we can bring them no solace with this historic overflight. What we have seen can bring solace to no member of the human race. Yet we have not witnessed desolation, but rather a weird and— if I may be forgiven a bizarre sort of aesthetic judgment—wonderful landscape of an entirely new form of life, its origin shrouded in secrecy, though the authorities themselves may not know. Speculation that the plague arose in a biological laboratory in San Diego, California has neither been corroborated nor denied by government authorities, and EBN has been unable to interview a potential key participant in the . . . uh . . . drama, famed neurosurgeon Dr. Michael Bernard, currently kept in sterile confinement near Wiesbaden, West Germany.

We are now transmitting direct-feed video and still pictures from our cameras and special real-time reconnaissance cameras aboard our aircraft. Some will be seen live; others are being processed and edited and will follow this historic live broadcast.

How can I begin to describe the landscape beneath us? A new vocabulary, a new language, may be necessary. Textures and forms hitherto unknown to biologists, to geologists, cover the cities and suburbs, even the wildernesses of North America. Entire forests have become gray-green . . . uh . . . forests of spires, spikes, needles. Through telephoto lenses we have seen motion in these complexes, elephant-sized objects moving by unknown means. We have seen rivers undergoing some sort of controlled flow, patterns unlike the flow of normal waterways. On the Atlantic Coast, most especially in the vicinity of New York and Atlantic City, for a distance of some ten to twenty kilometers the ocean itself has been coated with an apparently living blanket of shiny, glassy green.

As for the cities themselves—not a sign of normal living things, not a sign of human beings. New York City is an unfamiliar jumble of geometric shapes, a city apparently dismantled and rearranged to suit the purposes of the plague—if a plague can have a purpose. Indeed, what we have seen supports the popular rumors that North America has been invaded by some form of intelligent biological life—that is, intelligent microorganisms, organisms that cooperate, mutate, adapt and alter their environment. New Jersey and Connecticut show similar biological formations, what the journalists of this flight have come to call megaplexes, for want of any better word. We leave further refinements in nomenclature to the scientists.

We are now descending. The city of Chicago is in the state of Illinois, situated at the southern tip of Lake Michigan, a huge inland body of fresh water. We are now about one hundred kilometers from Chicago, moving southwesterly over Lake Michigan. Let's move the camera to show what we, the correspondents and scientists and crew aboard this flight, are seeing directly. This special high-detail visual display screen is now showing the surface of Lake Michigan, absolutely smooth, very much like the surface of the ocean around the seaboard metropolitan areas. The grid is, I assume, for mapping purposes. Pardon my finger, but I may point out these peculiar features, seen before in the waters of the Hudson River, these peculiar and quite vivid yellow-green circles, or atolls, with the extremely complex radiating lines like the spokes of a wheel. No explanation for these formations is known, though satellite pictures have occasionally shown extensions of the spokes racing to the shore to connect with topographic changes taking place on the land.

Pardon me? Yes, I'll move. We have, uh, been informed that some of these displays are classified, for our eyes only, as it were.

Now we have changed course and are swooping in an arc over Waukegan, Illinois. Illinois is renowned for its flatness, as well as for its automobiles, Detroit being in . . . no, Detroit is in Michigan. Yes. Illinois is renowned for its flat topography, and Chicago has been called the Windy City, because of winds blowing in from Lake Michigan. As we can see, the topography is now a network of ground very much like farmland, though instead of grids and squares, the divisions are ovoid—elliptical, I mean—or circular, with smaller circles filling in between larger circles. In the center of each circle is a mound, a sort of point reminiscent of the central cone in lunar craters. These cones—yes, I see, they are actually cone-shaped pyramids, with concentric steps or tiers rising along the outside. The tips of these cones are orange, rather like the flight suit I am wearing. Day-glo orange, very striking.

• • •

We have slowed considerably. The swing-wings have been deployed, and we now pass at a comparatively leisured pace over Evanston, north of Chicago. Not a *sign* of humanity wherever we look. We are all . . . er . . . quite nervous now, I believe even the U.S. Air Force officers and crew, for if anything were to go wrong, we would be deposited directly in the middle of . . . Yes, well we won't think about *that*. Lower and slower.

We have decided to pass over Chicago because of satellite and high-altitude reconnaissance aircraft photographs showing a concentration of biological activity around this once-great city. As Chicago was once the capital of the American heartland, now apparently it is serving as some kind of focus, a clearing house perhaps, for activity all around the country, from Canada to Mexico. Great pipeline-like structures can be seen flowing into Chicago from all directions. In some areas the pipelines open up into broad canals and we can actually see the rapid flow of a viscous green fluid . . . Yes. There. Can we . . . ? Well, later in the broadcast. The canals must be a half kilometer wide. Amazing, awesome.

Rumors from major centers of military intelligence in Wiesbaden and in London and Scotland point to another and very different center of activity on the West Coast of the United States. Details are not available, but apparently Chicago shares with Southwestern California the distinction of being prime points of interest for investigators and researchers. We will not be flying to the West Coast, however; our aircraft does not have the range without refueling, and there are no refueling points that far across the continent.

We are now experiencing some acceleration as we make several sharp turns. Passing over the suburb of Oak Park, where according to a map spread before us, not a single street or roadway can be identified. And now over Chicago itself, if I may judge by proportion perhaps just over Cicero Avenue, now out to the lake again, yes, that's Montrose Harbor and Lake Shore Drive and Lincoln Park, identifiable only by outline against the lake. More acceleration, a wide circle, over the area of the Museum of Science and Industry perhaps—we are all guessing here. And now I can see waterways, perhaps the original branches of the Ship Canal, and now we are down to approximately a thousand meters, a very perilous altitude, for we have no idea how high these biologicals may extend. Lord, I am frightened. We all are. We are now passing over . . . yes . . .

Jesus. Pardon me. They must have been the stockyards, Union Stockyards. That's what they must have been. We have just barely seen them, but the pilot has started us into a steep climb and we are now swinging due south. What we have seen . . .

Pardon me.

I am wiping my eyes, out of terror, awe, for I have seen nothing like this in all the hours we have been wandering over the nightmare land. Telephoto cameras showed us extensive detail of what must at one time have been the famed stockyards of Chicago. When we consider the enormous mass of living creatures—pigs, cattle—concentrated in those regions, perhaps we should not be surprised or shocked. But the largest moving creatures I have seen have been whales, and these exceeded in size the largest whale by I know not precisely how much. Great brown and white eggs, could they have been hovering? Perhaps just on the ground. Greater than dinosaurs, yet with no discernible legs, head, tail. Not without features, however, extensions and elongations, tended or surrounded by polyhedrons, that is, icosahedrons or dodecahedrons—with insect-like legs, straight not jointed, legs that had to be two or three meters thick. The ovoid creatures or whatever they were could have easily spread across a rugby field.

Yes, yes—we have been told . . . we have just been informed there are airborne life forms, living things and that we have narrowly missed a couple of them, resembling gigantic manta rays stretched out, gliders or bats, also white and brown. Flowing in a stream southwest, as if forming a squadron or flock. Excuse me. Excuse me.

Cut the sound. Cut the sound, dammit. And turn that camera off me.

(Pause of five minutes.)
We're back, and apologies for the delay. I am human and . . . well, at times liable to a touch of panic. I hope this will be understood. And I myself stand in amazement before the calm and expertise of the . . . uh . . . the officers and crew of this aircraft, professionals

all, damned good men. We have just passed over Danville, Illinois and will shortly . . . a few seconds from now be over Indianapolis. We have seen changes in the character of the landscape, or if I may call it a bioscape, below us, changes in color and shape, but we are at a loss to interpret what we see. It is as if we have passed over an entirely new planet, and while our two scientists have been taking readings and scribbling notes furiously, they are much too busy to pass on whatever theories or hypotheses they may have.

Indianapolis is below us, and as indecipherable, as mysterious and . . . beautiful and alien as the other megaplexes. Some of the structures here appear to be as tall as the buildings they replaced, some perhaps a hundred to two hundred meters tall, casting shadows now in the afternoon light. Soon time will reverse for us, as it were, as we head east, southeast, and the sun will set. The shadows lengthen on the bioscape, the atmosphere is remarkably clear— no industry, no automobiles . . . yet who can say what sort of pollution a living landscape might cause? Whatever pollution there is is not passed on to the atmosphere.

Yes.

Yes, that is confirmed by our scientists. When we passed low over Chicago, the readings indicated virtually pure air, smoke-free, pollution-free, and that is reflected in the pure colors of the horizon. The air is also moist and, for this time of year, unseasonably warm. Winter may not come to North America this year, for by now Chicago and the cities we have passed over should be blanketed by at least light snowfalls. No snow. There is rain, warm and in large drops—we have passed over areas of dense overcast; but no snow, no ice.

Yes. Yes. I saw it too. What looked like a fireball, a meteor of some sort perhaps, remarkable—And several more, apparently—

(Voices in the background, quite loud, sound of alarms)

My God. That was apparently a re-entry vehicle or vehicles in the upper atmosphere, just dozens of kilometers away. Detectors aboard the aircraft are screaming warnings about radiation. The pilots and officers have activated all emergency systems and we are now in a steep climb away from the area, with . . . yes, with yes . . . no, we are in a dive, presenting I believe a posterior profile to whatever the object was—

There is talk here that the fireball was a matches the profile of a re-entry vehicle a nuclear missile an ICBM perhaps and that it did not repeat did not of course how would we be here? *did not go off* and now—

(More voices, sounding puzzled; more alarms)

I believe we cannot pull out of the dive now. We have lost most instrumentation. The engines have quit and we are in a powerless dive. We still have radio communications but—

(End transmission RB-1H. End direct feed Lloyd Upton EBN. End scientific telemetry.)

34

Bernard lay on the cot, one leg off the side and the other crooked with his foot propped against a fold in the mattress. He hadn't shaved in a week, nor bathed. His skin was heavily marked with white ridges and his lower legs had grown prominences from his upper shins to the base of his toes. Even naked he looked like he was wearing bell-bottom trousers.

He didn't care. Except for his hour-long session with Paulsen-Fuchs and his ten minute physical each day, he spent much of his time on the cot, eyes closed, communing with the noocytes. The rest of the time he spent trying to crack the chemical language. He had received little help from the noocytes. The last conversation on the subject had been three days before.

/Your conception is not complete, not correct.

—It isn't finished yet.

Why not let your comrades proceed with the work? There is more that can be accomplished if you devote your attention inward.

—It would be simpler if you just told us how you communicated . . .

WISH we could be more *pure* with each other, but command clusters believe discretion is best now.

—Yes, indeed./

The noocytes, then, kept things from him—and from the researchers outside the chamber. Pharmek, in turn, kept things from Bernard now. Bernard could only guess their reasoning; he hadn't challenged them on Paulsen-Fuchs' slow reduction of news and research findings. In some ways, it hardly mattered; Bernard had more than he could do adjusting to the noocyte interactions.

The terminal was still on, still displaying data supplied to the computer three days ago. Red lines had completely replaced the scrolling green numbers now. Infrequently, they were joined by blue lines. The curve determined by their lengths smoothed out as, byte by byte, the chemistry was broken down into an intermediary mathematical language, which in the next phase would be translated into a kind of pidgin of formal logic notation and

English. But that next phase was weeks or months away.

Focusing his attention on the memory prompted an uncharacteristic noocyte interruption.

Bernard. You still work on our *blood music*.

Hadn't Ulam used that phrase once?

Is it that you WISH to join us on our level? We did not consider this possibility.

—I'm not sure what you're suggesting.

The part of you which stands behind all issued communication may be encoded, activated, returned. It will be like a DREAM, if we understand fully what that is. (ANNOTATION: You dream all the time. Did you know that?)

—I can become one of you?

We think that is a correct assessment. You already are one of us. We have encoded parts of you into many teams for processing. We can encode your PERSONALITY and complete the loop. You will be one of us—temporarily, should you choose. We can do it now.

—I'm afraid. I'm afraid you'll steal my soul from inside . . .

Your SOUL is already encoded, Bernard. We will not initiate unless we receive permission from all your mental fragments.

"Michael?" Paulsen-Fuchs' voice pulled him out of the conversation. Bernard shook his head and blinked at the viewing chamber window. "Michael? Are you awake?"

"I've been . . . awake. What is it?"

"A few days ago you gave us permission to have Sean Gogarty visit you. He is here now."

"Yes, yes." Michael stood. "In there with you? My eyes are blurry."

"No. Outside. I suspect you will wish to get dressed, clean up first."

"Why?" Bernard countered testily. "I'm not going to be a pretty sight no matter how often I shave."

"You wish to meet him as you are?"

"Yeah. Bring him in. You interrupted something interesting, Paul."

"We are all becoming just interruptions to you now, aren't we?"

Bernard tried to smile. His face felt stiff, unfamiliar. "Bring him in, Paul."

Sean Gogarty, professor of theoretical physics at Kings College, University of London, stepped up into the viewing chamber and shielded his eyes with one hand as he peered into the containment lab. His face was open, friendly, nose long and sharp, teeth prominent. He was tall and carried himself well, and his arms looked well-muscled under his Irish wool jacket. His smile faded and his eyes narrowed behind stylish aviator glasses as he saw Bernard. "Dr. Bernard," he said, his voice pleasantly Irish with a touch of Oxford.

"Dr. Gogarty."

"Professor, that is, just Sean, please. I like to eschew titles."

"Then I am Michael." *Am I?*

"Yes, well in your case . . . er . . . it'll be a bit harder to stick to that. I know of you, and I'm sure you've never heard of me, er, Michael." Again the smile, but without certainty, troubled. As if, Bernard thought, he expected a human being and met—

"Paul has briefed me on some of your work. You're a bit beyond me, Sean."

"Indeed. This thing, this incident in your country is as much beyond me, I'm certain. I have a few things I would like to talk out with you, Michael, and not just you."

Paulsen-Fuchs looked at Gogarty with some apprehension. No doubt this meeting was sanctioned by several governments, Bernard thought, or it never would have happened, but Paul was still on edge.

"My colleagues, then," Bernard gestured at Paulsen-Fuchs.

"Not your human colleagues, no," Gogarty said.

"My noocytes."

"Noocytes? Yes, yes, I understand. Your noocytes. Tielhard de Chardin would have approved of that name, I think."

"I haven't been thinking much about Tielhard de Chardin lately," Bernard said, "but he might not be a bad guide."

"Yes, well, I'm here just barely, by the scruff of the neck," Gogarty said, "and my time has been limited. I have a notion to propose to you, and I would like you and your small colleagues to pass judgment on it."

"How did you get detailed information about me, about the noocytes?" Bernard asked.

"Experts all over Europe are being approached. Someone came to me on a hunch. I hope it doesn't affect his promotion. I'm not highly respected by all my fellows, Dr. Bernard—Michael. My ideas are more than a touch far-out."

"Let's hear them," Bernard said, growing impatient.

"Yes. I assume you haven't heard much about Information Mechanics?"

"Not a whisper," Bernard said.

"I'm working in a very specialized area of that branch of physics—an area not yet recognized—the effects of information processing on space-time. I'll put it simply enough, because the noocytes may already know more than I and be better able to explain it to you—"

"Don't count on it. They relish complexity, and I don't."

Gogarty paused and sat absolutely still for several seconds. Paulsen-Fuchs glanced at him with fleeting anxiety.

"Michael, I have amassed a great deal of theoretical structure which supports the following assertion." Deep breath. "Information processing—more strictly, observation—has an effect on events occurring within space-time. Conscious beings play an integral role in the universe; we fix its boundaries, to a great extent determine its nature, just as it determines our nature. I have reason to believe—just an hypothesis so far—that we don't so much discover physical laws as collaborate on them. Our theories are tested against past observations both by ourselves—and by the universe. If the universe agrees that past events are not contradicted by a theory, the theory becomes a template. The universe goes along with it. The better the theory fits the facts, the longer it lasts—if it lasts at all. We then break the universe down into territories—our particular territory, as human beings, being thus far quite distinct. No extraterrestrial contact, you know. If there are other intelligent beings beyond the Earth, they would occupy yet other territories of theory. We wouldn't expect major differences between the theories of different territories—the universe does, after all, play a major role—but minor differences might be expected.

"The theories can't be effective forever. The universe is always changing; we can imagine regions of reality evolving until new theories are necessary. Thus far, the human race hasn't generated nearly the density or amount of information processing—computing, thinking, what have you—to manifest any truly obvious effects on space-time. We haven't created theories so complete that they pin down reality's evolution. But that has all changed, and quite recently."

Listen closely to the GOGARTY.

Bernard perked up and began to pay more attention.

"If I only had time to present my mathematics, my correlations with formal information mechanics and quantum electrodynamics . . . and if only you could understand!"

"I'm listening. We're listening, Sean."

Gogarty's eyes widened. "The...noocytes? Have they responded?"

"You haven't given them much to respond to. Do go on, Professor."

"Until now, the densest single unit of information processing on this planet was the human brain...slight nod to cetaceans, perhaps, but not nearly as much stimulus and processing going on, much more insular I'd say. Four, five billion of us, thinking every day. Small effects. Time stresses, little tremors as it were, not even measurable. Our powers of observation—our power to formulate effective theories—is not sufficiently intense to bring about the effects I've discovered in my work. Nothing in the solar system, perhaps not even the galaxy!"

"You are rambling, Professor Gogarty," Paulsen-Fuchs said. Gogarty gave him an irritated nod and fastened his eyes on Bernard's, pleading with him.

He speaks of interest.

"He's getting to the point, Paul, don't rush him."

"Thank you. Thank you very much, Michael. What I am saying is that we now have conditions sufficient to cause the effects I've described in my papers. Not just four, five billion individual cogitators, Michael, but trillions...perhaps billions of trillions. Most in North America. Tiny, very dense, focusing their attention on all aspects of their surroundings, from the very very small to the very large. *Observing* everything in their environment, and theorizing about the things they do not observe. Observers and theorizers can fix the shape of events, of reality, in quite significant ways. There is nothing, Michael, but information. All particles, all energy, even space and time itself, are ultimately nothing but information. The very nature, the *timbre* of the universe can be altered, Michael, right now. By the noocytes."

"Yes," Bernard said. "Still listening."

Something not stated...evidence...

"Two days ago," Gogarty said, becoming more animated, his face reddening with excitement, "the USSR apparently launched a full-scale nuclear strike on North America. Unlike the Panama strike, not one of the warheads went off."

Bernard looked at Paulsen-Fuchs first with pique, then amusement. He hadn't been told a thing about this.

"The USSR is not that bad at building warheads, Michael. There should have been holocaust. There wasn't. Now I have compiled several striking graphs from observations and information. One very important source was an American reconnaissance aircraft carrying scientists and reporters over North America, with a live broadcast going to Europe by satellite. The aircraft was in the middle of the United States when the strike was attempted. The plane apparently went down, but not because of the strike itself. Nobody is sure why it crashed, but the way its telemetry and communications were cut off . . . The timing, the queueing, fits my theory precisely. Not only that, but in places around the globe, very peculiar effects were felt. Radio silences, power cut-offs, meteorological phenomena. All the way out to geosynchronous orbit—two satellites separated by twelve thousand kilometers malfunctioned. I put the effects and coordinates of the incidents into our computer and it produced this profile of the four-space field." He lifted a blown-up photo of a computer image from his satchel.

Bernard squinted to see it more clearly. His vision suddenly sharpened. He could make out the grain of the photo paper. "Like a weightlifter's nightmare," he said.

"Yes, a bit twisty around the torus," Gogarty agreed. "This is the only figure that makes sense in light of the information. And no one can make sense of this figure—but me. I'm afraid it's made my stock jump a bit in the scientific marketplace. If I'm correct, and I believe I am, we are in for a lot more trouble than we think, Michael . . . or a lot less, depending on what sort of trouble you're anticipating."

Bernard could feel the diagram being intensely absorbed. The noocytes left off their constant tinkering with his mentality for seconds.

"You're giving my small colleagues a lot to think about, Sean."

"Yes, and their reactions?"

Bernard closed his eyes.

After several seconds had passed, Bernard opened his eyes again and shook his head. "Not a word," he said. "Sorry, Sean "

"Well, I'd not expected much "

Paulsen Fuchs looked at his watch. "Is that all, Dr. Gogarty?"

"No. Not quite. Michael, the plague cannot spread beyond North America. Or rather, beyond a circle of seven thousand kilometers diameter, if the noocytes are averaged out over that area of the globe."

"Why not?"

"Because of what I've been saying. There are too many of them already. If they were to expand beyond that radius, they would create something very peculiar—a portion of spacetime much too closely observed. The territory would not be able to evolve. Too many brilliant theorists, don't you see! There would be a kind of frozen state, a breakdown on the quantum level. A singularity. A black hole of thought. Time would be severely distorted and the effects would destroy the Earth. I suspect they have limited their growth, realizing this." Gogarty wiped his brow with a kerchief and sighed again.

"How did they prevent the warheads from detonating?" Bernard asked.

"I'd say they've learned how to create isolated pockets of observation, very powerful. They *delude* trillions of observers into establishing a small, temporary pocket of altered spacetime. A pocket where physical processes are sufficiently different to prevent warheads from detonating. The pocket doesn't last long, of course—the universe violently disagrees with it—but it lasts just long enough to prevent holocaust.

"There's one crucial question," he continued. "Are your noocytes in communication with North America?"

Bernard listened internally, and received no response. "I don't know," he said.

"They *can* be in communication, you know, without using radio or any such familiar means. If they can control the effects they have on the local manifold, they could create waves of subtly disrupted time. I'm afraid we don't have instruments sensitive enough to detect such signals."

Paulsen-Fuchs stood and tapped his watch meaningfully.

"Paul," Bernard said, "is that why my news has been cut back? Why I didn't hear about the Russian attack?"

Paulsen-Fucks didn't answer. "Is there anything you can do for Mr. Gogarty?" he asked.

"Not immediately. I—"

"Then we will leave you to your contemplation."

"Wait a second, Paul. What in hell is going on? Mr. Gogarty would obviously like to spend much more time with me, and I with him. Why all the limitations?"

Gogarty glanced between them, acutely embarrassed.

"Security, Michael," Paulsen-Fuchs said. "Little pitchers, you know."

Bernard's reaction was a sudden, short wry bark of a laugh. "Pleasant meeting with you, Professor Gogarty," he said.

"And you," Gogarty said. The viewing chamber sound was cut off and the two men departed. Bernard walked behind the lavatory curtain and urinated. The urine was reddish-purple.

You are not in charge of them? They command you?

—If you haven't figured it out by now, I'm quite mortal. What's with my piss? It's purple.

Phenyls and ketones being discharged. We must SPEND MORE TIME studying your hierarchic status.

"I'm low monkey," he said aloud. "Very low monkey now."

35

The fire crackled lustily and cast broad, dim tree-shadows across the historic old buildings of Fort Tejon. April Ulam stood facing away from the pit with arms wrapped around herself, her tattered gown rippling slightly in the chill evening breeze. Jerry poked the fire with a stick and looked at his twin. "So what did we see?"

"Hell," John said firmly.

"We saw Los Angeles, gentlemen," April said out of the gloom.

"I didn't recognize *anything,*" John said. "Not even like Livermore, or the farm fields. I mean—"

"There wasn't anything *real* there," Jerry finished for him. "Just all . . . spinning."

April advanced and pulled her gown away from her legs to sit on a log. "I think we should tell each other what we saw, as close as we can describe it. I'll begin, if you wish."

Jerry shrugged. John continued to stare into the fire.

"I think I recognized the outlines of the San Fernando valley. It's been ten years since I last visited Los Angeles, but I remember coming over the hills, and there's Burbank, and Glendale . . . I just don't remember what they looked like, back then. Hazy air. It was hot, not like now."

"The haze is still there," Jerry said. "But it doesn't look the same."

"Purple haze," John said, shaking his head and chuckling.

"Now if you agree that we saw the valley—"

"Yeah," Jerry said. "Maybe that."

"Then there was something *in* the valley, all spread out."

"But not solid. Not made of solid stuff," John said slowly.

"Agreed," April said. "Energy, then?"

"Looked like a Jackson Pollack painting all spun around," Jerry said.

"Or a Picasso," John said.

"Gentlemen, I'd agree, and amend a little—it looked a great deal like a Max Ernst to me."

"Don't know about him," Jerry said. "Something spinning in the middle. A tornado."

April nodded. "Yes. But what kind of tornado?"

John squinted and rubbed his eyes. "Spread out at the bottom, all kinds of spikes going out—like lightning, but not glowing. Like shadows of lightning."

"Touching," John said. "Then disappearing."

"A tornado dancing, perhaps," April suggested.

"Yeah," the twins said.

"I saw trains and disks weaving in and out, under the tornado," she continued. "Did you?"

They shook their heads in unison.

"And on the hills, lights moving, as if fireflies were crawling up to the skies." She had her exalted look again, staring dreamily over the fire. John wrapped his hands around his head and continued shaking it.

"Not real," he said.

"No, indeed. Not really at all. But it must have some connection with what my son did."

"Shit," John said.

"No," Jerry said. "I believe you."

"If it started in La Jolla, and spread all over the country, then where is it oldest and most established?"

"La Jolla," Jerry said, looking at her expectantly. "Maybe it got started at UCSD!"

April shook her head. "No, in La Jolla, where Vergil worked and lived. But all up and down the coast, it spread fast. So maybe all the way down to San Diego, it has united, come together, and made this place its center."

"Fuck it," John said.

April said, "We can't get to La Jolla, not with this in the way. And I've come here to be with my son."

"You're crazier than shit," John said.

"I don't know why you gentlemen were spared," April said, "but it's obvious why I've been."

"Because you're his mother," Jerry said, laughing and nodding as if at a great deduction.

"Exactly," April said. "So gentlemen, tomorrow we will drive back up and over the hill, and if you wish, you can join me, but I will go by myself if need be, and join my son."

Jerry sobered. "April, that *is* crazy. What if that's just something really dangerous, like a big electric storm or a nuclear power plant gone haywire?"

"There ain't any big nuclear power plants in LA," John said.

"But Jerry's right. It's just fucking crazy to talk about walking into that hell."

"If my son is there, it will not hurt me," April said.

Jerry poked the fire vigorously. "I'll take you there," he said. "But I won't go in with you."

John looked hard and seriously at his brother. "You're both bugfuck."

"Or I can walk," April said, determined.

Jerry stood with his hands on his hips, staring resentfully at his brother and April Ulam as they walked toward the truck. Sweet purple-pink fog spilled out of the LA basin and drifted at tree-top level over Fort Tejon, filtering the morning light and leaving everything without shadow, ghostly.

"Hey!" John said. "Goddammit, hey! Don't just leave me here!" He ran after them.

The truck crested the hills on the deserted highway and they looked down into the maelstrom. It looked very little different in daylight.

"It's like everything you've always dreamed, all rolled up at once," Jerry said, driving intently.

"Not a bad description," April said. "A tornado of dreams. Perhaps the dreams of everyone who's been taken by the change."

John clutched the dash with both hands and stared wide-eyed down the highway. "There's about a mile of road left," he said. "Then we got to stop."

Jerry agreed with a curt nod. The truck slowed.

At less than ten miles an hour, they approached a curtain of dancing vertical streams of fog. The curtain stretched for several dozen feet above the road and to each side, rippling around vague orange shapes that might have once been buildings.

"Jesus, Jesus," John said.

"Stop," April said. Jerry brought the truck to a halt. April looked at John sternly until he opened the cab door and stepped out to let her exit. Jerry put the shift lever into neutral and set the brake, then got out on the other side.

"You gentlemen are missing loved ones, aren't you?" April asked, smoothing her tattered gown. The maelstrom roared like a distant hurricane—roared, and hissed, and bellowed down a rain gutter.

John and Jerry nodded.

"If my Vergil's in here, and I know that he is, then they must be, too. Or we can get to them from here."

"That's crazier than shit," John said. "My wife and my boy can't be in there."

"Why not? Are they dead?"

John stared at her.

"You know they aren't. I know my son is not dead."

"You're a witch," Jerry said, less accusing than admiring.

"Some have said so. Vergil's father said so before he left me. But you *know*, don't you?"

John trembled. Tears rolled down his cheeks. Jerry stared at the curtain with a vague grin.

"Are they in there, John?" he asked his brother.

"I don't know," John said, sniffing and wiping his face with one arm.

April walked toward the curtain. "Thank you for your help, gentlemen," she said. As she entered, she became scrambled like a bad television picture, and then vanished.

"Look at that!" John said, trembling.

"She's right," Jerry said. "Don't you feel it?"

"I don't *know!*" John wailed. "Christ, brother, I don't know."

"Let's go find them," Jerry said, taking his brother's hand. He pulled gently. John resisted.

Jerry pulled again.

"All right," John said quietly. "Together."

Side by side, they walked down the few yards of highway and into the curtain.

36

Her leg cramped on the eighty-second level. With a twist and a cry, she fell on the stairs and knocked her head against the railing. One knee caught a stair edge just below the patella. The flashlight and radio flew from her hands onto the concrete landing. The bottle of water wedged between two stairs and burst open, soaking her and dribbling away as she watched, paralyzed with pain. It seemed hours—but was probably only minutes—before she could even pull herself up to the landing. She lay on her back, eyes sandy from needing to weep and having no tears.

A knot on her forehead, one leg that just wouldn't move right, little food and no water; scared, hurting, and with thirty more stories to go. The flashlight beam flickered and went out, leaving her in complete darkness. "Shit," she said. Her mother had deplored that word even more than taking the name of God in vain. Since they were not a particularly religious family, that was a minor infraction, odious only when used in front of those it would offend. But saying "shit" was the ultimate, an acknowledgment of bad manners, bad upbringing, or simply surrendering to the lowest emotions.

Suzy tried to stand and fell down again, her knee ripe with new agony. "Shit, shit, SHIT!" she screamed. "Get better, oh please get better." She tried to rub the knee but that only made it hurt worse.

She felt for the flashlight and found it. With a shake, it lit up again and she directed the beam around to reassure herself the brown and white sheets and filaments hadn't overtaken her. She looked at the door to the eighty-second floor and knew she wouldn't be able to climb stairs for some time, perhaps the rest of the day. She crawled to the door and glanced over her shoulder at the radio as she reached for the knob. The radio lay on the landing; it had come down hard when she fell. For a moment, she thought she might as well abandon it, but the radio meant something special to her. It was the only human thing she had left, the only thing that talked to her. She might be able to find another in the building, but she couldn't chance silence. Trying to keep her injured knee straight, she crawled back for it.

Getting past the heavy fire door resulted in more misery and more bruises when it slammed on her arm, but she finally lay back on the carpet of the elevator lobby, staring up at the acoustic ceiling overhead. She rolled onto her stomach, alert for anything moving.

Stillness, quiet.

Slowly, trying to conserve her strength, she crawled out of the lobby and around a corner.

Beyond a glass partition, the entire floor was covered with drafting tables, white enamel legs on beige carpet, black lamps arranged like so many birds with adjustable necks. The glass door had already been propped open with a rubber wedge. Hobbling past the desk and couches, she leaned on the nearest table, eyes bright with exhaustion and pain. There were blueprints on the drafting table beside her. She was in an architect's office. She looked at one drawing more closely. It laid out deck plans for a ship. So this was an office for people who designed ships. "What the hell do I care?" she asked herself.

She sat on a tall stool with locked casters. With one foot she labored for half a minute to unlock the casters, then rolled herself down an aisle between tables, using the table edges to push herself along.

Another long glass wall separated the drafting area from office cubicles. She stopped and stared. All the fear had gone now. She had run out of it. There might be more fear available the next morning, she thought, but for now she didn't miss it. She simply observed.

The cubicles were filled with things moving. They were so strange that for a time she hardly knew how to describe them to herself. Disks with snail feet crawled along the glass, their edges actually lighting up. Something fluid and shapeless, like a blob of wax or a lavalight, bobbed around in another cubicle, straining on black ropes or cables that stretched and sparkled; the blob fluoresced green wherever it struck glass or furniture. In the last cubicle, a forest of scaled sticks, like chicken legs, bent and swayed in an impossible breeze.

"It's crazy," she said. "It doesn't mean a thing. Nothing's happening because it doesn't make sense."

She rolled away from the cubicles, up against the far windows. The rest of the floor seemed clear—no crumpled clothing. Seen from across the floor, the cubicles resembled aquariums filled with exotic sea creatures.

Maybe she was safe. Usually whatever was in an aquarium didn't come out. She tried to convince herself she was safe, but it really didn't matter. For the moment, there wasn't anywhere else she could go.

Her knee was swelling, straining her jeans. She thought about cutting the jeans open, and then decided it was best simply to slide out of them. With a grunt, she let herself down from the stool and leaned back against a filing cabinet. Lifting her hips, balancing on one leg, she humped and bunched the jeans carefully past the swelling.

It wasn't very ugly yet, just puffy and purpling under the kneecap. She poked it and felt faint, not from pain, but simply because she was drained. There was nothing left of Suzy McKenzie now. The old world had gone first, until nothing remained but buildings, which without people were like skeletons without flesh. New flesh was moving in to cover the skeletons. Soon the old Suzy McKenzie would be gone, too, leaving nothing but a quizzical shadow.

She turned her face north, around the edge of the cabinet and over a low credenza.

There was the new Manhattan, a tent city with skyscrapers for poles; a city made of toy blocks with the blocks rearranged under blankets. Glowing warm mellow brown and yellow in the sunset. Newer York, filled with empty clothes.

Old Suzy dropped back on the carpet, cradled her head in her arms and pushed her hauntingly empty jeans under her knee to elevate it. "When I awake," she told herself, "I will be a Wonder Woman, shiny and bright. And I will know what's happening."

Down deep, however, she understood she would wake up normal enough, and the world would be the same.

"Not a good deal," she murmured.

In the dark, filaments grew silently over the carpet, reaching into the glass cubicles, subduing the buoyant creativity within.

37

—I belong to nobody. I am not what I once was. I have no past. I am cut loose and there is really nowhere to go but where they wish to take me.

—I am separated from the outside world physically, and now mentally.

—My work is done here.

—I am waiting.

—I am waiting.

Truly, you WISH to journey among us, be among us?

—I do.

He stares at the red and green and blue on the VDT. The figures lose all meaning for the moment, as if he is a newborn child. Then the screen, the table it rests on, the lavatory curtain beyond and the walls of the containment chamber are replaced by a silvery null.

Michael Bernard is crossing an interface.

He is encoded.

No longer conscious of all the sensations of being in a body. No more automatic listenings and responses to the slide of muscles past one another, the bubbling of fluids in the abdomen, the push and roar of blood and pounding of the heart. He no longer balances, tenses or relaxes. It is like suddenly moving from the city into the heart of a quiet cave.

At first, thought itself is grainy, discontinuous. If such a thing can be, he visualizes himself at the very basement of the universe, where all the atoms and molecules combine and separate, making silent noises at each other like scuttling shellfish on the bottom of the sea. He is suspended in silent, jerking activity, unable to critique his situation or even to be sure what he is. Part of his faculties are temporarily cut off. Then—jerk! He can critique, evaluate. Thought moves like a dissociation of leaves across a lawn in a breeze. Jerk! Now, like a sluggish flow of gelatin circling and setting up in a cold bowl.

Bernard's journey has not even begun yet. He is still caught in the interface, not big, not small. There is part of him still relying on his universe-sized brain, still pushing thought along cells instead of within cells.

The suspension becomes a drawn-out unconsciousness, thought pulled like a thread to fit a tiny needle's

eye————————————————————————————
————————————————————————
————————————————————
————————————————
————————————
————————
————
——
—

The small bursts upon him and his world is suddenly filled with action and simplicity. There is no light, but there is sound. It fills him in great sluggish waves, not heard but felt through his hundred cells. The cells pulse, separate, contract according to the rush of fluid. He is in his own blood. He can taste the presence of the cells making up his new being, and of cells not directly part of him. He can feel the rasping of microtubules propelling his cytoplasm. What is most remarkable, he can feel—indeed, it is the ground of all sensation—the cytoplasm itself.

This is now the basis of his being, the flow of electric sensation of pure life. He is aware of the knife-edge chemical balance between animation and dead jelly, with its roots in *order,* hierarchy, interaction. Cooperation. He is individual and, at the same time, he is each of the fellows of his team, the other hundred-cell clusters downstream and upstream. The downstream companions are as distant, as chemically isolated as if they were at the bottom of a deep well; the upstream companions are intense, rich.

He can no more puzzle the mechanisms of his thought than he could in his universe-sized brain. Thought rises above the chemistry, the interchanges within his cluster and the processes within his cells. Thought is the combination, the language of all interaction.

Sensation along the membranes of his cells is intense. It is here that he receives, feels the aura and pressure of huge molecular messages from outside. He takes in a plasmid-like data lump, *ases it, and pours information from it, absorbing it into his being, duplicating those parts which will be needed by others among his

companions. Now the lumps come rapidly, and as he breaks and
pours each one, each string of molecules a library, he finds bits
and pieces of Michael Bernard returning to him.

The huge Bernard is encompassed within a tiny hundred-cell
cluster. He can feel there is actually a human being on the level
of the noocytes—himself.

Welcome.

—Thank you.

He senses a fellow team member as a diversity of tastes, all
possible varieties of sweetness and richness. The camaraderie is
overwhelming. He loves his team (how can he love anything
else?). He is an integral part, in turn loved and necessary.

Abruptly, he tastes the wall of a capillary. He is part of the
research team, passing on information by manufacturing nucleic
acid packets.. Absorbing, re-making, passing on, absorbing...

Extrude. Push through.

That is his instruction. He will leave the capillary, enter the
tissue.

Leave a portion stuck out into the data flow.

He pushes between the capillary cells—support cells, not themselves noocytes—and lodges in the wall. Now he waits for data
in the form of structured proteins, hormones and pheromones,
nucleic acid strings, data perhaps even in the form of *tailored*
cells, viruses or domesticized bacteria. He needs not only basic
nutrients, easily available from the blood serum, but supplies of
the enzymes which allow him to absorb and process data, to think.
These enzymes are supplied by *tailored* bacteria which both
manufacture and deliver.

The blood is a highway, a symphony of information, instruction. It is a delight to process and modify the rich broth. The
information has its own variety of tastes, and is like a living thing,
liable to change in the blood unless it is carefully monitored,
trimmed of accretions, buffed. Words cannot convey what he is
doing. His whole being is alive with the chatter of interpreting
and processing.

He feels the dizzying spiral of recursion, thinking about his
own tiny thought processes—molecules thinking about molecules,
keeping records of themselves—applying words that until now
have had no place in this realm. Like bringing God's word for a
tree down to the tree and speaking it, watching the tree blossom
in blushing confusion.

**You are the power, the gentle power, the richest taste of all
... the ultimate upstream message.**

His fellows approach him, cluster around his appendage in the blood, crowd him. He is like an initiate suddenly inspired with the breath of God in a monastery. The monks gather, starved for a touch, a sign of redemption and purpose. It is intoxicating. He loves them because they are his team; they are more than loving to him, because he is the Source.

The command clusters know that he is, himself, part of a greater hierarchy, but this information has not made it down to the level he now occupies. The common clusters are still in awe.

You are the flow of all life. You hold the key of *opening* and *blocking*, of pulse and silence.

—Farther, he said. Take me farther and show me your lives.

38

"Suzy. Wake up."

Suzy's eyes fluttered open. Kenneth and Howard stood over her. She blinked and looked around at the blue plaster walls of her bedroom, the sheets pulled up to her neck. "Kenny?"

"Mom's waiting."

"Howard?"

"Come on, Seedling." That's what Kenneth had always called her. She pushed the blankets down, then pulled them back up; she still had on her blouse and panties, not her pajamas.

"I have to get dressed," she said.

Howard handed her the jeans. "Hurry up." They left the bedroom and shut the door behind them. She swung her legs over the edge of the bed and stuck them into the pants legs, then stood and tugged them higher, zipping and buttoning. Her knee didn't hurt. The swelling had gone down and everything seemed fine. Her mouth tasted funny. She looked around for the flashlight and radio. They were on the floor by the bed. Picking them up, she opened the door and stepped into the hall. "Kenny?"

Howard took her arm and gently nudged her toward their mother's bedroom. The door was closed. Kenneth turned the knob and opened it and they stepped into the elevator. Howard pushed the button for the restaurant and lounge.

"I knew it," she said, shoulders slumping. "I'm dreaming." Her brothers looked at her and smiled, shaking their heads.

"No, you're not," Kenneth said. "We're back."

The elevator smoothly lifted them the remaining twenty-five floors.

"Bull," she said, feeling the tears on her cheeks. "It's cruel."

"Okay, the part about the bedroom, the house—that's a dream. Some stuff down there you probably don't want to see. But we're here. We're with you again."

"You're dead," she said. "Mom, too."

"We're different," Howard said. "Not dead."

"Yeah, what are you, then, zombies? Goddammit."

"They never killed us," Kenneth said. "They just . . . dismantled us. Like everybody."

"Well, almost everybody." Howard pointed at her and they grinned.

"You lucked out, or missed out," Kenneth said.

She was scared now. The elevator door opened and they stepped out into a fancy mirrored hall. Lights reflected into infinity on either side. *The lights were on. The elevator worked.* She had to be dreaming, or she was finally and totally crazy.

"Some died, too," Kenneth said solemnly, taking her hand. "Accidents, mistakes."

"That's only part of what we know, now," Howard said. They walked between the mirrors, past a huge geode cut open to show amethyst crystals, past a monumental lump of rose quartz and a sliced nodule of malachite. Nobody met them at the maitre d's station. "Mom's in the restaurant," he said. "If you're hungry, there's plenty of food up here, that's for sure."

"The power's on," she said.

"Emergency generator in the basement. It ran for a while after the city's power stopped, but no more fuel, you know? So we found more fuel. They told us how to work it, and we turned it on before fetching you," Howard said.

"Yeah. It's hard for them to reconstruct lots of people, so they only did Mom and us. Not the building maintenance supervisor or the others. We did all the work. You've been asleep for a while, you know."

"Two weeks."

"That's why your knee's better."

"That, and—"

"Shh," Kenneth said, holding up his hand to caution his brother. "Not all at once." Suzy looked between them as they guided her into the restaurant.

It was late afternoon. The city, clearly visible from the restaurant's broad picture windows, was no longer wrapped up in the brown and white sheets.

She couldn't recognize any landmarks. Before, she could pick out at least the hidden shapes of buildings, the valleys of streets and the outlines of neighborhoods.

Not the same place.

Gray, black, dazzling marble white, arranged in pyramids and many-sided polyhedrons, some as translucent as frosted glass. Slabs hundreds of feet high marched off like dominoes along what had once been West Street from Battery Park all the way to Riverside Park. All the shapes and masses of the buildings of Manhattan had been dropped into a bag, shaken, rearranged, and repainted.

But the structures weren't concrete and steel any more. She didn't know what they were.

Alive.

Her mother sat behind a broad table heaped high with food. Salads lay in bowls along the front, a thick ham partially sliced rose from the middle, trays of olives and sliced pickles taking up the sides, cakes and desserts the rear. Her mother smiled and slid out from her seat behind the table, holding out her arms. She was dressed in an expensive Rabarda gown, long sleeves draped with beaded detailing and fringe, and she looked absolutely terrific. "Suzy," her mother said. "Don't look so upset. We're back to visit."

She hugged her mother, feeling solid flesh, and gave up on the thought it was a dream. It was real. Her brothers hadn't picked her up at the house—that couldn't have been real, could it?—but they *had* taken her up the elevator and here she was with her mother, warm and full of love, waiting to feed her daughter.

And over her mother's shoulder, out the window, the changed city. She couldn't imagine that, could she?

"What's going on, Mother?" she asked, wiping her eyes and standing back, glancing at Kenneth and Howard.

"The last time I saw you, we were in the kitchen," her mother said, giving her the once-over. "I wasn't very talkative then. Lots of things were happening."

"You were sick," Suzy said.

"Yes . . . and no. Come sit. You must be very hungry."

"If I've been asleep two weeks, I should have starved to death," she said.

"She still doesn't believe," Howard said, grinning.

"Shh!" her mother said, waving him off. "You wouldn't believe, would you, either of you?"

They admitted they probably wouldn't.

"I *am* hungry, though," Suzy admitted. Kenneth pulled out a chair and she sat before an immaculate table setting of fine china and silver.

"We probably made it too fancy," Howard said. "Too much like a dream."

"Yeah," Suzy said. She felt punch-drunk, happy, and she didn't care what was real any more. "You clowns overdid it."

Her mother heaped her plate with ham and salads and Suzy pointed to the mashed potatoes and gravy.

"Fattening," Kenneth said.

"Tsk," Suzy replied. She lifted the first forkful of ham and chewed on it. Real. Bite of tooth on fork, real. "You know what happened?"

"Not everything," her mother said, sitting beside her.

"We can be a lot smarter now, if we want to be," Howard said. For a moment Suzy felt hurt; did he mean her? Howard had always been ashamed of his grades, a hard worker but not in the least brilliant. Still, he was smarter than his slow sister.

"We don't even need our bodies," Kenneth said.

"Slower, slower," her mother admonished them. "It's very complicated, darling."

"We're dinosaurs now," Howard said, picking at the ham from where he stood. He made a face and let go of the slice he had lifted.

"When we were sick . . ." her mother began.

Suzy put down her fork and chewed thoughtfully, listening not to her mother, but to something else.

Healed you
Cherish you
Need

"Oh, my God," she said quietly around her mouthful of ham. She swallowed and looked around at them. She lifted her hand. White lines lay across the back, extending beyond her wrist to form faint networks beneath the skin of her arm.

"Don't be afraid, Suzy," her mother said. "Please don't be afraid. They left you alone because they couldn't enter your body without killing you. You have an unusual chemistry, darling. So do a few others. That's not a problem anymore. But it's your choice, honey. Just listen to us . . . and to them. They're a lot more sophisticated now, honey, much smarter than when they entered us."

"I'm sick now, too, aren't I?" she asked.

"There are so many of them," Howard said, sweeping his arms out across the view, "that you could count every grain of sand on the Earth, and every star in the sky, and still not reach their number."

"Now listen," Kenneth said, bending close to his sister. "You always listen to me, don't you, Seedling?"

She nodded like a child, slow and deliberate.

"They don't want to hurt, or kill. They need us. We're a small part of them, but they need us."

"Yes?" she said, her voice small.

"They love us," her mother said. "They say they come from us, and they love us like . . . like you love your cradle, the one in the basement."

"Like we love Mom," Kenneth said. Howard agreed earnestly.

"And now they give you the choice."

"What choice?" Suzy said. "They're inside me."

"The choice whether to continue like you are, or to join us."

"But you're like me again, now."

Kenneth knelt beside her. "We'd like to show you what it's like, what they're like."

"You're brainwashed," she said. "I want to be alive."

"We're even more alive, with them," her mother said. "Honey, we're not brainwashed, we're convinced. We went through some very bad stuff at first, but that's not necessary now. They don't destroy anything. They can keep everything inside them, in memory, but it's better than memory—"

"Because you can *think* yourself into it, and be there, just like it was—"

"Or will be," Howard added.

"I still don't know what you mean. They want me to give up my body? They're going to change me, like they did you, like the city?"

"When you're with them, you won't need your body any more," her mother said. Suzy looked at her in horror. "Suzy, honey, we've been there. We know."

"You're like a bunch of Moonies," she said softly. "You always warned me Moonies and people like that would take advantage of me. Now it's you trying to brainwash *me*. You feed me and make me feel good and I don't even know you're my mother and brothers."

"You can stay the way you are, if that's what you want," Kenneth said. "They just thought you'd like to know. There's an alternative to being alone and afraid."

"Will they leave my body?" she asked, holding up her hand.

"If that's what you want," her mother said.

"I want to be alive, not a ghost."

"That's your decision?" Kenneth asked.

"Yes," she said firmly.

"Do you want us to leave, too?"

She felt the tears again and reached for her mother's hand. 'I'm confused," she said. "You wouldn't lie to me, would you? You're *really* my mother and Kenny and Howard?"

They nodded. "Only better," Howard added. "Listen, sis, I wasn't the smartest fellow in town, was I? Good-hearted, maybe, but sometimes a real rock quarry. But when they came into me—"

"Who are *they?*"

"They came from us," Kenneth said. "They're like our own cells, not like a disease."

"They're cells?" She thought of the blobby things—she forgot their names—she had seen under the microscope in high school. That scared her even more.

Howard nodded. "Smart, too. When they came into me, I felt so strong—in the mind. I could think and remember all sorts of things, and I remembered stuff I hadn't even lived through. It was like I was talking on the phone with zillions of brilliant people, all friends, all cooperating—"

"Mostly," Kenneth said.

"Well, yeah, they argue sometimes, and we argue, too. It's not cut and dried. But nobody hates anybody because we're all duplicated hundreds of thousands, maybe millions of times. You know, like being Xeroxed. All across the country. So like, if I die here, now, there's hundreds of others tuned in to me, ready to become me, and I don't die at all. I just lose this particular me. So I can tune in to anybody else, and I can be anywhere else, and it becomes impossible to die."

Suzy had stopped eating. Now she stopped picking at the food with her fork and put the utensil down. "That's too heavy for me right now," she said. "I want to know why I didn't get sick, too."

"Let them answer this time," her mother said. "Just listen to them."

She closed her eyes.

Different people
Some like you
Died/disaster/end
Set aside, conserved
Like parks these
People/you
To learn.

The words did not just form alone in her mind. They were accompanied by a clear, vivid series of visual and sensual journeys, across great distances, mental and physical. She became aware of the differences between cell intelligence and her own, the different experiences now being integrated; she touched on the forms and thoughts of people absorbed into the cell memories; she even felt the partially saved memories of those who had died before being absorbed. She had never felt/seen/tasted anything so rich.

Suzy opened her eyes. Already, she was not the same. Something in her had been bypassed—the part that made her slow. She wasn't completely slow now, not all the way through.

"See what it's like?" Howard asked.

"I'm going to think about it," she said. She pushed the chair back from the table. "Tell them to leave me alone and not make me sick."

"You've told them already," her mother said.

"I just need time," Suzy said.

"Honey, if you want, you can have *forever*."

39

Bernard floats in his own blood, uncertain with whom he is communicating. The communication is carried up the stream of blood by flagellates, adapted protozoans capable of high speed in the serum. His replies return by the same method, or are simply cast into the blood flow.

Everything is information, or lack of information.

—How many of me are there?

That number will always change. Perhaps a million by now.

—Will I meet them? Integrate with them?

No cluster has the capacity to absorb the experiences of all like clusters. That must be reserved for command clusters. Not all information is equally useful at any given time.

—But no information is lost?

Information is always lost. That is the struggle. No cluster's total structure is ever lost. There are always duplications.

—Where am I going?

Eventually, above the *blood music*. You are the cluster chosen to re-integrate with BERNARD.

—I *am* Bernard.

There are many BERNARD.

Perhaps a million others, thinking as he thought now, spreading through the blood and tissue, gradually being absorbed into the noocyte hierarchy. A million changing versions, never to be re-integrated.

You will meet with command clusters. You will experience THOUGHT UNIVERSE.

—It's too much. I'm frightened again.

FRIGHTENED is impossible without hormonal response of macro-scale BERNARD. Are you truly FRIGHTENED?

He searches for the effects of fear and does not find them.

—No, but I should be.

You have expressed interest in hierarchy. Adjust your processing to *************.

The message is incomprehensible to his human mind, embedded in the biologic of the noocyte cluster, but the cluster itself

199

understands and prepares for the entry of specific data packages.

As the data comes in—slender coiled strings of RNA and gnarled, twisted proteins—he feels his cells absorb and incorporate. There is no way of knowing how much time this takes, but he seems to almost immediately comprehend the experience of the cells rushing past in the capillary. He feeds off their recently shed experience-memories.

By far the greatest number are not mature noocytes, but normal somatic cells either slightly altered to prevent interference with noocyte activity, or servant cells with limited functions specified by simple biologic. Some of these cells do the bidding of command clusters, others ferry experience memory in hybridized or polymerized clumps from one location to another. Still others carry out new body functions not yet assumable by untailored somatic cells.

Still lower in the scale are domesticized bacteria, carefully tailored to perform one or two functions. Some of these bacteria (there is no way to connect their type with any he knows by human names) are small factories, flooding the blood with the molecules necessary to the noocytes.

And at the bottom of the scale, but by no means negligible in importance, are tailored phage viruses. Some of the virus particles act as high-speed transports for crucial information, towed by flagellate bacteria or slimmed-down lymphocytes; others wander freely through the blood, surrounding the larger cells like dust clouds. If somatic cells, servants or even mature noocytes have abandoned the hierarchy—rebelled or malfunctioned drastically—the virus particles move in and inject their package of disruptive RNA. The offending cells soon explode, casting out a cloud of more tailored virus, and the debris is cleaned away by various noocyte and servant scavengers.

Every type of cell originally in his body—friend or foe—has been studied and put to use by the noocytes.

Dislodge and follow the trail of the command cluster. You will be interviewed.

Bernard feels his cluster move back into the capillary. The walls of the capillary narrow until he is strung out in a long line, his intercellular communications reduced until he feels the noocyte equivalent of suffocation. Then he passes through the capillary wall and is bathed in interstitial fluid. The trail is very distinct. He can "taste" the presence of mature noocytes, a great many of them.

It comes to him suddenly that he is, in fact, still near his brain, possibly still *in* his brain, and that he is about to meet one of the researchers responsible for breaking through to the macro-scale world.

He passes through crowds of servant cells, information-bearing flagellates, noocytes waiting for instructions.

I am about to be introduced to the Grand Lunar, he tells himself. The thought and accompanying mental chuckle is passed into his experience data almost immediately, extruded and hastily retrieved by a servant cell, and carried away to the command cluster. Even more rapidly, a response comes to him.

BERNARD compares us with a MONSTER.

—Not at all. I'm the monster here. Either that, or the situation itself is monstrous.

We are nowhere near to understanding the subtleties of your thought. Have you found the *downloading* informative?

—So far, very informative. And I admit I feel humble here.

Not like a supreme command cluster?

—No. I am not a god.

We do not understand GOD.

The command cluster was much larger than a normal noocyte cluster. Bernard estimated it held at least ten thousand cells, with a commensurately greater thinking capacity. He felt like a mental midget, even with the difficulty of making judgments in the noocyte realm.

—Do you have access to my memories of H.G. Wells?

Pause. Then. **Yes. They are quite vivid for not being pure experience memories.**

—Yes, well they come from a book, an encoding of an unreal experience.

We are familiar with *fiction*.

—I feel like Cavour in *The First Men in the Moon*. Speaking with the Grand Lunar.

The comparison may be appropriate, but we do not comprehend it. We are very different, BERNARD, far more different than your comparison with the unreal experience would suggest.

—Yes, but like Cavour, I have thousands of questions. Perhaps you don't wish to answer all of them.

To keep your fellow macro-scale HUMANS from knowing all we might do, and trying to stop us.

The message was just unclear enough to show Bernard that the command cluster was still unable to completely encompass the reality of the macro-scale.

—Are you in touch with the noocytes in North America?

We are aware there are other, far more *powerful* concentrations, in much better circumstances.

—And . . . ?

No response.

Then, **Are you aware that your *enclosing space* is in jeopardy?**

—No. What sort of jeopardy? You mean the lab?

The lab is surrounded by your fellows in *uncertain hierarchy relationship*.

—I don't understand.

They wish to destroy *the lab*, and presumably all of us.

—How do you know this?

We are able to receive RADIO FREQUENCY TRANSMISSIONS in several LANGUAGES *encodings*. Can you stop these attempts? Are you in a position of hierarchy INFLUENCE?

Bernard puzzles over the request.

We have memory of the TRANSMISSIONS.

—Then let me hear them.

He can taste the passage of a flagellate, intersecting the messenger of the command cluster, returning with a packet of data. Bernard's cluster absorbs the data.

He "listens" to the transmissions now in memory. They are not of the best quality, and most of them are in German, which he poorly understands. But he can understand enough to realize why Paulsen-Fuchs has been looking worse and worse of late.

The Pharmek facility is surrounded by camps of protesters. The countryside all the way out to the airport is dotted with them; the protesters number perhaps half a million, and more are arriving by bus, automobile or on foot every day. The army and police do not dare break them up; the mood throughout West Germany, and most of Europe, is very ugly.

—I have no power to stop them.

PERSUASION?

Another inner chuckle.—No; I'm what they want destroyed. And you.

You are far less influential in your realm than we are here.

—Oh, yes, of course.

For a long period, no messages issue from the command cluster.

There is even less time. We are transferring you now.

He feels a subtle shift in the voice as he is moved by flagellates away from the command cluster. **Follow.** He realizes that a group of clusters has broken away from the command cluster. They are communicating with him, and their voice seems oddly familiar, more direct and accessible.

—Who is guiding me?

The response is chemical. An identifying string is brought to him by a flagellate, and suddenly he knows he is being guided by four clusters of primary B-lymphocytes, the earliest versions of the noocytes. Primary B-lymphocytes are accorded a place in most command clusters, and treated with great respect; they are the precursors, even though their activities are limited. They are primitive in both meanings of the word; less sophisticated in design and function than recently created noocytes, and the ancestors of all.

You may enter THOUGHT UNIVERSE.

The voice fades in and out like a bad telephone connection. Choppy, incomplete.

****

The sensation of being in a noocyte cluster ended abruptly. Now Bernard was neither embodied nor shrunk to the noocytes' scale. His thoughts simply *were*, and the place where they *were* was excruciatingly beautiful.

If there was any extension in space, it was illusory. Dimensions seemed to be defined by subject; information relevant to his current thinking was close at hand, other subjects were farther away. The overall impression was of a vast, many layered library, arranged in a sphere around him. He shared this center with another presence.

Humans, human form, the presence said. A scurry of information surrounded Bernard, giving him arms, legs, a body and face. Beside him, apparently sitting in a reclining chair, was a wispy image of Vergil Ulam. Ulam smiled without passion or conviction.

"I am your cellular Vergil. Welcome to the inner circle of the command clusters."

"You're dead," Bernard said, his voice an imperfect approximation.

"So I understand."

"Where are we?"

"Roughly translating the noocyte descriptive string, we are in a Thought Universe. I call it a noosphere. In here, all we experience is generated by thinking. We can be whatever we wish, or learn whatever we wish, or think about anything. We won't be limited by lack of knowledge or experience; everything can be brought to us. When not used by the command clusters, I spend most of my time here."

A granite dodecahedron, its edges decorated with gold bars, formed between them. It rolled this way and that for a moment, then addressed Vergil's pale, translucent form. Bernard did not understand the communication. The dodecahedron vanished.

"We all take characteristic shapes here, and most of us add textures, details. Noocytes don't have names, Mr. Bernard; they have sequences of identifying amino acids chosen by codons from the introns of ribosomal RNA. Sounds complicated, but really much simpler than a fingerprint. In the noosphere, all active researchers must have definite identifying symbols."

Bernard tried to find traces of the Vergil Ulam he had met and shaken hands with. There didn't seem to be many. Even the voice lacked the accent and slight breathlessness he remembered. "There's not very much of you here, is there?"

Vergil's ghost shook its head. "Not all of me was translated to the noocyte level before my cells infected you. I hope there's a better record somewhere. This one is hardly adequate. I'm only about one third here. What *is* here, however, is cherished and protected. Shape of honored ancestor, vague memory of creator." Its voice faded in and out, omitting or sliding over certain syllables. The image moved sparingly. "The hope is they will connect with noocytes back home, find more of me. Not just fragments of a broken vase."

The image became more transparent. "Must go now. Supplements coming. Always part of me here; you and I, we're the models. I suspect you have precedence now. Be seeing you."

Bernard stood alone in the noosphere, surrounded by options he hardly knew how to take advantage of. He held his hand out toward the surrounding information. It rippled all around him, waves of light spreading from nadir to zenith. Ranks of information exchanged priorities and his memories stacked up around him like towers of cards, each represented by a line of light.

The lines cascaded.

He had been thinking

****

"Just another day for you, isn't it?" Nadia turned and stepped gracefully onto the courtroom escalator.

"Not the most pleasant," he said. Down they went.

"Yes, well, just another." She smelled of tea roses and something else quiet and clean. She had always been beautiful in his eyes, no doubt in the eyes of others; small, slender, black-haired, she did not draw immediate stares, but a few minutes alone in a room with her and there was no doubt: most men would want to spend many hours, days, months.

But not years. Nadia was quickly bored, even with Michael Bernard.

"Back to business, then," she said halfway down. "More interviews."

He did not respond. Nadia, bored, became a baiter.

"Well, you're rid of me," she said at the bottom. "And I am rid of you."

"I'll never be rid of you," Bernard said. "You always represented something important to me." She swiveled on her high heels and presented the rear of an immaculately tailored blue suit. He grabbed her arm none too gently and brought her around to face him. "You were my last chance at being normal. I'll never love another woman like I did you. You burned. I'll like women, but I'll never commit to them; I'll never be naive with them."

"You're babbling, Michael," Nadia said, lips tightening on his name. "Let me go."

"Like hell," he said. "You have one and a half million dollars. Give me something in return."

"Fuck off," she said.

"You don't like scenes, do you?"

"Let go of me."

"Cool, dignified. I can take something now, if you want. Take it out in trade."

"You bastard."

He trembled and slapped her. "For the last of my naivete. For three years, the first wonderful. For the third a royal misery."

"I'll *kill* you," she said. "Nobody—"

He brought his leg around behind her and tripped her. She fell back on her ass with a shriek. Legs sprawled, hands spread on stiff arms behind her, she looked up at him with lips writhing. "You—"

"Brute," he said. "Calm, cold, rational brutality. Not very different from what you put me through. But you don't use physical force. You just provoke it."

"Shuttup." She held out her hand and he helped her to her feet.

"I'm sorry," he said. Not once, during their three years together, had he ever struck her. He felt like dying.

"Bullshit. You're everything I said you were, you bastard. You miserable little *boy*."

"I'm sorry," he repeated. The crowds of people in the hall watched them warily, murmuring disapproval. Thank God there were no reporters.

"Go play with your toys," she said. "Your scalpels, your nurses, your *patients*. Go ruin their lives and just *stay away from me*."

****

An older memory.

"Father." He stood by the bed, uncomfortable at the reversal of roles, no longer the doctor but now a visitor. The room smelled of disinfectant and something to hide the smell of disinfectant, tea-roses or something sweet; the effect was that of a mortuary. He blinked and reached out for his father's hand.

The old man (he *was* old, looked old, looked worn out by life) opened his eyes and blinked. His eyes were yellow, rheumy, and his skin was the color of French mustard. He had cancer of the liver and everything was failing piece by piece. He had requested no extraordinary measures and Bernard had brought his own lawyers in to consult with the hospital management, just to ensure his father's wishes were not ignored. (Want your father dead? Want to ensure he will die more rapidly? Of course not. Want him to live forever? Yes. Oh, yes. Then I won't die.)

Every couple of hours he was brought a powerful painkiller, a modern variation on the Brompton's cocktail that had been in favor when Bernard had begun his practice.

"Father. It's Michael."

"Yes. My mind is clear. I know you."

"Ursula and Gerald say hello."

"Hello to Gerald. Hello to Ursula."

"How are you feeling?"

(Like he's going to die, you idiot.)

"I'm a junkie now, Mike."

"Yes, well."

"Have to talk now."

"About what, Father?"

"Your mother. Why isn't she here?"

"Mother's dead, Father."

"Yes. I knew that. My mind is clear. It's just . . . and I'm not complaining, mind you . . . it's just that this hurts." He took hold of Bernard's hand and squeezed it as hard as he could—a pitiful squeeze. "What's the prognosis, son?"

"You know that, Father."

"Can't transfer my brain for me?"

Bernard smiled. "Not yet. We're working on it."

"Not soon enough, I'm afraid."

"Probably not soon enough."

"You and Ursula—doing okay?"

"We're settling things out of court, Father."

"How's Gerald taking it?"

"Badly. Sulking."

"Wanted to divorce your mother once."

Bernard looked into his father's face, frowning. "Oh?"

"She had an affair. Infuriated me. Taught me a lot, too. Didn't divorce her."

Bernard had never heard any of this.

"You know, even with Ursula—"

"It's over with, Father. We've *both* had affairs, and mine is turning out pretty serious."

"Can't own a woman, Mike. Wonderful companions, can't own them."

"I know."

"Do you? Maybe you do. I thought, when I found out about your mother's lover, I thought I would die. It hurt almost as much as this does. I thought I owned her."

Bernard wished the conversation would take another direction. "Gerald doesn't mind going off to school for a year."

"But I didn't. I was just sharing her. Even if a woman only has you for a lover, you share her. She shares you. All this concern with fidelity, it's a sham, a mask. Mike. It's the record that counts. What you do, how well you do it, how dogged you are."

"Yes, Father."

"Say." His father's eyes widened.

"What?" Bernard asked, taking his hand again.

"We stayed on together thirty years after that."

"I never knew."

"Didn't need to know. I was the one who needed to know, to accept. That's not all that's on my mind. Mike, remember the cabin? There's a stack of papers up in the loft, under the bunk."

The cabin in Maine had been sold ten years before.

"I was doing some writing," his father continued after swallowing hard and painfully. His face wrinkled up and he made a bitter moue. "About when I was a doctor."

Bernard knew where the papers were. He had rescued them and read them during his internship. They were now in a file in his office in Atlanta.

"I have them, Father."

"Good. Did you read them?"

"Yes." And they were very important to me, Father. They helped me choose what I wanted to do in neurology, the direction I wanted to take—Tell him, tell him!

"Good. I've always known about you, Mike."

"What?"

"How much you loved us. You're just not demonstrative, are you? Never have been."

"I love you. Loved mother."

"She knew. She was not unhappy when she died. Well." He made the face again. "I have to sleep now. You sure you can't find a good young new body for me?"

Bernard nodded. *Tell him.*

"The papers were very important to me, Father. Dad."

He hadn't called him Dad since he had been thirteen. But the old *(old)* man didn't hear. He was asleep. Bernard picked up his coat and valise and left, passing the nurse's station to inquire—out of habit—when the next medication would be.

His father died at three o'clock the next morning, asleep and alone.

****

And farther . . .

Olivia Ferguson, the same wonderfully smooth eighteen years old as he, her first name echoing her complexion, her plush dark hair pressing against the Corvette's neck rest, turned her large green eyes on him and smiled. He glanced at her and returned the smile and it was the most wonderful evening in the world, it was *fine;* the third time he had taken a girl out on a date. He was, wonder of wonders, a virgin—and this night it didn't seem to matter. He had asked her out near the bell tower on the UC Berkeley campus as she stood near one of the twin bronze bears, and she had looked at him with real sympathy.

"I'm engaged," she had said. "I mean, it couldn't be anything—"

Disappointed, and yet ever-prepared to be gallant, he had said, "Well, then it'll just be an evening out. Two people on the town.

Friends." He hardly knew her; they shared an English class. She was the loveliest girl in the class, tall and composed, quiet and assured yet not in the least distant. She had smiled and said, "Okay."

And now he felt the freedom, released from the obligation of pursuit; the first time he felt on equal footing with a woman. Her fiance, she explained, was in the Navy, stationed at the Brooklyn Naval Yard. Her family lived on Staten Island, in a house where Herman Melville had once stayed a summer.

The wind blew her hair without mussing it—miraculous, wonderful hair which (in theory) would be delightful to feel, run his hands through. They had been talking since he picked her up at her home, an apartment she shared with two women near the old white Clairemont Hotel. They had driven across the Golden Gate into Marin to eat at a small seafood restaurant, the Klamshak, and talked there—about classes, about plans, about what getting married was all about (he didn't know and didn't even bother to fake sophistication). They had both agreed the food was good and the decor not in the least original—cork floats and nets on the wall, filled with plastic lobsters and a weary-looking dried blowfish, an old holed dory perched out front on shell-strewn sand. Not once did he feel awkward or young or even inexperienced.

He thought, as they drove back across the bridge, In other circumstances, I'm sure we'd fall in love with each other. I'm positive we'd be married in a few years. She's terrific—and I'm not going to do anything about it. The sensation he felt at this was sad and romantic and altogether wonderful.

He knew that if he pressed her, she would probably come up to his apartment with him, and they would make love.

Even though he hated and despised being a virgin, he would not press her. He would not even suggest it. This was too perfect.

They sat in the 'vette outside the converted old mansion where she lodged and discussed Kennedy, laughed about their fears during the missile crisis, and then held hands and just looked at each other.

"You know," he said quietly, "there are times when . . ." He stopped.

"Thank you," she said. "I just thought you would be good on a date. Most men, you know—"

"Yeah. Well, that's me." He grinned. "Harmless."

"Oh, no. Not harmless. Not in the least."

Now was the turning point. It could go one way, or the other.

He flashed on her olive-colored body and knew it was smoothly, youthfully perfect. He knew that she would go with him to his apartment.

"You're a romantic, aren't you?" she said.

"I suppose I am."

"I am too. The silliest people in the world are romantics."

He felt heat in his face and neck. "I love women," he said. "I love the way they talk and move. They're enchanting." He was going to open up now, and regret it later, but what he felt was too true and undeniable, especially after this evening. "I think most men should feel a woman is, like, sacred. Not on a pedestal, that sort of thing. But just too beautiful for words. To be loved by a woman, and—That would just be incredible."

Olivia looked through the windshield, a smile flickering on her face. Then she looked down at her purse and smoothed her calf-length blue dress with her hands. "It'll happen," she said.

"Yeah, sure." he nodded. But not between us.

"Thank you," she said again. He held her hand, and then reached up to caress her cheek. She rubbed against his hand like a kitten and tugged on the door handle. "See you in class."

They hadn't even kissed.

—What has happened to me since? Three wives—the third because she looked like Olivia—and this distancing, this standing apart. I have lost far too many illusions.

There are options.

—I don't understand.

What would you wish to revise?

—If you mean go back, I don't see how.

It is all possible here, in Thought Universe. Simulations. Reconstructions from your memory.

—I could live out another life?

When there is time.

—With the real Olivia? She . . . where was she, is she?

That is not known.

Then I'll pass. I am not interested in dreams.

There are more memories within you.

—Yes . . .

****

But where did they fit, where did they come from?

Randall Bernard, twenty-four, had wed Tiffany Marnier on the seventeenth of November, 1943, in a small Kansas City church.

She wore a silver-beaded silk and white lace gown that her mother had worn for her wedding, no veil, and the flowers had been blood-red roses. They had—

They sipped a cup of wine between them and exchanged their vows and broke a piece of bread and the minister, a Theosophist who would by the end of the 1940s be a Vedantist, pronounced them equal in the eyes of the Deity, and now united by love and common regard.

The memory was tinted, like an old photograph, and not good on details. But it was there and he hadn't even been born, and he was seeing it, and then seeing their wedding night, marveling in the quick glimpses of his own creation and how so little had changed between man and woman, marveling at his mother's passion and pleasure, and his father's doctorly, precise, knowing skill, even in bed a doctor—

And his father went off to war, serving as a corpsman in Europe, moving with Patton's U.S. Third Army through the Ardennes and crossing the Rhine near Coblenz—sixty-five miles in three days— and his son watched what he could not possibly have seen. And then he watched what his father could not possibly have seen:

A soldier in plus-fours stepping into the dark, dank hallway of a brothel in Paris; not his father, not anybody he knew—

Very dim, but clear in outline, a woman rocking a child in orange sunlight coming through an isinglass window—

A man fishing with cormorants in a gray early morning river—

A child staring out of a barn loft at a circle of men in the yard below, slaughtering a huge black and white wide-eyed bullock—

Men and women doffing their long white robes and swimming in a muddy river surrounded by red stone bluffs—

A man standing on a cliff, horn bow in hand, watching a herd of antelopes cross a hazy grass plain—

A woman giving birth in a dark underground place, lit by tallow lamps, watched by smeared, anxious faces—

Two old men arguing about impressed balls of clay in a circle drawn in sand—

—I don't remember these things. They aren't me, I didn't experience them—

He broke free of the flow of information. With both hands, he reached up to red-glowing circles over his head, so warm and attractive.—Where did they come from? He touched the circles and felt the answer in his hundred-cell body.

Not all memory comes from an individual's life.

—Where, then?

Memory is stored in neurons—interactive memory, carried in charge and potential, then downloaded to chemical storage in cells, then downloaded to molecular level. Stored in introns of individual cells.

The insight was almost agonizing in its completeness and intensity.

Symbiotic bacteria and transfer virus—naturally occurring in all animals and specific for each species—are implanted with molecular memory transcribed from the intron. They exit the individual and pass on to another individual, 'infect,' transfer the memory to somatic cells. Some of the memories are then returned to chemical storage status, and a few return to active memory.

—Across generations?

Across millennia.

—The introns are not junk sequences...

No. They are highly condensed memory storage.

Vergil Ulam had not created biologic in cells out of nothing. He had stumbled across a natural function—the transfer of racial memory. He had altered a system already in existence.

—I do not care! No more revelations. No more insights. I've had enough. What happened to me? What did I become? What good is revelation when it's wasted on a fool?

He was back in the framework of Thought Universe again. He looked around at the images, the symbolic sources of different branches of information, then at the rings over his head. They glowed green now.

You are DISTRESSED. Touch them.

He reached up and touched them again.

With a jerk, he stretched out into the interface and began to integrate with the macro-scale Bernard; up the tunnel of dissociation, into the warm darkness of the lab. It was night—or at least sleeping time.

He lay on his cot, barely able to move.

We can no longer hold your body form.

—What?

You will be withdrawn into our realm again soon, within two days. All your work in the macro-scale must be completed by that time.

—No...

We have no choice. We have held off long enough. We must transform.

"No! I'm not ready! This is too much!" He realized he was screaming and held both hands to his mouth.

He sat up on the edge of the cot, his grotesquely ridged face dripping sweat.

40

"Are you going to leave again? Just go away?" Suzy held on to Kenneth's hand. He stopped before the elevator. The door opened.

"It's tough just being human again, you know?" he said. "It's lonely. So we'll go back, yes."

"Lonely? What about how I'll feel? You'll be dead again."

"Not dead, Seedling. You know that."

"Might as well be."

"You could join us."

Suzy started trembling. "Kenny, I am *afraid*."

"Look. They left you, like you asked, and they're letting you go. Though what you'll do out there, I don't know. The city's not made for people any more. You'll be fed and you'll live okay, but ... Suzy, everything's changing. The city will change more. You'll be in the way ... but they won't hurt you. If you choose, they'll set you aside like a national park."

"Come with me, Kenny. You and Howard and Mom. We could go back—"

"Brooklyn doesn't exist any more."

"Jesus, you're like a ghost or something. I can't talk sense to you."

Kenny pointed to the elevator. "Seedling—"

"Stop calling me that, goddammit! I'm your sister, you creep! You're just going to leave me out there—"

"That's your choice, Suzy," Kenneth said calmly.

"Or make me a zombie."

"You know we're not zombies, Suzy. You felt what they're like, what they can do for you."

"But I won't be *me* anymore!"

"Stop whining. We all change."

"Not that way!"

Kenneth looked pained. "You're different than you were when you were a little girl. Were you ever afraid of growing up?"

She stared at him. "I am still a little girl," she said. "I'm slow. That's what everybody says."

"Were you ever afraid of not being a baby? That's the difference. Everybody else is still locked into being babies. We're not. You could grow up, too."

"No," Suzy said. She turned away from the elevator. "I'm going back to talk to Mom." Kenny grabbed her by the arm.

"They're not there anymore," he said. "It's a real strain, being rebuilt like this."

Suzy gaped at him, then ran into the elevator and leaned against the back wall. "Will you come down with me?" she asked.

"No," Kenneth said. "I'm going back. We still love you, Seedling. We'll watch over you. You'll have more mothers and brothers and friends than you'll ever know. Maybe you'll let us be with you, sometime."

"You mean, inside me, like them?"

Kenneth nodded. "We'll always be around. But we aren't going to rebuild our bodies for you."

"I want to go down now," she said.

"Going down, then," Kenneth said. The elevator doors started to close. "Good-bye, Suzy. Be careful."

"KennnNETHHH!" But the door closed and the elevator descended. She stood in the middle of the floor and ran her fingers through her long, stringy blond hair.

The door opened.

The lobby was a webwork of gray, solid-looking arches supporting the upper mass of the tower. She imagined—or perhaps remembered what they had shown her—the elevator shaft and the restaurant deck being all that remained of the original tower, left specially for her.

Where will I go?

She stepped on the gray and red speckled floor—not carpet, not concrete, but something faintly resilient, like cork. A brown and white sheet—the last she saw of that particular substance— slid down over the elevator door and sealed it with a hissing noise.

She walked through the webwork of arches, stepping over cylindrical humps in the red and gray surface, leaving the shadow of the transformed tower and standing in half-clouded daylight.

The north tower stood alone. The other tower had been dismantled. All that remained of the World Trade Center was a single rounded spire, smooth and glossy gray in some areas, rough and mottled black in others, with a hint of webwork in patterns pushing up through the outer material.

From the transformed plaza, covered with feathery treelike

fans, to the waterfront, there was nothing more than twenty feet tall.

She walked between the fans, waving gently on their shiny red trunks, down to the shore. The water was a solid, gelatinous green-gray, no waves, smooth as glass and just as shiny. She could see the pyramids and irregular spheres of Jersey City, like a particularly weird collection of children's blocks and toys; the reflection in the solid river was vivid and perfect.

The wind sighed pleasantly. It should have been cold or at least cool, but the air was warm. Already her chest hurt with not crying. "Mother," she said, "I just want to be what I am. Nothing more. Nothing less." Nothing more? Suzy, that's a lie.

She stood by the shore for a long time, then turned and began her hike into Manhattan Island.

41

To Bernard, the ridiculous environment he had lived in for so many weeks seemed the lesser of two realities.

He did little work now. He lay back on the bed, keyboard under his arm, thinking and waiting. Outside, he knew, the tension was building. He was the focus.

Paulsen-Fuchs could not prevent two million people from getting at him, destroying him and the lab. (Villagers with torches; he was both Dr. Frankenstein and the monster. Ignorant frightened villagers doing God's work.)

In his blood, his flesh, he carried part of Vergil I. Ulam, part of his father and mother, parts of people he had never known, people perhaps thousands of years dead. Within, there were millions of duplicates of himself, sinking deeper into the noocyte world, discovering the layers and layers of universes within the biologic: old, new and potential.

And yet—where was the insurance policy, the guarantee that he wasn't being deceived? What if they were simply conjuring false dreams to make him quiescent, to drug him for the metamorphosis? What if their explanations were all sugar-coated phrases meant to reassure? He had no evidence the noocytes lied—but then, how could one tell when something so alien lied, or if "lie" was even an accessible concept for them?

(Olivia. She had broken her engagement, he learned much later, two months after their single date. They had smiled at each other on the last day of class—and passed out of each other's lives. He had been—what? Shy, inept? Too romantic, too in love with that single lovely and Petrarchan night? Where was she—in the North American biomass?)

And even if he accepted what he had been told, he had certainly not been told everything. A million questions remained, some idle, most crucial. He was still, after all, an individual (wasn't he?) anticipating a virtually unknown experience.

The command clusters—the researchers—none answered him now.

In North America—what happened to all the *bad* people whose memories were preserved by the noocytes? They were, to be sure,

suspended from the world in which they had been *bad* just as
surely as if they were in prison—far more suspended. But being
bad meant bad thinking, being *evil* meant being a cancer cell in
the society, a dangerous and inexplicable screw-up, and he was
not just thinking of ax murderers. He was thinking of politicians
too greedy or blind to know what they were doing, white collar
sharpies who had swindled the life's savings from thousands of
investors, mothers and fathers too stupid to know you shouldn't
beat your children to death. What happened to these people and
to the millions of screw-ups, *evil* screw-ups, in human society?

Were all truly equal, duplicated a million times, or did the
noocytes exercise a little judgment? Did they quietly *delete* a few
personalities, *edit* them out . . . or alter them?

And if the noocytes took the liberty of altering the real screw-
ups, perhaps fixing them or immobilizing them some way, going
into their thought processes and using a kind of grand consensus
of right thinking as a pattern for corrections—

Then who was to say they weren't altering others, people with
minor problems, people with all the complexes of little screw-ups
and errors and temporary nastiness . . . things all humans have.
Occupational hazards of being human. Of living in a tough universe, a *different* universe than the ones the noocytes inhabited.
If they did correct and edit and alter, who could say they were
good at it? Knew what they were doing, and retained workable
human personalities afterward?

What did the noocytes do with people who couldn't handle the
change, who went crazy—or who, as was hinted, died incom-
pletely assimilated, leaving partial memories, like Vergil's partial
in Bernard's own body? Did they cull and weed here, too?

Was there politics, social interaction, in the noosphere? Were
humans given an equal vote with noocytes? Humans had, of course,
become noocytes—but were the genuine, the original noocytes
more or less well regarded?

Would there be conflict, revolution?

Or would there be profound quiet—the quiet of the grave,
because of a deletion of the *will* to resist? Not an important thing,
free will, for a rigid hierarchy. Was the noosphere a rigid hierarchy,
lacking in dissent or even comment?

He didn't think so.

But could he know for sure?

Did they really respect and love humans as masters and crea-
tors, or did they simply suck them in, chew them up, digest the
information needed and send the rest into entropy, forgotten, dis-

organized, *dead?*

Bernard, do you now feel the fear of Big Change? The completely different—sublime, or hellish—as opposed to the difficult, often hellish *status quo?*

He doubted that Vergil had ever thought these things out. He may not have had time, but even allowing him the time, Vergil simply did not think such things through. Brilliant in the creation, slovenly in the consideration of consequences.

Wasn't that true of every creator?

Didn't anyone who changed things ultimately lead some people—perhaps many people—to death, grief, torment?

The poor human Prometheuses who brought fire to their fellows.

Nobel.

Einstein. Poor Einstein and his letter to Roosevelt. Paraphrase: "I have loosed the demons of Hell and now you must sign a pact with the devil or someone else will. Someone even nastier."

Curie, experimenting with radium; how responsible was she for Slotin, over four decades later?

Did Pasteur's work—or Salk's, or his own—save the life of a man or woman who ultimately went on to wreak havoc, to turn bad, to really and truly screw up? Undoubtedly.

And did the victims ever think, "Sue the bastard!"

Undoubtedly.

And if such thoughts were heeded, such questions asked, wouldn't all parents slaughter their children while they slept in the cradle?

The old cliche—Hitler's mother, aborting herself.

So confusing.

Bernard rocked back and forth between sleep and nightmare, coming down hard on the side of nightmare, and lifting up on another swing to a kind of ecstasy.

Nothing will ever be the same again.

Good! Wonderful! Wasn't it all badly flawed anyway?

No, perhaps not. Not until now.

Oh, Lord, I am driven to prayer. I am weak and incapable of making these judgments. I do not believe in you, not in any form that has been described to me, but I must pray, because I am in dread, in unholy fear.

What are we giving birth to?

Bernard looked down at his hands and arms, swollen and covered with white veins.

So ugly, he thought.

42

The food appeared on top of a waist-high, grayish spongy cylinder at the end of a high-walled cul-de-sac.

Suzy looked down at the food on the plate, reached out to touch the apparent fried chicken, and drew her finger back slowly. The food was warm, the cup of coffee was steaming, and it looked perfectly normal. Not once had she been served something she didn't like and not once had there been too much, or too little.

They were watching her closely, keeping track of her every need. She was being tended like an animal in a zoo, or at least that was the way she felt.

She knelt down and began to eat. When she had finished, she sat with her back to the cylinder, sipping the last of the coffee, and pulled her collar up. The air was getting colder. She had left her coat in the World Trade Center—or what the north tower had become—and for the past two weeks, hadn't felt any need for it. The air had always been comfortable, even at night.

Things were changing, and that was disturbing—or exciting. She wasn't sure which.

To tell the truth, Suzy McKenzie had been bored much of the time. She had never been much on imagination, and the stretches of rebuilt Manhattan she had traveled had not appealed to her much. The huge canal-pipes pumping green liquid from the river into the interior of the island, the slow-moving fan-trees and propellor-trees, the expanses of glassy-silver bumps, like collections of road reflectors, spread over hundreds of acres of irregular surface—none of these things had interested her for more than a few minutes. They had no relation to her. She could not begin to understand what they were for.

She knew it should all have been fascinating, but it wasn't *human*, and so she didn't much care.

People interested her; what they thought and did, who they were, how they felt about her and she about them.

"I hate you," she said to the cylinder as she returned her plate and cup to its top surface. The cylinder swallowed them and

)wered out of sight. "All of you!" she shouted at the walls of the
ul-de-sac. She wrapped her arms around herself for warmth and
icked up the flashlight and radio. It would be dark soon; she'd
ave to find a place to sleep, perhaps play the radio for a few
1ore minutes. The batteries were weakening, even though she
ad played it sparingly. She walked out of the cul-de-sac and stared
t a forest of fan-trees climbing a steep reddish-brown mound.

On top of the mound was a many-faceted black polyhedron,
ach facet sporting a silvery needle about a yard long. There were
1any others like it on the island. She hardly noticed them now.
Valking around the mound took about ten minutes. She entered
shallow valley the length of a football field, its sides lined with
ently curving black pipe as thick as her waist. The pipe vanished
1 a dimple at the end of the valley. She had slept in such junctions
efore. She walked to the end of the valley and knelt down near
1e depression. She ran her hands over the surface of the dimple;
was quite warm. She could lie here for the night, under the
ipes, and be fairly comfortable.

The sky glowed brilliant purple to the west. The sunsets were
sually orange and red, subdued; the horizon had never looked so
lectric.

She turned on the radio and pulled the speaker close to her ear.
he had turned down the volume to conserve the batteries, even
1ough she suspected that was ineffective. The short wave trans-
1itter in England, ever-faithful, came on immediately. She ad-
1sted the knob and bunched deeper under the pipes.

". . . riots in West Germany have centered around the Pharmek
acilities housing Dr. Michael Bernard, suspected carrier of the
lorth American plague. While the plague has not yet spread any-
vhere in the world but North America, tensions run high. Russia's
ealed borders and . . ." The signal slid and she readjusted.

". . . famine in Roumania and Hungary, now in its third week,
nd no relief in sight . . ."

". . . Mrs. Thelma Rittenbaum, noted Battersea psychic, reports
1at she has had dreams of Christ appearing in the middle of North
.merica, raising the dead and preparing an army to march on the
est of the world." (A shaky woman's voice on a tape of poor
uality spoke a few unintelligible words.)

The rest of the news was about England and Europe; Suzy
njoyed this most of all, since occasionally it seemed the world
light be normal, or at least recovering. There was no hope for
er home; she had given up hope weeks ago. But other people,

elsewhere, might be leading normal lives. That was comforti
to think about.

Not that anybody, anywhere, knew or cared about her.

She turned the radio off and curled up tighter, listening to t
hiss of liquid flowing in the pipes, and low, deep groans fro
someplace far below.

She slept, surrounded by blackness with patches of stars sho
ing between the outlines of the pipes. And when, in the midd
of a warm dream about shopping for clothes, she awoke—

Something was wrapped around her. She stroked it drowsily
soft, warm, like suede. She fumbled with the flashlight and flick
it on, running the circle of light across her covered legs and hip
The covering was pliable, light blue with indefinite green stripes—
her favorite colors. Out from under the covering, her arms a
head were cold. She was too sleepy to question; she pulled t
cloak high and slipped back into her dreams. This time, she w
a young girl, playing in the street with friends from years ag
friends who had since grown up and in many cases, moved awa

Then, one by one, the buildings were torn down. They a
watched as men with huge sledgehammers came along and knock
the brownstones down. She turned to see how her friends we
reacting and they were all grown up, or grown old, receding fro
her and calling for her to follow. She began to cry. Her shoes we
stuck to the pavement and she couldn't move them. When all t
buildings were gone, the neighborhood was a level lot, plumbi
sticking up in the air, a toilet leaning crazily on a pipe where son
upper floor must have once been.

"Things are going to change again, Suzy." Her shoes loosen
and she turned to see Cary, embarrassingly naked.

"Jesus, aren't you cold?" she asked. "No—it wouldn't matte
You're just a ghost."

"Well, I suppose," Cary said, smiling. "We just all wanted
warn you. You know? It's all going to change again, and we wante
to give you a choice."

"I'm not dreaming, am I?"

"Nah." He shook his head. "We're in the blanket. You can ta
to us when you're awake, too, if you want."

"The blanket . . . all of you? Mom and Kenny and Howard?"

"And lots of others, too. Your father, if you want to talk
him. It's a gift." he said. "Sort of a going-away present. We a
volunteered, but then there's a lot more of me, and all the other
than we strictly need."

"You're not making sense, Cary."

"You'll make it. You're a strong girl, Suzy."

The dream background had become nebulous. They both stood in orange-brown darkness, the distant sky brightening to orange as if there were fires on the horizon. Cary looked around at the surroundings and nodded. "It's the artists. There are so many artists, scientists, I kind of feel lost. But I'm going to be one of them soon as I decide. They give us time. We're honored, Suzy. They know we made 'em and they treat us real good. You know, back there," he gestured at the darkness, "we could live together. There's a place where all of 'em think. It's just like real life, the real world. It can be the way it used to be, or the way it's going to be. Any way you want."

"I'm not joining, Cary."

"Nah. Didn't think you would. I didn't really have any choice, when I joined, but I don't regret it. I wouldn't have ever been as much in Brooklyn Heights as I am now."

"You're a zombie, too."

"I'm a ghost." He smiled at her. "Anyway, part of me's going to stay with you, if you want to talk. And another part's going away when they change."

"It's going back the way it was?"

He shook his head. "It'll never be the same. And . . . look, I don't understand all this, but it won't be too long before there's another change. Nothing's ever going to be the same."

Suzy looked at Cary steadily. "You think being naked would tempt me?"

Cary looked down at his image. "Never thought about it," he said. "Shows you how casual I'm getting. Can't you change your mind?"

She shook her head firmly. "I'm the only one who didn't get sick," she said.

"Well, not the only one. There's about twenty, twenty-five. They're being taken care of, as best we can."

She preferred being unique. "Thanks a lot," she said sarcastically.

"Anyway, wear the blanket. When the change comes, wrap up in it real tight. There'll be a lot of food left over."

"Good."

"I guess you're going to wake up now. I'll get out of the way. You can see us when you're awake, too. For a while."

Suzy nodded.

"Don't throw it away," he warned. "Otherwise you'll get hurt."

"I won't."

"Well." He reached out and touched her crossed arms with spread palm.

She opened her eyes. Dawn was pale orange-gray above th pipes. The surface of the dimple and the pipes themselves wer cold.

Suzy wrapped the blanket tighter and waited.

43

Paulsen-Fuchs stood in the observation chamber, leaning forward on the table, eyes lowered. He had had enough of staring at what lay on the cot in the containment lab.

Bernard had lost his human form in the early morning. The cameras had recorded the transformation. Now, a gray and dark brown mass lay on his bed, portions extending to the floor on two sides. The mass moved fitfully, sometimes experiencing a short, violent shudder.

Before he had been confined to one position, Bernard had picked up the portable keyboard and carried it with him to his coat. The telephone cord-wire issued from the side of the mass. The keyboard itself was somewhere under, or within.

And Bernard was still sending out messages, though he could not speak. The monitor in the control lab recorded a steady flow of words, Bernard's record of his transformation.

Most of what came from the keyboard was virtually unintelligible. Perhaps Bernard was very nearly a noocyte himself.

The transformation didn't make Paulsen-Fuchs' decision any easier. The protesters—and the government, by not exercising authority to prevent them—had demanded that Bernard be killed, that the containment lab be completely sterilized.

They were over two million strong, and if their demands were not carried out, they would destroy Pharmek brick by brick. The army had said it would not protect Pharmek; the police had abrogated their responsibility as well. There was nothing Paulsen-Fuchs could do to stop them; only fifty employees were left on the grounds, the others having been evacuated for their own safety.

Many times he had considered simply leaving the facility, going to his home in Spain and isolating himself completely. Forgetting what had happened, what his friend Michael Bernard had brought with him into Germany.

But Heinz Paulsen-Fuchs had been in business too long to simply retreat. As a very young man, he had watched the Russians enter Berlin. He had put aside all vestiges of his unenthusiastic Nazi past, tried to be as nondescript as possible, but he had not retreated. And during the years of occupation, he had worked at three different jobs. He had stayed in Berlin until 1955, when he and two other men had started Pharmek. The company had nearly gone bankrupt in the wake of the thalidomide panic; but he had not retreated.

No: he would not abrogate responsibility. He would flip the switch that would send sterilizing gases into the containment lab. He would instruct the men with the torches who would enter and finish the task. That would be defeat, but he would at least stay, and not hide out in Spain.

He had no idea what the protesters would do once Bernard was dead. He walked slowly from the observation chamber, into the control lab, and sat before the monitor on which Bernard's message was appearing.

He ran it back to its beginning. He could read fast enough to catch up with the words. He wanted to review what Bernard had already said, to see if he could make sense of more of it.

Bernard's final electronic diary entries, beginning 0835

> *Gogarty. They will be gone in weeks.*
>
> *Yes, they* do *communicate. Minor kinsmen. Outbreaks of the "plague" we are not even aware of—Europe, Asia, Australia—people without symptoms. Eyes and ears, gathering, learning, reaping the inconsiderable crop of our lives and history. Marvelous spies.*
>
> *Paul—racial memory. Same mechanism as biologic. There are many lives in each of us; in the blood, in the tissue.*
>
> *Burden on local space-time. Too many. Gogarty. Push right through . . . they cannot help it. Must take advantage. We—you—of course cannot perhaps would not want to stop them.*
>
> *They are the grand achievement*
>
> Th.y love. They *cooperate. They have discipline, yet are free; they know death, but are immortal.*
>
> *They now know me, thru and thru. All my thoughts and motives. I am a theme in their art, their wonderful living *fictions*. They have duplicated me a million times over. Which of me writes this? I do not know. There is no longer an original.*
>
> *I can go off in a million directions, lead a million lives (and not just in the *blood music*—in a universe of Thought,*

Imagination, Fantasy!) and then gather my selves together, hold a conference, and start all over again. Narcissism beyond pride, propinquitous, far grander than simply living forever. (They have found her!)

Each of them can have a thousand, ten thousand, a million counterparts, depending on their quality, their functions. None needs die, but in time all or nearly all will change. In enough time, most of the million me's will bear no resemblance to the present me, for we are infinitely variable. Our minds work on the infinite variety of life's foundations.

Paul, I wish you could join us.

We are aware of the pressures on you.

(Text break 0847-1023)

Not tapping keys. Into the keyboard, into the electronics. Know you must destroy.

Wait. Wait until 1130. Give an old friend that long.

I do not like my old self, Paul. I have given it up, most of it. Pruned away withered pieces. Relived and reshaped whole sections of my 52 years. One could become a saint here, or explore a multitude of sins. What saint can not know sin?

(Text break 1035-1105)

Gogarty.

CGATCATTAG (UCAGCUGCGAUCGAA) *Name now.*

Gogarty. Amazing Gogarty! Far too dense, far too much seeing theorizing, far too much being. They know in NA. Down to the smallest, they have peered in NA. Telling us, preparing. All go together. Afraid deathly wonderfully afraid the finest fear, Paul, not felt in the gut but wondered in thought, nothing like it. Fear of freedom beyond the constraints now, and seeming wonderfully free already. So much freedom we must *change to accommodate. Unrecognizable.*

Paul 1130 that much time.

1130 1130 1130!

Such a rush of feeling for the old, affection chick for egg man for mother student for school

Diverging. Some other takes the writing.

Meeting myselves. Command clusters coordinate. Celebration. So much, so rich! Three of me stay to write, already very different. Friends back from vacation. Drunk with experience freedom knowing

Olivia, waiting . . .

> *And Paul this is* backwater *noocyte slum not like NA*
> *Brief. Coming. New Year!*
> NOVA

(end text 1126.39)

Heinz Paulsen-Fuchs read the final words on the VDT and raised his eyebrows. Hands on the arm of his chair, he looked at the clock on the wall.

1126.46

He glanced at Dr. Schatz and stood. "Open the door," he said. She reached out to the switch and opened the door to the observation room.

"No," he said. "To the lab."

She hesitated.

1126.52

He ran to the console, shoved her unceremoniously aside and flipped the three switches in rapid succession, fumbling the last and repeating.

1127.56

The three-layer hatch began its ponderous slide.

"Herr Paulsen-Fuchs—"

He slid in through the foot-wide gap, into the outer isolation area, still chill with released vacuum, into the high-pressure area, ears popping and, into the inner chamber.

1129.32

The room was filled with fire. Paulsen-Fuchs thought for a moment that Dr. Schatz had begun some mysterious emergency cleansing, had unleashed death in the chamber.

But she had not.

1129.56

The fire cleared, leaving a smell of ozone and something twisting lens-like in the air over the cot.

The cot was empty.

1130.00

44

Suzy felt the queasiness and put down her plate. "Is it now?" she asked the empty air. She pulled the cloak tighter. "Kenny, Howard, is it now? Cary?"

She stood in the middle of a smooth circular arena, the gray wood cylinder behind her. The sun was moving in irregular circles and the air seemed to shimmer. Cary had told her about what would happen the night before, while she slept; told as much as she would understand. "Cary? Mother?"

The cloak stiffened.

"Don't go!" she screamed. The air grew warm again and the sky seemed covered with old varnish. The clouds smoothed into oily streaks and the wind picked up, driving between the pillar-covered mound on one side of the arena and the spiked polyhedron on the other. The polyhedron's spikes glowed blue and quivered. The polyhedron itself sectioned into triangular wedges; light leaked from between the wedges, red as molten lava.

"This is it, isn't it?" she asked, crying. She had seen so much in dreams the past week, had spent so much time with them, that she had become confused over what was real and what was not. Answer me!"

The cloak shivered and moved up in a hood over her head. The hood sealed itself under her chin and wrapped her forehead in a thin, translucent white layer. Then it grew around her fingers and formed gloves, down to her legs and feet, wrapping her tight but allowing her to move as freely as before.

The air smelled sweetly of varnishes, fruits, flowers. Then of warm fresh bread. The cloak slapped around her face and she tried to scratch at it with her fingers. She rolled on the ground until the voice in her ears told her to stop. She lay flat in the middle of the arena, staring upward through the transparency.

Be quiet. Be still. It was her mother's voice, stern but gentle. You've been a very willful young girl, the voice said, and you've refused everything we've offered. Well, I might have done the same. Now I ask one more time, and decide quickly. Do you wish to go with us?

"Will I die if I don't?" Suzy asked, voice muffled.

No. But you'll be alone. Not one of us is staying.

"They're taking you away!"

What Cary said. Did you listen, Seedling? That was Kenneth
She struggled to tear the cloak away.

"Don't leave me."

Then come with us.

"No! I can't!"

No time, Seedling. Last chance.

The sky was warm electric orange-yellow and the clouds ha
thinned to tangled ragged threads. "Mother, is it safe? Will I b
afraid?"

It's safe. Come with us, Suzy.

Her mouth was paralyzed, but her mind seemed to crackle an
come apart. "No," she thought.

The voices stopped. For a time all she saw was racing lines o
red and green, and her head hurt, and she felt like she woul
vomit.

The air glittered high above. The ground of the arena shrun
beneath her, the surface crazing and breaking up.

And for a dizzy moment, she was in two places at once. Sh
was with *them*—they had taken her away, and even now she spok
to her mother and brothers, to Cary and her friends . . .

And she was in the crumbling arena, surrounded by the tattere
remnants of the pillared mound and the spiked polyhedron. Th
structures were falling apart, as if made of sand at a beach, dryin
and collapsing under the sun.

Then the feeling passed. Her queasiness was over. The sky wa
blue, though bits and pieces of it hurt to look at.

The cloak fell away from her and was indistinguishable from
the dust of the arena.

She stood and brushed herself off.

The island of Manhattan was as level and empty as a cooki
sheet. To the south, clouds billowed thick and dark gray. Sh
turned around. Where the food cylinder had been, dozens of ope
boxes haphazardly filled with cans now rested. On top of th
nearest box was a can-opener.

"They think of everything," Suzy McKenzie said. In minutes
the rain began to fall.

TELOPHASE

FEBRUARY, THE NEXT YEAR

45

Camusfearna, Wales

The winter of burning snow had hit England hard. This night, the velvet-black clouds obscured the stars from Anglesey to Margate, scattering luminous blue and green flakes on land and sea. When the flakes touched the water, they were immediately extinguished. On land, they piled in a gently glowing cloak which pulsed like bellowsed coals if stepped upon.

Against the cold, electric heaters, thermostats and furnace regulators had for months proven unreliable. Catalytic heaters burning white gas were popular until no more could be had, and then they were at a premium, for the machines that made them proved equally unreliable.

Antique coal stoves and boilers were resurrected. England and Europe slipped quickly and quietly back to an earlier, darker time. It was useless to protest; the forces at work were, to most, unfathomable.

Most houses and buildings simply remained cold. Surprisingly, the number of people sick or dying continued its decline, as it had throughout the year.

There were no outbreaks of virulent disease. No one knew why.

The wine, beer and liquor industries had not fared well. Bakeries radically altered their product lines, most switching over to production of pasta and unleavened breads. Microscopic organisms the world around had changed with the climate, as unreliable as machinery and electricity.

In eastern Europe and Asia, there was starvation, which put paid to (or confirmed) ideas about acts of God. The world's greatest cornucopias no longer existed to spill forth their groceries.

War was not an option. Radios, trucks and automobiles, planes and missiles and bombs, were just not reliable. A few Middle Eastern countries carried on feuds, but without much enthusiasm. Weather patterns had changed there, too, and for a period of weeks, burning snow fell on Damascus, Beirut and Jerusalem.

Calling it the winter of burning snow summed up everythin
that had gone wrong, was going wrong; not just the weather.

Paulsen-Fuchs' Citröen sputtered along the rugged single-lan
macadam road, snow chains grinding. He carefully nursed i
prodding the accelerator, braking gently on a slippery incline
trying to keep the machine from giving up altogether. On th
bucket seat next to him, a bag of paperback mystery novels an
a smaller bag wrapped around a bottle had been stuffed into
picnic basket.

Few machines worked very well any more. Pharmek had bee
closed for six months because of severe maintenance problems
At first, people had been brought in to replace the machines, bu
it had soon become apparent that the factories could not operat
with people alone.

He stopped by a wooden post and rolled his window down t
get a clear view of the directions. *Camusfearna*, a handcarve
board declared; two kilometers straight ahead.

All of Wales seemed covered with phosphorescent seafoam
Out of the black sky came galaxies of brilliant flakes, each charge
with mysterious light. He rolled the window up and watched flake
fall on his windshield, flashing as the wipers caught them an
pushed them aside.

The headlights were off, even though it was night. He coul
see by the snowglow. The heater made ominous gurgles and h
urged the car on.

Fifteen minutes later, he made a right turn onto a narrow, snow
shrouded gravel road and descended into Camusfearna. The tin
inlet held only four houses and a small boatdock, now locked i
jagged, crusty sea-ice. The houses with their warm yellow light
were clearly visible through the snow, but the ocean beyond wa
as black and empty as the sky.

Last house on the north side, Gogarty had said. He missed th
turn, rolled roughly over frozen sod and grass, and backed up
regain the road.

He hadn't done anything half this insane in thirty years. Th
Citröen's motor chuffed, snarled and stalled barely ten meters fro
the old, narrow garage. Snowglow swirled and dreamed.

Gogarty's dwelling was a very old plastered and white-washe
stone cottage, shaped like a brick—two stories topped with a slat
shingle roof. On the northern end of the house a garage had bee
appended, ribbed metal sheet and woodframe also painted white
The garage door opened, adding a dim orange-yellow square t

the universal blue-green. Paulsen-Fuchs pulled the bottle from the bag, stuffed it into his coat and climbed out of the car, boots making little pressure-waves of light in the snow.

"By God," Gogarty said, coming to meet him. "I didn't expect you to try the journey in this weather."

"Yes, well," Paulsen-Fuchs said. "The craziness of a bored old man, no?"

"Come on in. There's a fire—thank God wood still burns! And hot tea, coffee, whatever you want."

"Irish whiskey!" Paulsen-Fuchs cried, clapping his gloved hands together.

"Well," Gogarty said, opening the door. "This is Wales, and whiskey's scarce everywhere. None of that, regrettably."

"I brought my own," Paulsen-Fuchs said, pulling a bottle of Glenlivet from beneath his coat. "Very rare, very expensive."

The flames crackled and snapped cheerily within the stone fireplace, supplementing the uncertain electric lights. The interior of the cottage was a jumble of desks—three of them in the main room—bookcases, a battery-powered computer—"Hasn't worked in three months," Gogarty said—an etagiere filled the seashells and bottled fish, an antique rose and velvet daybed, a manual Olympia typewriter—now worth a small fortune—a drafting table almost hidden beneath unrolled cyanotypes. The walls were decorated with framed eighteenth century flower prints.

Gogarty took the tea kettle off the fire and poured out two cups. Paulsen-Fuchs sat in a worn overstuffed chair and sipped the gunpowder brew appreciatively. Two cats, an orange tabby with spiky fur and a pug-nosed black long-hair, sauntered into the room and stationed themselves before the fire, blinking at him with mild curiosity and resentment.

"I'll share a whiskey with you later," Gogarty said, sitting on a stool across from the chair. "Right now, I thought you'd like to see this."

"Your 'ghost'?" Paulsen-Fuchs asked.

Gogarty nodded and reached into his sweater pocket. He removed a folded piece of brilliant white paper and handed it to Paulsen-Fuchs. "It's for you, too. Both our names. But it arrived here two days ago. In the mail box, though there hasn't been mail delivery for a week. Not out here. I posted my letter to you in Pwllheli."

Paulsen-Fuchs unfolded the letter. The paper was unusual, buff-textured and almost blindingly white. On one side was a neatly handwritten message in black. Paulsen-Fuchs read the message and looked up at Gogarty.

"Now read it again," Gogarty said. The message had been short enough that most of it remained in his memory. The second time he read it, however, it had changed.

> *Dear Sean and Paul.*
> *Fair warning to the wise. Sufficient. Small changes now, big coming. VERY big. Gogarty can figure it out. He has the means. The theory. Others are being alerted. Spread the word.*
>
> > *Bernard*

"Every time, it's different. Sometimes more elaborate, sometimes very concise. I've taken to recording what it says each time I read it." Gogarty held out his hand and rubbed his fingers. Paulsen-Fuchs handed him the letter.

"It's not paper," Gogarty said. He dipped it in his tea cup. The letter did not absorb, nor did it drip upon removal. He held it in both hands and made a vigorous tearing motion. Though he carried the motion through, the letter remained in one piece, on one hand, having passed through the other hand in some unobvious fashion. "Care to read it again?"

Paulsen-Fuchs shook his head. "So it is not real," he said.

"Oh, it's real enough to be here whenever I want to read it. It's just never quite the same, which leads me to believe it isn't made of matter."

"It is not a prank."

Gogarty laughed. "No, I think not."

"Bernard is not dead."

Gogarty nodded. "No. Bernard went with his noocytes, and I believe his noocytes are in the same location as the North American noocytes. If 'location' is the proper word."

"And where would that be? Another dimension?"

Gogarty shook his head vigorously. "My goodness, no. Right here. Right down where everything begins. We're macro-scale, of course, so when we investigate our world, we tend to look outward, to the stars. But the noocytes—they are microscale. They have a hard time even conceiving of the stars. So they look inward. For them, discovery lies in the very small. And if we can assume that the North American noocytes rapidly created an advanced civilization—something that seems obvious—then we can assume ey found a way to investigate the very small."

"Smaller than themselves."

"Smaller by an even greater factor than our smallness compared
a galaxy."

"You are talking about quantum lengths?" Paulsen-Fuchs knew
tle about such things, but he was not totally ignorant.

Gogarty nodded. "Now it so happens that the very small is my
ecialty. That's why I was called up for this noocyte investigation
the first place. Most of my work deals with lengths smaller
an ten to the minus thirty-third centimeters. The Planck-Wheeler
ngth. And I think we can look to the submicroscale to discover
ere the noocytes went, and why."

"Why, then?" Paulsen-Fuchs asked.

Gogarty pulled out a stack of papers filled with text and equa-
ns written by hand. "Information can be stored even more com-
ctly than in molecular memory. It can be stored in the structure
space-time. What is matter, after all, but a standing-wave of
formation in the vacuum? The noocytes undoubtedly discovered
s, worked with it—have you heard about Los Angeles?"

"No. What about it?"

"Even before the noocytes disappeared, Los Angeles and the
astline south to Tijuana vanished. Or rather, became something
se. A big experiment, perhaps. A dress rehearsal for what's
ppening now."

Paulsen-Fuchs nodded without really comprehending and leaned
ck in the chair with his cup. "It was difficult getting here," he
id. "More even than I expected."

"The rules have changed," Gogarty said.

"That seems to be the consensus. But why, and in what fash-
n?"

"You look tired," Gogarty said. "Tonight, let's just relax, enjoy
e warmth, not stretch our minds beyond reading the letter a few
ore times."

Paulsen-Fuchs nodded and laid his head back, closing his eyes.
es," he murmured. "Much harder than I thought."

The snow had stopped by sunrise. Daylight returned the fields
d banks to unassuming whiteness. The black snow clouds had
ssipated into harmless-looking gray puffs gliding on the west-
ard wind. Paulsen-Fuchs awoke to the smell of toast and fresh
ffee. He lifted himself up on his elbows and rubbed his tousled
ir. The couch had served well; he felt rested, if travel-grimed.

"How about hot water for a shower?" Gogarty asked.

"Wonderful."

"Shower-room is a bit cold, but wear these slippers, stay the wood slats, and it shouldn't be too awful."

Feeling much refreshed, and certainly more alert—the shower room had been *very* cold—Paulsen-Fuchs sat down to breakfast. "Your hospitality is remarkable," he said, chewing toast and cream cheese liberally slathered with marmalade. "I feel most guilty for the way you were treated in Germany."

Gogarty pursed his lips and waved the admission away. "Think nothing of it. Strain on everyone, I'm sure."

"What does the letter say this morning?"

"Read for yourself."

Paulsen-Fuchs opened the dazzling sheet of white and ran his fingers along the sharply defined letters.

Dear Paul and Sean,
Sean has the answer. Stretching of the theory,
observation too intense. Black hole of thought.
Like he said. Theory fits, universe is shaped.
Not other way. Too much theory, too little
flexibility. More coming. Big changes.

Bernard

"Remarkable," Paulsen-Fuchs said. "The same piece of whatever-it-is?"

"As far as I can tell, the very same."

"What does he mean this time?"

"I think he's confirming my work, though he isn't being very clear. If, that is, the note reads the same way to you as it does to me. You'll have to record what you've read for us to be sure."

Paulsen-Fuchs wrote down the words on a sheet of paper and handed them to Gogarty.

The physicist nodded. "Much more explicit this time." He put down the paper and poured Gogarty more coffee. "Very evocative. He seems to be confirming what I said last year—that the universe really has no underpinnings, that when a good hypothesis comes along, one that explains the prior events, the underpinnings shape themselves to accommodate and a powerful theory is born."

"Then there is no ultimate reality?"

"Apparently not. Bad hypotheses, those that don't fit what happen on our level, are rejected by the universe. Good ones, powerful ones, are incorporated."

"That seems most confusing for the theoretician."

Gogarty nodded. "But it lets me explain what's happening to our planet."

"Oh?"

"The universe doesn't stay the same forever. A theory that works can determine reality for only so long, and then the universe must ring a few changes."

"Upset the apple cart, so we do not become complacent?"

"Yes indeed. But reality can't be *observed* to change. It has to change at some level not being fixed by an observation. So when our noocytes observed anything and everything to the smallest possible level, the universe was unable to flex, to reshape itself. A kind of strain built up. They realized they could no longer conduct themselves in the macro-scale world, so they . . . well, I'm not at all sure what they did. But when they departed, the strain was suddenly released and caused a snap. Things are out of kilter now. The change was too abrupt, so the world has been shifted unevenly. The result—a universe that is inconsistent with itself, at least in our local vicinity. We get burning snow, unreliable machines, a gentle kind of chaos. And it may be gentle because—"

He shrugged. "More cracked pottery, I'm afraid."

"Let's hear it."

"Because they're trying to save as many of us as they can, for something later."

"The 'Big Changes.'"

"Yes."

Paulsen-Fuchs regarded Gogarty steadily, then shook his head. "I am too old," he said. "You know, being in England has reminded me of the war. This is what England must have been like during the . . . you called it the 'Blitz.' And what Germany became toward the end of the war."

"Under siege," Gogarty said.

"Yes. But we humans are very delicately balanced, chemically. You think the noocytes are trying to keep mortality rates down?"

Gogarty shrugged again and reached for the letter. "I've read this thing a thousand times, hoping there would be some clue to that question. Nothing. Not a hint." He sighed. "I can't even hazard a guess."

Paulsen-Fuchs finished his toast. "I had a dream last night, rather vivid," he said. "In that dream, I was asked how many handshakes I was from someone who lived in North America. Is that meaningful, do you suppose?"

"Ignore nothing," Gogarty said. "That's my motto."

"What does the letter say now? You read."

Gogarty opened the paper and carefully recorded the message. "Pretty much the same," he said. "Wait—one word added. 'Big changes *soon*.'"

They went for a walk in the intermittent sunshine, boots crunching and squeaking in the snow, compressing it to ice. The air was bitterly cold but the wind was slight. "Is there hope that it will all flex back, return to normal?" Paulsen-Fuchs asked.

Gogarty shrugged. "I'd say yes, if all we were dealing with were natural forces. But Bernard's notes aren't very encouraging, are they?"

"I am ignorant," Gogarty said suddenly, exhaling a cloud of vapor. "How refreshing to say that. Ignorant. I am as subject to unknown forces as that tree." He pointed to a bent and gnarled old pine on a bluff above the beach. "It's a waiting game from here."

"Then you did not invite me here so that we could seek solutions."

"No, of course not." Gogarty experimentally tapped a frozen puddle with his foot. The ice broke, but there was no water beneath. "It just seemed Bernard wanted us here, or at least together."

"I came here hoping for answers."

"Sorry."

"No, that is not strictly true. I came here because I have no place in Germany now. Or anywhere else. I am an executive without a company, without a job. I am free for the first time in years, free to take risks."

"And your family?"

"Like Bernard, I have shed various families over the years. Do you have a family?"

"Yes," Gogarty said. "They were in Vermont, last year, visiting my wife's parents."

"I am sorry," Paulsen-Fuchs said.

When they returned to the cabin, consuming more cups of hot coffee and laying a fresh fire in the grate, Bernard's note read:

Dear Gogarty and Paul—
Last message. Patience. How many handshakes are you from someone now gone? One handshake. Nothing is lost. This is the last day.

Bernard

They both read it. Gogarty folded it and put it in a drawer for safe-keeping. An hour later, feeling a tingle of premonition, Paulsen-Fuchs opened the drawer to read the letter again.

It was not there.

46

London

Suzy leaned out of the window and took a deep breath of the cold air. She had never seen anything so beautiful, not even the glow of the East River when she had crossed the Brooklyn Bridge. The burning snow was simple, entrancing, an elegant coda announcing the end of a world gone mad. She was sure of that much. In the nine months she had spent in London, in her small apartment paid for by the American Embassy, she had watched the city come to a shuddering, spasmodic halt. She had hidden away in her apartment, peering out the window, seeing fewer and fewer cars or lorries (such a fun word), more and more people walking, even as the bright snow deepened, and then—

Fewer people walking, more, she supposed, staying inside. An American consular official came to see her once a week. Her name was Laurie (not quite like the trucks) and sometimes she brought Yves, her fiance, whose name was French but who was an American by birth.

Laurie *always* came, bringing Suzy her groceries, her children's books and magazines, bringing news—what there was of it. Laurie said the "airwaves" were becoming more and more difficult. That meant nobody was getting much use out of their radios. Suzy still had hers, though it hadn't worked since she dropped it while climbing on to the helicopter. It was cracked and didn't even hiss but it was one of the only things that was hers.

She pulled back from the window and shut her eyes. It hurt every time she remembered what had happened. The sense of loss, standing in the middle of empty Manhattan, feeling foolish. The helicopter landing a couple of weeks later, and taking her back to the huge aircraft carrier off the coast . . .

Then they had sailed her across the ocean to England and found her an apartment—a flat—in London, a nice small place where she felt okay most of the time. And Laurie came and brought things Suzy needed.

But she hadn't come today, and she never came after dark. The snow was very thick and very bright. Pretty.

Strangely, Suzy didn't feel at all lonely.

She closed the window to shut out the cold air. Then she stood before the long mirror that hung on the inside of her wardrobe door and looked at the bright snowflakes melting and dimming in her hair. That made her smile.

She turned and looked into the dark wardrobe interior. The steam pipes rattled, just like at home. "Hello," she said to the few clothes in the wardrobe. She pulled out a long dress she had worn to the American Ball six months ago. It was a wonderful emerald green and she looked very good in it.

She hadn't worn it since, and that was a shame.

She stood by the radiator and took off her robe, then unzipped and unlatched the back and stepped into the dress. Gown, she corrected herself.

Didn't one get to meet the queen only in a gown? That made sense.

She pulled it up over her shoulders and fitted her breasts into the cups sewn in. Then she zipped it up as high as she could and stood before the wardrobe again, turning back and forth, all but her face, smiling at herself.

She had been very popular at the embassy in the first few months. Everybody liked her. But they had stopped asking her over because the embassy was quite a distance away, and traffic was messier and messier.

Actually, Suzy thought as she looked at the pretty girl in the mirror, she wouldn't mind dying right now.

It was so beautiful outside. Even the cold was beautiful. The cold felt differently than it used to in New York, and not because it was English cold. Cold everywhere felt differently, she imagined.

If she died, she could go up into the burning snow, higher into the dark clouds, dark as sleep. She could go looking for Mother and Cary and Kenneth and Howard. They probably weren't in the clouds, but she knew they weren't dead—

Suzy frowned. If they weren't dead, then how could she find them by dying? She was so stupid. She hated being stupid. She had always hated it.

And yet—Mother had always told her that she was a wonderful person, and did as well as she could (though there was always better to aspire for). Suzy had grown up liking herself, liking others, and she didn't really want to become somebody else, or *something* else—just to—

She didn't want to change just to be better. Though there was always better to aspire for.

It was very confused. Everything was changing. Dying would be changing. If she didn't mind that, then—

The snow was making a sound outside. She listened at the window and heard a pleasant drone like bees in a field of flowers. A warm sound for a cold sight.

"How strange," she said. "Yes, how strange, how strange." She began to sing the words but the song was silly and didn't say what she was feeling, which was—

Accepting.

Perhaps it wasn't the snow making the sound, but a wind. She wiped the condensation from the window and went back to the bed to turn out the light so she could see better. If the snow was blowing one way or another, then it was wind making the sound. It didn't sound like wind.

Accepting, and lonely.

Where was Laurie? Where everybody was. Inside, staring out at the snow, just like her. But Laurie probably had Yves with her. It wasn't good to be lonely on the—

she unexpectedly sobbed and gulped it back

yes, it *was* she could feel it

—the last night of the world.

"Whew," she said, spreading the gown and sitting on one of the table chairs. She wiped her eyes. That had snuck up on her. She was just being crazy. Stupid, as always.

Not afraid, though.

Accepting.

The wardrobe door creaked and she turned to look at it, half expecting to see Narnia behind the clothes. (She had liked the apartment—the flat—right away because of the wardrobe.)

It was snowing inside the wardrobe. Flecks of light moved over the clothes. She shivered and stood up slowly, straightened out her gown, and one step at a time approached the wardrobe. Confetti light played over the interior, the wood at the back, the clothes, even the hangers.

She pulled the door open wider and looked at herself in the mirror. Behind the glass, she was surrounded by bright bubbles of light, like millions of ginger ale sparkles.

Suzy leaned forward. The face in the mirror was not hers, exactly. She touched her lips, then reached up and met finger tips—cold, glassy—with the image.

The cold and glassy faded. The finger tips became warm.

Suzy backed away until she came up against the chair.

The image stepped out of the mirror, smiling at her.

Not just herself. Her mother, too. Her grandmother. And maybe great grandmother, and great-great. Mostly Suzy, but them, also. All in one. They smiled at her.

Suzy reached behind to zip the dress higher. The image held her arms open and she was mostly Suzy's mother and Suzy ran forward and buried her face in her mother's shoulder, against the green velvety strap of the gown. She didn't cry.

"Let's use the wardrobe," she said, her voice muffled.

The image—more Suzy now—shook her head and took Suzy by the hand. Then Suzy remembered. When the transformed city had gone away, leaving her stranded—after she had refused to go with Cary and everybody else—she had felt *twinned.*

They had copied her. Xeroxed her.

Taken the copy with them, just in case.

And now they had brought her back to meet the original Suzy. The copy had changed, and changed wonderfully. She was all Suzy, and all her mother, and all the others individually, but *together.*

The image led Suzy toward the rear wall of the flat, away from the window. They stood up on the bed, smiling at each other.

Ready? the image asked silently.

Suzy looked back over her shoulder at the buzzing snow, then felt the warm, solid grip. How many handshakes from someone in America?

Why, no handshake at all.

"Are we going to be slow, where we're going?" Suzy asked.

No, the image mouthed, entirely Suzy now. Suzy could see it in her eyes. Cary had been right. They fixed people.

"Good. I'm awful tired of being slow."

The image held up her hand, and together they ripped away the wallpaper. It was easy. The wall just opened up and the paper just curled away.

There was snow beyond the wall, but not like the snow beyond the window. This snow was far more beautiful.

There must have been a million flakes for everyone alive. Everyone dancing together.

"We're not going to use the wardrobe?" Suzy asked.

It doesn't go where we're going, the image said. Together, they hunkered down, get ready, get set—

And sprang from the bed, through the opening in the wall.

The building trembled, as if somewhere a big door had slammed. In the night, the burning flakes of snow danced their Brownian dance. The black clouds above became transparent and Suzy saw all directions at once. It was a delightful and scary way to see.

The storm abated just before dawn. The earth was very quiet as the hemisphere or darkness passed away.

The day began fitfully, casting a long gray-orange glow on the waveless ocean and still land. Concentric rings of light fled from the dimming sun.

Suzy looked a long ways outward. (She was so tiny, and yet she could see everywhere, see very *big* things!)

The inner planes cast long shadows through an enveloping haze. The outer planets wavered in their orbits, and then blossomed in kaleidoscopic splendor, extending cold luminous arms to welcome their prodigal moons home.

The Earth, for the space of a long, trembling sigh, held together in the maelstrom. When its time came, the cities, towns and villages—the homes and huts and tents—were as empty as shed cocoons.

The Noosphere shook loose its wings. Where the wings touched, the stars themselves danced, celebrated, became burning flakes of snow.

INTERPHASE

THOUGHT UNIVERSE

Michael Bernard, nineteen and yet not, sat in the Klamshak opposite Olivia. Over their booth hung the weary blowfish and plastic lobster and cork floats, not very original.

She had just told him about the break-up of her engagement.

He looked down at the table, sensing a very different potential between them now. The way had been cleared.

"Good dinner," Olivia said, folding her hands behind her plate, strewn with oyster shells and shrimp tails. "Thank you. I was very glad when you called."

"I just felt silly," Bernard said. "I acted like a real ninny last time."

"No. You were very gallant."

"Gallant. Hm." He laughed.

"I'm okay. It was a shock at first, but . . ."

"It must have been."

"You know, when he told me, I just thought of coming back to school and getting on with things. Like breaking an engagement was nothing at all. It only hurt when he left. And when I thought of you."

"Will you give me another chance?"

Olivia smiled. "Only if you can keep me feeling as good as I do now."

> **Nothing is lost. Nothing is forgotten.**
> **It was in the blood, the flesh,**
> **And now it is forever.**